Parting her lips just a little, she pressed them to his. His lips _were_ soft.

But then his hands were on her shoulders and he gently pushed her away.

In that horrifying moment, Aisly realized that she had completely misread his attention.

"I want to. You're so lovely. But it wouldn't be fair."

His voice was so gentle and his eyes so soft that she wanted to run and hide. The way her body was responding to him was nothing but wrong. And yet, for some strange reason, she felt close to this foreigner, closer than she'd felt to anyone in a long time. She was just so lonely. That was why.

"I'm sorry," she whispered and moved back a bit.

He caught her wrist before she could get far. "Never apologize for touching me." It wasn't an admonishment, precisely. His voice was warm and if she didn't know better—he _was_ an injured man—it was textured with longing.

Author Note

Some books start with a character or event in history. Some start with a what-if. This is a what-if story. What if two people meet and fall madly in love, neither of them knowing that they are supposed to be enemies? What if by the time they do find out, it's too late to change their minds and hearts, but the world wants to keep them apart?

This is how Magnus and Aisly's story started for me. Magnus is a noble warrior bound by his duty but with a soft heart. The last thing he needs is a woman who challenges that loyalty. Aisly is focused and fiercely independent and has already been burned by one bad relationship. The last thing she needs is another man in her life. Yet from almost the first moment they meet, they recognize a part of themselves in the other. They'll have to work through their own insecurities, while the world tries to keep them apart, to find their happily-ever-after.

I hope you enjoy reading their romance as much as I enjoyed writing it. Thank you so much for reading.

HARPER
ST. GEORGE

In Bed with the
Viking Warrior

HARLEQUIN® HISTORICAL

Recycling programs
for this product may
not exist in your area.

ISBN-13: 978-0-373-36867-9

In Bed with the Viking Warrior

Copyright © 2016 by Harper St. George

Printed in U.S.A.

Harper St. George was raised in rural Alabama and along the tranquil coast of northwest Florida. It was this setting, filled with stories of the old days, that instilled in her a love of history, romance and adventure. In high school she discovered the romance novel, which combined all of those elements into one perfect package. She lives in Atlanta, Georgia, with her husband and two young children. Visit her website: harperstgeorge.com.

Books by Harper St. George

Harlequin Historical

Viking Warriors

Enslaved by the Viking
One Night with the Viking
In Bed with the Viking Warrior

Outlaws of the Wild West

The Innocent and the Outlaw

Digital Short Stories

His Abductor's Desire
Her Forbidden Gunslinger

Visit the Author Profile page at Harlequin.com.

For my parents. Thanks for all the babysitting
so I could get this book finished!

As always, thank you to Tara Wyatt and Erin Moore
for being there for me when the writing gets
hard. Thank you to Brenna Mills for reading my
unpolished drivel. Special thanks to Michelle Styles
for her advice and sharing her historical knowledge.
You all are the best. I can't even say how much
I appreciate the help. And a big thank you to my
editor, Kathryn Cheshire, for helping this story shine!

Chapter One

Smoke filled his nose, burning his lungs as he breathed it in, almost suffocating him until he blew it out in a long wheeze that left him dizzy and nauseated. But his body was so starved for air that he breathed in again almost immediately. A cough tore through his chest, wrenching him sideways, though he could barely move because his arms were caught under an unidentified weight. Slowly he opened his eyes, the heaviness of an extremely long sleep making even that simple task difficult and causing his head to feel muddled and full of cobwebs.

An orange blaze filled his vision and he closed his eyes against the sharp pain that stabbed through his temple. Belatedly, he became aware of the heat warming his body, almost blistering in its intensity because he was far too close to the fire. Turning his head away, he forced his eyes open again only to stare into a pair of grotesque eyes, their lids open wide, the irises clouded over, unseeing. Dead eyes. He'd seen dead eyes before. A tangled memory of dead bodies came to him. He moved his head away as far as his body would allow to see the rest of the face. The head's mouth was open in a silent scream.

He opened his own mouth to call to someone, but nothing came out save a hoarse cry of anguish. He jerked back but was caught by that same unidentifiable weight as before. Only now he knew. Now, as he looked around him, as he took in the sheer magnitude of the eyes staring at him, he knew what that weight was.

He was in a death pile. Slain warriors had been stripped of their clothing, their identity, and piled high to be burned. It would save the hassle of burying the bodies and keep the vultures at bay.

He had no memory of how he'd come to be here. No memory of a battle and he didn't recognise the men. The only thing he knew with any real certainty was that he wasn't dead, but he would be if he didn't get away. Wrenching hard on his arm, he managed to pull it free from the man lying on it. The force of the movement made him roll to the side, landing in a heap on the dirt next to the bodies. He lay there for a moment, fingers pressed to the ground as he tried to get his bearings.

Taking stock of his body, he made sure that all of his limbs were in good working order. Aside from some scratches, everything seemed to work. He was nude, but he'd have to deal with that later. It hurt to breathe, though. Now that he was opposite the fire, he could take his first breath of fresh air. It still burned going in. Pushing himself up to his knees, he groaned as a wave of pain moved through his head. His hand went to his forehead and found a crusty gash there. The blood had matted in his hair.

He pulled his hand away and the world went dim before it tilted and started to spin. He had to press a hand back to the ground to stop himself from toppling over. Now that he was aware of the injury, a constant pounding had begun in his skull and wouldn't let up. A wave of nausea moved through him and he groaned as he fell forward, retching into the dirt. Nothing but bile came up.

He ran a hand over his chest and it felt grainy, as if his skin was covered in a fine powder. Bringing his fingers to his nose, he smelled cold ashes. How long had he been asleep? What battle had got him here? Trying to remember only made his head feel clouded and dark, so he stopped trying to remember. Ignoring the lurch in his belly, he forced his head up to look around the clearing just to make sure no one was there. Right now he needed to get to safety. Whoever was in charge of these bodies probably wouldn't be happy to see him alive when they returned.

A path led away from the fire through the trees. He'd go the opposite way, through the forest, and put as much distance as he could between himself and this certain death. But he couldn't stop himself from taking one last look at the dead. If he'd battled with them, one of them should at least look familiar, but he didn't recognise any of the faces he could see. They were strangers. Walking around the pile of men—there were at least a score of them, maybe more—prodding as he went, he hoped one of them would still be alive, but their flesh had already hardened.

Dead flesh. Dead eyes. There was nothing but death here.

Glancing around the clearing again, he saw nothing he could take with him. Their clothing had all been taken, burned probably or scavenged by the victors. There were no weapons. The large fire caught his gaze again, the bright light making his eyes water.

Turning, he made his way through the woods, stumbling from tree to tree as he fought to keep himself upright. His legs were weak and he was having trouble keeping his balance, probably from the head wound. He needed to find somewhere safe to rest for a couple of days. And he needed water to cure his parched throat.

The night was cloudy, obscuring the stars from him. Not that it mattered. He didn't know where to go, where he'd come from, his own name. Trying to call up memories left him with a dark void. Frustration threatened to make his head pound harder, but he pushed the thoughts away. Right now he needed to find safety to recover. The rest would come once he'd had a chance to heal. It had to.

Up ahead the sound of water rushing over rock made his heart pick up speed in his chest and his legs gained new strength as he followed the sound. The back of his throat tingled at the very thought of water as his legs powered him forward to reach it. Pushing away from the final large oak that bordered the stream, he slid down the muddy embankment and landed in the stream, the smooth pebbles at the bottom biting into the soles of his feet. He lunged face forward into the stream, drinking in the cool water as if he hadn't had a drink in years.

Even though it was cold, it burned going down and he tasted smoke. Before he could stop it or fight against it, his stomach heaved, expelling the water and leaving him in a knot of agony, his hands pressed to his head as the world swam around him. Falling back against the bank of the stream, he lay still, the water freezing as it knifed through his flesh, but he was afraid that the cold was the only thing keeping him conscious, so he wouldn't chance leaving it just yet. When he opened his eyes, blackness hung around the periphery of his vision, but he refused to give in to it and forced himself to sit up. This time when he drank, he cupped it in his hands and took small sips, just enough to ease the ache.

'Halt!'

The word came out of nowhere, splintering his mind with a thousand shards of pain. It was followed by others spoken in a harsh, tangled string that he couldn't even begin to unravel. A single man ran towards him, emerging from the forest at the exact spot near the ancient oak that he himself had. He must have followed him from the death pile. It was too dark to see clearly, but he was dressed in a dark-coloured tunic, with a sword held in both hands across the front of his torso.

He had no choice but to fight the man, but with no weapon, armour or even clothing, he was at a distinct disadvantage. Rising to his feet, he gritted his teeth, determined to keep himself steady as he backed into the stream to lure the man down the embankment. There was no way he could fight an opponent with a sword bare-handed on solid ground and win, especially not while injured. The freezing water came up to mid-thigh, where he stopped, daring the man to come forward.

The man stopped at the edge of the water, sword raised high, but still too far away to pose an immediate threat should he choose to attempt a strike. He spoke again, this time slower and with venom. It took a moment for his mind to catch up to the words, especially because the man spoke them in a way that sounded wrong. With an accent. 'You die tonight, Magnus. You won't cheat death again.'

Magnus. His own name? The word was meaningless to him, not causing so much as a flicker of recognition. The gash had addled him…that was certain.

'Who are you?' he asked, his own voice rough and un-recognisable. It bothered him how he'd had to turn the words over and over in his mind before speaking them to make sure they'd come out correctly.

The man laughed, his eyes gleaming in the dim light of the moon. 'You've gone daft. It's all right, Magnus. I've come to put you down.'

He moved further back into the stream, making his opponent move forward. The man grimaced when the freezing water soaked through his trousers and lunged to try to swipe at him with his sword, saving himself the trouble of walking further into the water. He lunged to the side, but although the move saved him from the sword, it made him dizzy and the world made a horrify-ing lurch. He grabbed on to the only thing of substance he could find. The man's wrist.

He yanked, pulling his opponent off his feet and into the water with him. The man still kept his grip on the sword, though, and quickly found purchase on the stream bed in his booted feet, but he swiped out with his leg, catching the man at the bend of his knee. The force top-pled them both over, but he quickly gained the upper hand, his grip strong on the man's wrist to keep the sword from becoming a threat, while pressing his knee into the man's stomach.

Freeing a hand, the man swiped out with a fist, catch-ing him in his temple just below the gash and opening it up again. Fresh, warm blood poured down into his eye and clouded his vision. The man spoke, but the sound was drowned out by the ringing in his ears. He refused to give in to his weakness, though. This was it. Either he won this fight or his life was over. And he refused to be dragged back to that pile of death.

Letting go of the man, he transferred his grip to the man's tunic to hold him, then brought his fist back for a well-aimed strike to his nose. The crack of bone and a cry of pain greeted him and on instinct the man dropped his sword. He took the advantage and fell forward, pushing the man underwater. It wasn't a noble victory, as he'd much rather finish a fight with his fist or a weapon, but already the rush of strength he'd had at the beginning of the fight was beginning to wane. The man fell under his weight, taking in a mouthful of water as he went under. His opponent thrashed and he simply had to hold on until he went limp a few moments later.

His arms were shaking as he dragged the man to shore. If nothing else, he'd solved the problem of his clothing. Taking a moment to clean the stinging blood from his eye, he quickly stripped the man of his tunic and leggings. There was an emblem sewn near the top, a crest of some kind, and he thought he should know what it meant, but he didn't. Shaking his head, he tamped down his frustration as he retrieved the sword from the bottom of the stream and then donned the clothing. They were snug on him. The tunic pulled too tight across his shoulders and the trousers were a bit short for his liking, but the boots fit well, even soaked through as they were.

Once he was done, he took hold of the man and dragged him back to the stream. Taking a grip on the man's upper arm, he pulled him floating behind him as he walked downstream. There were bound to be more enemies around from the battle and he needed to at least attempt to hide the body, in case anyone came looking for the man, they wouldn't be sure of his direction. It would give him a better chance to escape, and if he could stay in the stream as he fled without succumbing to the cold, then they'd never track him.

He walked for over an hour before his shivering forced him to consider leaving the water. At least the cold had stopped his bleeding. Taking the body to a natural alcove created by two dead trees near shore, he pushed it inside and gave it one last glance. The man's head was shaved. He touched a hand to his own beard and shoulder-length hair. He should probably cut it. Whoever this man was, whatever his station, he would have to appear to be like him, particularly if he was wearing his clothing. The man's knife was stashed in his boot. He'd have to take care of that later. Right now he had to get as far away as he could.

He left the stream a little while later when he came to a section of wide, flat rocks that he hoped would hide his footprints from any trackers come morning. Taking one last drink of water, he stepped out on to the shore and made his way into the woods. The night air was freezing now that he was soaked. More reason to keep walking. If he stopped now, as wet as he was, he'd catch his death by morning. The world continued to come in and out of focus for him as he walked, sometimes stumbling into trees and over foliage, sometimes falling to the ground and momentarily losing consciousness only to rouse himself and force his legs to carry him onward.

Finally, near dawn, his body revolted and he fell to the ground in a heap. When he tried to rise, the ground came crashing up to meet him again and his head cracked against the earth, sending pain splintering through his entire body. He had to rest before he made his injuries worse. Raising his head enough to find a large spruce with limbs low towards the ground, he crawled to it and took cover in the needles. He couldn't even take the sword from the scabbard across his shoulder as darkness crept over him.

It seemed he had just closed his eyes when he awoke with a start. His heart threatened to pound out of his chest, but he stayed very still, aware that one wrong move could mean death. Fluttering drew his attention to a bush just past the reaches of the pine's branches, where two brown finches rolled together briefly in a brawl before one flew off, chased by the other. The sun was high in the sky.

He sighed in relief and lowered his forehead to the ground. He was still in the same position in which he'd collapsed. Dew covered his already soaking wet clothing and his warm breath came out in a puff of vapour as it mixed with the cool air. The first hard freeze was just weeks away, at most. That didn't leave him very much time to figure out who he was and where he belonged.

Magnus.

The unfamiliar name twisted and turned itself over in his mind, but it wouldn't stick. If it was his name, wouldn't he recognise it? Just thinking about it made his head ache even more. Pushing himself to a sitting position, he had to wait for the world to right itself before he could open his eyes. His hand automatically went to the gash on his forehead and he grimaced at how tender and swollen it was. Another knot graced the back of his head, thanks to his fall. There was nothing he could do for the wounds now, though, not when there was every chance he was being chased by his captors.

His fingers moved to the tangled mess of hair. It was caked with blood and fell past his shoulders. If he came upon anyone, he couldn't risk looking like a wild marauder covered with blood, so he'd have to cut it. All of the men in the death pile had longer hair and beards. Pulling the knife from the strap on his borrowed boots, he set about sawing through the length of his hair. It fell away in dark blond strands turned red with blood. When that was done, he scraped away his beard, though he wasn't able to make it a close shave with the crude knife.

On shaking legs, he made his way back to the stream and took a long drink before dousing his head with the cold water until much of the remaining blood had been washed away. He couldn't risk getting himself too clean and reopening the wounds. He needed all of his strength to get away.

Drawing in a shaking breath, he rose to his feet and entered the icy depths of the stream. If they found his tracks leading to the tree, perhaps they'd continue onward in that direction in their search for him.

He continued in the stream throughout the rest of the day, only getting out when he couldn't bear its cold any longer. When night fell, he found another tree and collapsed in exhaustion. He needed food, but that would be a task for tomorrow.

Chapter Two

Aisly blinked back the threat of tears and attacked the dirt again with her spade, attempting to uproot the larkspur. The stubborn thing refused to break free of the soil. She'd already been gone for a large portion of the morning, and with the long trek back home, she didn't have time to waste. The girls should almost be finished with the vestment hems she'd left them. The thick cord-and-line pattern was one they had mastered months ago, but if she didn't get back soon, her young apprentices would be out playing in the morning sun and she'd never get them back inside to finish their work. A whole day would be lost.

A whole day she couldn't afford to lose, because she'd be late on the order. The abbess was already fond of implying that Aisly's charges bordered on sinfulness, even suggesting that a more devout woman might view it as a privilege to do God's work for the abbey. She'd have no qualms about deducting for tardiness. Aisly didn't know if her embroidery qualified as God's work. She simply knew that it was her only means to earn a living.

A means that was closer to slipping away from her with every day that passed.

That was the real reason for her tears, the reason she hacked at the root viciously until it finally gave way, causing her to fall backward with a thud. The real reason she'd had to come into the forest today, instead of waiting until the commission was finished. She hadn't wanted anyone to see her tears. Her menses had begun that morning, a reminder that there would be no child, nothing at all to bind her to the home she had grown to love and to depend on for her livelihood. Nothing at all to keep her father-in-law from evicting her from her late husband's home. There had been a marriage agreement giving her the right to her home. She had signed it the day she married him with Lord Oswine looking on, but she hadn't found it in Godric's things. Without Wulfric's generosity, or a child to bind her to the property, she'd be homeless and without a means to earn a living.

Gathering her composure, she searched amongst the foliage for her discarded knapsack. Tears were foolishness that accomplished nothing, so she did her best to blink them back. It didn't bear thinking about Godric's dreadful father following through on his threat. Not yet anyway. She had months before he could even attempt it and there was no reason to believe that the elders would agree with him.

Even if the elders did agree with him, they would have to sway Lord Oswine. After her parents had died of ague, he had become the guardian of Aisly and her brother. Though the guardianship had meant they'd been more like servants than his children, he'd taken his responsibility for them very seriously. He'd attended her wedding and had overseen the signing of the contract.

Finding the hide bag amongst the dead leaves on the ground, she stuffed the plant inside and tied the drawstring. It was probably foolish to try to take the plant home and hope it took root, but she needed it so that she could practise dyeing her thread come the spring. It would save her coin if she could dye her own. Tying the spade to the knotted belt at her waist, she retrieved Godric's old sword from the ground beside her and set off for home.

The cold metal beneath her fingers made her feel secure in a way her late husband never had, though it was only the sword he'd used as a boy, not the sword he'd used as a warrior. That sword had been confiscated by the Danes when he'd gone to talk with them at their settlement and been killed. A move that had cost her their savings when the Danes had come to demand recompense for the fire he'd allegedly set that had destroyed a few of their houses. She'd even had to give them her tapestries, the wool in storage and most of her sheep when her coin hadn't been enough. The sheep had been the least of her worries, at least she still had milk, but the wool had been put aside so that she could weave cloth through the winter to sell in the spring. That had stung.

Yet it was the loss of the tapestries that hurt the most. Her mother had made them. Though her mother had been a well-known embroideress in the villages surrounding Heiraford, and the tapestries were worth quite a bit of coin, Aisly missed them because they'd been the only reminder she had of her mother. Having lost her at the age of eight, her thoughts of the woman were sometimes clouded. The only true memories she had were the hours spent learning the stitches from her mother's patient hand, and then after her death attempting to recreate the embroidery in those tapestries. Then one day the Danes had come and taken that last connection to her mother. There had been no warning, just a brutal knock on her door one morning telling her what her husband had done and that he was dead. Moments later they'd taken what had been most precious to her.

Some days she almost felt remorse that she mourned the tapestries more than her own husband. Life as a widow was infinitely better than life as Godric's wife. A few weeks of freedom and she'd already vowed to herself that she'd never marry again and suffer under the rule of another tyrant. To keep that vow she'd have to learn to protect herself. Her brother, Alstan, was one of Lord Oswine's best warriors and she'd convinced him to spend a few hours teaching her how to properly wield the sword. With so little training, she knew that she had a lot to learn yet, but already the grip felt comfortable in her hand. While not as heavy as the other sword and unlikely to inflict bone-crushing injury to an attacker, the small sword would suffice for protection.

With both hands, she could hold it steady and her arms didn't shake the way they had when she'd first picked it up a few weeks ago. As she walked back home through the forest, she gave a couple of test strikes and parries. The blade sliced cleanly through the air. Perhaps with time she could actually take on an opponent. Smiling at the thought, she set her gaze on a knot on a tree in front of her and swung in a circle, bringing the blade to a rest against the knot. Perfect.

Her mood improving, Aisly spent the next few moments of her walk finding various brown leaves and limbs to swipe at and following through with triumph. It wasn't much, but at least she was doing *something* to help retain

the Danes at the settlement, who stole the village's sheep and crops as if it were their right. At summer's end two maidens had gone missing, taken by the rebels. The Danish settlement had refused to help find them.

Aisly had no doubt that this man was part of that rebel group. The one time she'd seen officials from the Danish settlement, they'd looked…well, official. Their leaders had appeared well kept and had ridden with at least an outward display of respect through her village. This man looked like a heathen, dirty and dangerous. He didn't look like them at all. He looked ready to pounce on her and tear her apart.

Taking a shaking breath, she slipped in her frantic attempt to move up to the solid ground of the forest. The sword fell to the mud as she grabbed at the ground to push herself upright. The Dane took the advantage and splashed through the shallow water towards her. Heart pounding in her chest, she quickly decided that her only choice was to face him on the banks of the stream. Gathering the sword with both hands, she righted herself as best she could. The white of his teeth flashed above his full beard, which hung in twin braids down his chest, as he sneered at her attempt. As he came closer, she could see the dark, horizontal lines engraved in his teeth. Just how she'd heard the rebels marked themselves. The men who had come to her door had not had those markings. He didn't even draw a weapon as he came towards her, so sure was he that he didn't need it.

The very thought made a dangerous surge of anger come over her, fuelling her strength so that she raised the sword high above her head. His stride was long, so she figured it would take him only ten paces to reach her. She counted off each one in her head. When he was two paces away, he'd be close enough to reach with a swinging sword while still being far enough away that he wouldn't grab her. Catching him at that precise moment of vulnerability would be her only chance.

Eight.

Her fingers clenched tight, readying to strike.

Seven.

Her feet worked to gain solid footing, soles grinding down into the mud.

Six.

She took in a long breath. She'd let it out with the strike. He saw it and, taking it for fear, sneered at her.

Five.

A flash of movement just over the Dane's shoulder drew her eye. It was a man coming from the trees. He walked deliberately towards the Dane with his sword poised in front of him. Eyes wide, she forced herself to look back at the Dane and count.

Four.

Before she could check herself, she glanced back at the newcomer. Whether he was friend or foe she couldn't tell, but he brought a finger to his lips and his eyes demanded silence. Then he tightened both hands on the large sword he swung up past his shoulders. Her lips working in silent debate, she could only stare back at the Dane coming for her. He was close enough now that she could see the mottled blue of his irises.

Three.

She tightened her fingers again and prayed for strength. The rebel Dane let out a sound that was almost inhuman. A growl.

Two.

Something must have caught his eye, or perhaps it was

her own glance to the approaching man, but the Dane turned in time to deflect the stranger's raised sword. She watched in horror as the Dane lunged at the man. Every instinct she possessed told her that she should run and put as much distance between this fight to the death and herself as she could, but her feet stood rooted in the mud and rocks.

They were evenly matched in size, both with broad, muscled frames. But the rebel Dane moved in a clumsy, lumbering manner, while the stranger appeared graceful, his feet barely seeming to touch the ground as he moved in a circle around his opponent, putting himself between her and danger. But just as the Dane growled again and reached for his sword, the stranger lunged forward. The growl turned into a great bellow as the Dane's eyes widened in pain and he crumpled to the ground.

Keeping a tight grip on her sword, she let her gaze dart to the stranger, uncertain if he was now an enemy instead of her saviour. He watched the Dane until it was clear he wasn't an immediate threat, then stared back at her with deep brown eyes, bloody sword at his side. Despite the fact that he wasn't making a move towards her, she couldn't decide if he meant her any harm. There was no menace in his gaze. But then, Godric had taught her how that could change in an instant.

'Nay! Don't come any closer,' she warned when he took a tentative step forward.

Tilting his head a bit and furrowing his brow, he stared back at her. He still didn't say a word as he gestured to the man at his feet. Aisly stepped back to put even more space between them and gave him a nod, watching him disarm the fallen Dane. A wave of nausea threatened now that the danger was past and her arms began to shake from holding the sword for so long. He glanced at her as he gently tossed the man's sword up on to the forest floor, away from them both. His own sword rested on the muddy bank of the stream at his feet. The Dane's knife quickly followed and then the man held his hands aloft to show her that he held no weapons.

Finally able to take a steady breath, she lowered her arms but kept the sword in front of her and allowed herself a careful study of the man. He wasn't a Dane. Or at least she didn't think he was. He was tall, big like them, but his hair was odd. It was dark blond but had been cut in awkward tufts as if he'd taken to it himself with a knife. His beard was barely there, just mere scruff on the lower half of what was a very handsome face. A gash crusted over with blood ran from the centre of his forehead and disappeared into his hair above his ear. It looked to be a few days old and in need of attention. It was angry and pink around the edges and swollen badly. The flesh around his eye on that side was puffy and discoloured.

He wore no chain mail and his brown tunic was rather plain except for a bit of embroidery around the top and an emblem that might have been a bird on the shoulder that seemed vaguely familiar. It wasn't a Dane's tunic. She'd seen something similar on a mercenary once, but this man didn't seem Frankish. Of course, there were other lands.

'Who are you?' she asked.

His brow furrowed again as he studied her mouth, making her think he didn't understand her words. 'What is your name?' she asked again, keeping her voice steady.

When he still didn't answer, she worried that perhaps she'd been wrong and he wasn't a mercenary at all. She'd seen them before and they knew her language. They had to know it if they were to earn a living. If he didn't know her language, then he was truly a foreigner and one who had no business here. She scanned the edges of the forest looking for others like him and tightened her grip on the sword, raising it again. He wouldn't be alone if he was here for nefarious reasons.

'Nay.' He reached out towards her but stopped short of putting himself any closer to her. 'I won't hurt you.' His voice was rough as if his throat had been damaged and he spoke in a halting accent. A quick glance showed his neck appeared fine and uninjured. 'I don't know who I am.' He gestured to his head injury.

He did appear badly injured. Aside from the gash and swelling, now that she studied him closer, his flesh held an unnatural pallor and a fine sheen of sweat beaded on his skin. She'd once heard of a man who had been kicked by an ox and had forgotten how to talk, but could such a blow make someone forget his identity completely? 'You don't know your own name?'

He swallowed once before giving a quick shake of his head that caused him to close his eyes as if in pain and his whole body to waver. When he opened them again, their intensity caught her gaze and held tight. 'I only know that this man was going to kill me and you gave me an advantage. Thank you.'

Satisfied that he wasn't a threat, she lowered the sword and said, 'You saved me. I should be thanking you.'

'He wouldn't have been a danger to you had I not led him here.' The husk of his injured voice was not entirely unpleasant as it raked across her senses. 'I'll be on my way. There could be others following me and I don't want to put you in more danger.'

He retrieved his sword and took a few wary steps

backwards before giving her a nod and turning away. As he walked back the way he had come, she noticed that his graceful steps had deserted him. He walked heavily as if he was exhausted and stumbled once, though he caught himself quickly. He meant to continue on his way as if he hadn't just saved her life. Despite herself, she admired his shoulders as he slung the sword into the scabbard strapped between his shoulder blades. They were broad under his tunic and thick like a warrior's. And his hand around the sword's grip was large and strong. A warrior's hand, marked with small white scars near the knuckles.

'Wait!'

He paused and turned only his head to look at her, giving her a view of his uninjured profile. It was a fine profile. She didn't want to think about why the sight of his handsome brow and strong nose made her stomach clench pleasurably.

'You should rest before moving on.'

'I'll be fine. I'd be in your debt if you could tell me where I am.'

How could such a strong warrior not know where he was? The idea was baffling. 'The stream leads to the River Tyne, a few leagues down the way, I assume. We are near my village, Heiraford.' She'd never been further than the few miles it took to reach Lord Oswine's manor and the occasional visit to the abbey. The Danish settlement was just south of that, where the Tyne forked with another river, but she wasn't sure it was necessary to mention that to the stranger, as he'd been headed north. When the man only nodded his thanks, she continued, 'Did that Dane harm you? You're badly injured.'

But he ignored her question and swayed a bit when he turned forward, his feet slipping on the rocks. Fearing that he'd fall and injure himself even worse, she pushed her sword into its short scabbard at her waist and ran forward to his side, slipping an arm around his lower back. The muscle there was solid and dense.

'When did you last eat?'

He exhaled roughly. A laugh? 'I'm uncertain,' he admitted. 'I awoke two evenings past after having been injured. I can only assume I ate that day.'

'And you have no memory of that man? No idea why he would want you dead?'

He gave her a wry grin, flashing white teeth. 'One would think I'd remember the brute, but there's nothing familiar about him.'

She took a deep breath and pondered for a moment the wisdom of inviting him into her home. He was injured and he *had* saved her. But everyone had been wary of strangers since the attacks had begun. Helping him was the right thing to do—he clearly needed it—but the village elders wouldn't agree. She couldn't afford to stir up any trouble with them.

Nay, it was best to do what was right. 'Come with me. You saved me. A meal is the least I can do.'

Before she realised what he meant to do, his hand came up so that his fingers very lightly touched her jaw. A pleasurable heat prickled through her from the simple touch. 'I refuse to put you in further danger, fair one.'

So unexpectedly pleasant was the touch that she moved her head away just enough to break contact. But she couldn't look away from his eyes. They were a rich brown with tiny flecks of gold in their depths. It took her a moment to gather her words. 'I won't be in danger. My home and village are just through the trees there. We have warriors for protection.' Nodding back towards the m   on the ground, she said, 'The rebel Danes have been plaguing us for months. Thank you for making it one less.'

He seemed so hesitant to accept that she took the choice from him and affixed herself to his side again, her arm going back around his back. 'At least stay for a meal and a bit of rest. You need your strength.' If it were only a meal, she could bring it to him outside the gates and then he could be gone before Wulfric and the other elders even found out about him. That would make things simpler. No explaining why a strange man who could possibly be an enemy was in her home. No worrying that Wulfric would use him as an excuse to take her home from her.

'Aye, I could use a meal. Many thanks, fair one.' He put his arm around her shoulders, tucking her against his side.

They made a strange pair as they walked slowly towards her village. Aisly sent up a silent prayer that she wasn't making a huge mistake.

Chapter Three

Magnus.

As he put his arm around the woman at his side, the name pounded through his skull. It didn't fit any more now than it had the first time he'd heard it, but he was becoming more certain that it was his name. There would be no reason for his captor to lie about it, particularly when he'd had no notion that his memories were addled. A twinge of guilt threatened to plague him at his lie, but he put it out of his mind. There was no need to reveal his name to the woman when he had no idea where he was or even who he was. Instinct told him to reveal nothing for his own safety, at least until he was sure these people weren't enemies.

He was certain the head wound had festered and he was fevered. His choice was simple. Either die slowly over the next several days or risk her village. At least if he risked her village, he would stand a chance. And if he died, he would die with the fair maiden at his side. He glanced down at the woman, his gaze catching on the way she caught her plump bottom lip between her teeth as she helped him navigate a small incline. His arm tightened around her, tucking her soft, well-formed body closer to his side.

Once they were safely up the hill, his gaze travelled the curve of her cheekbone to her eyes. Long, dark golden lashes framed the light green gems. She felt his gaze on her and glanced up just to blush and look away. He continued his perusal, across the light sprinkling of flecks of colour that swept across her face from cheekbone to cheekbone, finally stopping to admire the little bit of reddish hair he could see shining from beneath her headrail. She was lovely.

The vivid, mossy green of her eyes met his again and this time she didn't look away immediately. They were kind and gentle as they swept over his face before she dragged them away. He had to force himself to turn his attention to the trees around them, needing to stay vigilant.

It bothered him how hard he had to turn the words over in his head before he found the ones he wanted to say. Her language was certainly not his native one. 'How far is your village?' They had moved further into the forest, away from the stream.

'It's a bit of a walk. We'll stop frequently if you need to rest,' she hurried to reassure him.

Stifling his laugh, Magnus shook his head but stopped when it made his head ache. The woman had no qualms about wounding his pride. 'I can make the walk, fair one. I merely wondered why you'd be alone so far from safety.'

'I'm hardly alone. I brought my sword.'

He didn't want to say how the sword hadn't saved her from the Dane.

'You think I couldn't have handled him.' It wasn't a question.

'I think he was more than twice your size. Do you have no man to protect you?'

The question made her step falter, but then she continued onward without looking at him. 'Nay, I do not need a man.' Her jaw clenched as she stared ahead.

What would make a woman so young think she didn't want a man in her life? The question was interesting, but he didn't press her further. Instead, he focused on putting one foot in front of the other without falling, his gaze scanning the forest for any sign of warriors. They walked in silence for a while, her softness fitting so naturally against him that he allowed himself to relish it. Apparently it had been a while since he'd enjoyed the nearness of a woman. Finally she stiffened beneath his arm, becoming more alert, meaning they must be getting close to the village.

Pulling away from her earned him a puzzled frown, but he wouldn't let anyone else know the true extent of his injuries. He couldn't count on anyone to keep him safe, though he believed the woman would try. He trusted her.

'Your village?' he asked, spotting a break in the trees far ahead. A wall made of earth and wood rose up tall on the far side of a clearing. The thought that it was easily scalable teased the edges of his mind. His memory might be gone, but his warrior instincts were intact.

The straw of a thatched roof could be seen just above the edge of the wall. It would make an excellent target for an archer with an arrow dipped in pitch. Trying to be mindful of his head wound, he turned his head left, then right to look for the sentries who must have seen them by now and saw no one. Though the movement caused black spots to dance before his vision, making him stumble with the next step, almost toppling the poor woman beneath him.

She stifled a cry of surprise and he did his best to land on his other side, jarring his bruised ribs and grimacing as his head roiled with pain. It was a moment before the roaring in his ears died down and he could hear her speaking to him. It was a moment more before he could concentrate enough on her strange words to make sense of them. The grey at the edges of his vision cleared enough that he could see her lovely face as she stared down at him, her brow furrowed in concern.

'Please don't die. Please don't die. Please don't die.' She spoke the words like a mantra.

He couldn't say why she reduced him to a grinning fool, but the smile spread across his face just the same. It was as if now that he was so close to death, the complexities of life had ceased to matter. Somehow his hand found its way to her cheek. He saw his thumb caressing her cheekbone before he actually felt the sensation of her silken skin. 'I'll not die. Not yet.'

Her smile was mesmerising in its beauty. He wondered if he'd found a nymph intent on leading him to his death, but he admitted that he'd happily follow her. He'd already followed her this far into the unknown.

'That's my village.' She nodded towards the wall, though her gaze never broke with his. 'It's only a little further.'

'I'll stay here. If there are others after me, I won't lead them to you in the village. It's not safe.'

She frowned. 'We'll be safer inside the walls.'

Shaking his head, he grimaced at the inevitable pain and stilled. 'It's close to the stream. There are no fortifications. Nothing stands between you and danger.'

'There is a wall.' She frowned. 'We're not that close to the stream and there are men always posted on lookout.'

'It's too low—that wall is no match for determined warriors. If there are sentries, they should have seen us already.'

She chewed her bottom lip and gave him a searching glance. She was wondering how he'd know that and he couldn't blame her. The need to run niggled at the edge of his mind, but it failed to give strength to his body and clarity to his vision. There was no help for it. He was at the mercy of her warriors, which was why he wouldn't go inside the walls.

'We've only approached through the back way and I know where they hide, so I avoided them.' He glanced at her face at that admission and she gave him a shy smile. 'I thought it might be best if others don't know of your presence right away.'

'Am I in danger from them? A danger to you?'

'I vow no one will harm you while you're in my home.' Their eyes met and held and Aisly had to struggle to take a breath. Something about this stranger affected her more than it should. She didn't know him at all, but she felt safe inviting him into her home. The danger in that would come from the elders, not the man himself.

He broke the stare, looking back towards the wall of her village. 'I believe you, fair one. It's not my intention to make things difficult for you, but it's best I stay outside. I'll be on my way after the meal you've offered. If you could just bring it out, I'd be grateful.'

She ignored the casual endearment and the fact that she liked it. 'My name is Aisly. And I fear you won't be going anywhere for a while in your condition.' Whether he realised it or not, his wound was grievous. She was amazed that he'd made it two whole days without falling into the deep sleep that could sometimes claim people after such an injury. That sleep usually led to death and it would happen to him soon if she couldn't figure out how to get nourishment into him quickly. Even that might not be enough. If only the warriors would see things her way and allow her to care for him before they tried to determine if he was a threat to the village.

'I just need a short rest. I'll recover quickly.' He grinned at her.

Typical warrior, refusing to admit to his weakness even when it was to his detriment. Even through the layers of his tunic and undershirt, the heat from his body had been unnatural and a touch to his temple confirmed her fears. He was feverish and wouldn't last more than another day on his own, and that was if more of those rebel Danes weren't after him.

'You need sleep and a meal. Stay here. I'll go and get you some food and a dressing for your wound.'

He agreed and reached for the sword strapped to his back. When his face twisted in pain, she reached around to unfasten the scabbard so that he could lie back. He smiled at her again as he sat back against a tree trunk and held the sword tight to his chest with both hands. The way he looked at her, so intense, so admiring, made something flutter deep in her belly.

'Many thanks, fair one.'

She opened her mouth to remind him again that her name was Aisly but decided to let it pass. Rising to her feet, she gave him one last lingering glance. 'Please stay here. Don't try to go.'

'You have my vow.' His eyes were already half-lidded,

making her wonder if that deep sleep would claim him before she could get back to him.

Turning abruptly, she hurried through the woods so that she could approach the gate from the front. It wouldn't do to have anyone wondering why she was meandering around behind the village, just in case someone got suspicious. She'd tell them about the stranger later, after she had done the minimum to help him.

Pausing a moment at the tree line, she smoothed a hand down her headrail and then her skirt to make sure she didn't look as harried as she felt. A quick glance at the sun confirmed it was nearing midday. A glance to the left showed movement in the fields. Men and women would still be there for a bit, so it'd be less likely for anyone to question her coming and going. Taking a breath, she took off at a sedate pace across the field towards the open gates. A warrior leaned back against one of the doors that had been blackened from a skirmish with the rebel Danes. He'd been one of the men who had served under Godric but hadn't been at the settlement that deadly day just over two months ago. She gave him a smile and he nodded before turning back to the warrior at his side.

No one was loitering about just inside the shadow of the walls. The autumn harvest required almost everyone to work, which was a great help to her just then. She breathed easier as she skirted around behind the row of small houses that lined the wall. In the small spaces separating each one, she could see Cuthbert's hall in the centre of the village. Though most of the warriors were helping in the fields, some of the warriors were sparring. They wouldn't bother her, but she didn't want to chance drawing their notice, either, so she stayed mostly hidden until she made her way past the hall and the expanse of land around it.

The blacksmith's shop was also in the centre of the village; the constant fire meant it needed to be away from the wall. Once she passed it, she was sure the stone forge would help hide her from view of the hall, so she moved back on to the path. She was just in time to see the tow-headed curls of her best apprentice, Bryn, disappearing around a corner. Squeals of children's laughter followed. It seemed her apprentices had run off, but she was glad of it for once.

Now that she was close to home and didn't feel like such an interloper, she hurried her pace. Her home was one of the larger houses situated in the western section of the village. Her plot of land was large enough for a small garden, the corral for the few sheep she kept and the structure that held her wool. The thought of it empty now still made her angry. The Danes had come close to ruining all hope of her gaining her independence.

But there was still a sliver of hope. If nothing else, she could ask Lord Oswine for help. There was always hope.

Hurrying inside, she found her home empty. The girls had finished the pieces they had been embroidering and left them neatly folded on the table in front. Resolving to check their work later, she rushed past the hearth in the centre of the house and placed the pack with the plants on the table where she prepared her meals to be dealt with later. The day was turning unseasonably warm, but the plaster walls still held in the cold of the previous night, so she added two pieces of wood to the fire. Then she filled a large bowl with stew simmering in the pot over the fire and placed it inside the basket she used in the garden. She covered it with another bowl to help contain any spills and grabbed a long length of linen, before grabbing her flagon of water and adding it to the basket.

The entire walk back to the stranger, she said prayers that she would find him alive. People were starting to trickle in from the fields, but she kept her gaze averted in the hopes that none of them would offer more than a greeting. The warriors at the gate were so accustomed to her coming and going that they barely gave her a glance. She still waited until she crossed the field and reached the forest before turning in the stranger's direction.

She walked as fast as she could without sloshing the stew all over the basket. When she finally saw his form in much the same position as she'd left him propped beneath a fir, she sent up a prayer of thanks. He wasn't asleep as she'd anticipated and he hadn't left. He was watching her through slitted eyes, a faint smile on his lips despite his pallor. He looked horrible. A fine sheen of sweat now dotted his forehead and his skin seemed even paler than before. But, somehow, he was still striking.

Sinking to her knees beside him, she opened her basket. 'I've brought some food.'

His eyes widened as she lifted out the bowl and his nostrils flared as he caught the scent. 'The gods have sent you to save me.' The soft smile lingered on his lips.

Gods? She'd heard the Northmen believed in gods. Her heart pounded, but she didn't comment on it as she brought the bowl to his mouth for him to drink. It wasn't until he'd taken a fair amount and leaned his head back to take a breath that she asked, 'What do you know of gods?'

He shook his head, wincing and stopping, because he'd forgotten the pain it caused. 'I don't know. I don't know of any gods. I spoke before I thought.'

He seemed genuinely unaware. Keeping her hands on

the outside of his, she guided the bowl back to his mouth so he could drink down a bit more. She used the opportunity to get a closer look at the ugly gash on his head. It had definitely festered and was pink and swollen at the edges. It should have been sewn up, but it was probably too late for that now.

'I've brought some linen and water to clean your wound, but it needs a poultice.'

He pulled back after taking a healthy drink. 'I told you, I'll not stay.'

She bit the inside of her lip to keep from pointing out that he didn't have much of a choice. She'd wager he wouldn't be able to make it more than a handful of steps. 'Then I should at least attempt to clean the grime from your wound before you go.'

His deep brown gaze caught hers again, warming her. 'Aye, I'd be grateful.' Then he brought the bowl back to his lips and his eyes never wavered from hers.

When a delightful shiver ran through her, she broke his stare to take out the linen and rip it in half. Retrieving the flagon of water from the basket, she pulled out the stopper with a pop and wet a wadded half of cloth. He gave a barely perceptible nod when she raised it in question, so she gently pressed it to his wound. The soft moan deep in his throat tugged at her heart.

She chewed her bottom lip as she gingerly moved the cloth around the edges of the wound, working her way inward as far as she dared to without causing him more pain. Except it was fairly well crusted over and not hurting him was impossible. 'I'm sorry,' she whispered, as she cleaned the area around the wound. Once that was done, she had no choice but to attempt to clean the wound itself. 'This may hurt,' she warned.

He didn't answer, so she chanced a glance down and found his eyes watching her, studying her. Swallowing against an unexpected feeling of breathlessness, she turned her attention back to her task. He didn't so much as grimace when she started to clean the wound in earnest and he didn't look away from her face.

It was a delicate task to clean the grime while making sure it didn't start bleeding again. But after a few minutes she was satisfied that she'd done all that she could. She'd have to see Edyth about a poultice, if she could convince him to agree to come home with her. Discarding the soiled linen, she folded the clean linen and wet it through. The flesh around the eye under his injury was an angry blue and swollen. 'Let's keep this over your eye for a while. I hope the cool water will help the swelling.'

He'd finished the stew and placed the bowl on the brown pine needles that were his pallet. When she put the linen in place, his hand came up to cover hers. She almost gasped at the strange pleasure that skittered up her arm, before pulling her hand away. Her gaze jerked to his and she knew he'd felt it, too. He was studying her with a puzzled look.

'You should at least rest before you move on.'

He nodded, a slight move, but he didn't speak as he continued to watch her. His body was sagging against the tree more now than when she'd first come upon him. His eyelids were heavier and she knew that it would be but moments before sleep overtook him. She only hoped that he'd wake up.

She began to cautiously repack the items in the basket, but when she moved to set it aside, his eyes didn't follow her. 'Stranger,' she called. He found her then, but he seemed to have trouble focusing, blinking several times. 'Rest and I'll keep vigil.'

The command hardly mattered because his large body was already sliding down to the ground. She lurched forward and barely managed to put her hands under him to break his fall, before she gently placed his head on the pine needles.

He took a deep, shaky breath, his brow furrowing a bit before he spoke again. 'You should tell your warriors about the Dane. If there are more of them close behind, you could be in danger.'

Now that he was almost unconscious, she hoped to wait. While she didn't think the men in her village would harm him, she wanted to give him a few hours to rest and regain strength from the nourishment, before bringing that hurdle to them. Did he sense that he wouldn't be waking up soon?

He must have seen her hesitation, because he grabbed her wrist and his eyes opened wider in entreaty. 'Promise you'll tell them.' His words were slightly slurred.

'Aye, I'll tell them.' She nodded and clenched her fist tight.

His chest rose and fell in deep, even breaths and she wondered how long that would hold true. His body was on fire.

Chapter Four

The sun was sinking low on the horizon and the foreigner hadn't shown any signs of waking up. She'd poked, prodded and even talked to him, but he hadn't moved. His breathing had become ragged and slow, which was when she finally convinced herself that he wasn't going to wake up. At least not that day.

Aisly had hoped that after his rest he'd be able to at least walk inside the village with her. She had wanted to get him settled in her home before presenting him to the others. That wasn't going to happen, though. Reluctantly she'd left him in the forest and once again had made her way to the village. This time going straight to Cuthbert's hall, where she paused and took a deep breath before going inside.

Bollocks. She'd forgotten that today was the day the council met.

The sight of her father-in-law, Wulfric, standing at the end of the long room sent a shiver down her spine and stopped her just inside the door. He wore a brown tunic cinched with a hide belt just below his protruding belly. His dark beard, shot through with silver, was parted in the middle and hung down to his chest. The hair above his lip was shaved, making it that much easier to see the flash of his teeth as he sneered at the young man on his knees before him. Others sat on benches clustered near them in the far end of the room, but every eye was on Wulfric and his victim.

'Did you not swear an oath on your twelfth year to uphold the laws of this land?' His voice seemed to bounce off the walls, easily filling the room.

She barely heard the young man's softer 'aye'. But something familiar about its cadence caught her ear. Looking closer, she saw that it belonged to Beorn, a man who lived in a cottage near her own. He wasn't a warrior, but a hard-working field worker who'd only just managed to gather the coin needed to marry his sweetheart a few months ago.

'Thievery is against the law of this land. I am told you stole a sheep. The wool was found in your home. Your wife...'

With this he gestured, and Aisly realised that the woman she had come to call a friend stood off to the side, silently sobbing.

'She was there in the home with the wool. It's obvious she knew—'

At this Beorn interrupted. 'Nay, she knew nothing. I never told her where it came from.'

'And yet she never suspected, never questioned.' The sneer never left Wulfric's face. The man seemed to get pleasure from tormenting those beneath him. Godric had often behaved the same.

'She had no reason to suspect. I'd never told her about my debts.'

Aisly chewed lightly on her bottom lip and clenched

her arms against her stomach. Rowena had only recently learned that she was with child. What would happen to them? Aisly knew that the young man's debt had been to Godric. She didn't know the specifics, because Godric had never told her, but she suspected it had to do with her late husband's proclivity for games of chance. That meant that the man's debts had fallen to her and she hadn't called them due. She'd wanted to when the Danes had taken all her coin, but she knew that the couple didn't have the ability to pay.

Searching amongst the men for Cuthbert, their chief's familiar shock of white hair, or his brother Arte's rotund body, she didn't find them. Wulfric hardly ever met to address grievances without them present, but it wasn't unheard of. Her father-in-law was the one the villagers all came to for their disputes.

Wulfric flicked his hand as if the man's words meant nothing. 'It matters not. She is your kin and as such will suffer along with you. I've no doubt that your thieving tendencies have infected her. You'll be taken to Lord Oswine with a recommendation to be relocated—'

'Wait!' Aisly heard her own voice call out before she could stop herself. All heads turned towards her and the brief reaction she'd entertained of running out the door fled. It didn't stop her cowardly rabbit heart from beating like that of a cornered animal.

Wulfric clenched his jaw and she had no doubt that vein in his temple that she was so well acquainted with throbbed as he set his eyes on her. She swallowed against the sudden dryness of her mouth and moved forward a few steps.

'I— Is that necessary, Wulfric? I never called the debt

due. Can't the wool be returned to its owner and this all forgotten?'

'It wasn't your debt to call, my dear.' The momentary shock that had crossed his face at her daring to interrupt was gone, replaced by a sneer.

'It was owed to Godric, so it's now mine.' Her voice grew stronger and she tightened her fists at her sides.

'Not everything that was my son's is yours.' A distinct thread of bitterness laced his words. 'I was listed on the debt, it reverted to me. I called it due.'

'They are indebted to you, yet you are the one with the power to level punishment on them for the debt?' It seemed an unfair advantage.

'Aye. I have that power. Is there something you are trying to say, Aisly?'

She sucked in a deep breath while her heart tried to beat its way from her chest. Wulfric had made it clear from the very first that he didn't approve of his son's marriage to a mere servant. He'd also made it known to others that he didn't want her to stay in his son's home. Now wasn't the time to provoke him, but there was something blatantly unfair about what was happening before her.

'Nay, Wulfric. I am only asking for you to be merciful. His wife is with child and I've never heard of either of them stealing. Perhaps it was one instance of poor judgement. If they return the wool, then nothing has been lost.'

Wulfric gave a short bark of laughter. 'The sheep is still gone. It's not only wool they took. And even if it were returned, the theft happened. It won't erase the crime or the need for the punishment. Actions done, Aisly, cannot be undone.' He gave her a vicious look that made her think those words were somehow meant for her and a chill crept down her spine. Then he dismissed her with a glance and turned his attention to the man kneeling before him.

'Perhaps I could pay the debt,' she insisted. 'How much is due? As I recall, it's fairly low.'

The amount he stated was so absurdly high she wondered if he'd made it up. She wouldn't have had that much coin had the Danes from the settlement not raided her coffers. Correctly assuming she couldn't pay, Wulfric turned his attention back to the man kneeling before him. He raised his hands high and wide as he made a show of it, delighting in the audience.

Aisly searched the room again for someone to help, but it was a fruitless search. No one save Cuthbert or Arte would dare to oppose him. Turning on her heel, she hurried from the room. The foreigner needed help and Cuthbert was the only one she'd trust to see to him. She'd also mention Beorn's dilemma. The older man was kind and fair, where Wulfric was cold and deceitful. Perhaps he'd intervene. She rushed back out to the gates and almost ran into Cuthbert as he made his way towards the village from the fields.

'We'll take him to my hall. I'll have Edyth look him over.' Cuthbert stared down at the fallen warrior as if he was afraid to touch him. Two of his warriors had come with them back to the tree where she'd left the foreigner, but judging from the disparity in their size and the fact that the stranger would be a dead weight, she didn't think they'd be enough to carry him inside.

As their chieftain, she'd always found Cuthbert to be wise and just, but she didn't trust the others. The thought of leaving her foreigner at the mercy of the warriors who slept in Cuthbert's hall made her stomach turn. 'I'd prefer to take care of him myself.' She kept her voice strong and full of confidence, though a quiver of doubt moved through her. The foreigner was big. A glance confirmed that his thigh, clearly bulging against the confines of his trouser leg, was as large as both of hers put together. He'd easily overpower her if he so chose.

Cuthbert gave a quick shake of his head. 'We cannot trust this man.'

'Nay, we can't, but I saw him kill that rebel Dane with my own eyes. He's not one of them.' She'd relayed the story to Cuthbert and the warriors as they'd walked back into the forest. Though she'd left out how long she'd sat with him and the strangely gentle way he'd treated her. 'He had plenty of opportunity to harm me if that was his intention.'

'He appears too wounded to try to harm you,' one of the warriors said.

They hadn't seen him. They hadn't seen how easily he'd moved to fight the rebel. If he'd wanted to, he could've killed her as well. There'd been no malice in his eyes, nothing to make her think he would harm her. She was intimately familiar with that look. The first time she'd seen it was two months after marrying Godric. She'd been busy with a commission and hadn't noticed how late the day had become. He'd come home with a friend expecting to find roasted meat, only to get pottage. He'd not struck her…not that time…but the desire had been there in his eyes.

'He'll need constant care and rest. The hall isn't the appropriate environment for that.' The warriors distrusted all foreigners and the simple truth was she didn't trust his care to them. For some reason, she felt a sense of ownership where he was concerned. Perhaps it was because she'd found him, or that he'd saved her. She really didn't want to examine it too closely.

Cuthbert cut a glance at her before staring back down at the warrior. 'I'd have to leave a warrior to guard you. I can't spare the men, not after the massacre.' It had been mere weeks since the confrontation that had killed Godric and his warriors, but a retaliation was always a possibility.

'But we need him to recover. That's a mercenary's tunic. He could prove useful.' Aisly was grasping at anything to make him important to them, though she wasn't sure why that was so important to her. She hadn't even known this man when she awakened that morning. But he *had* saved her life.

The warrior who had spoken before leaned down to examine the embroidered figure on the stranger's tunic. 'Aye, it's a mercenary tunic. But it's possible he's a Dane. He has their look.'

'We'll need to question him,' Cuthbert said. 'The fact remains that he killed the rebel Dane, so he very well could be useful to us. Dane or not, if we could buy his loyalty, he'll prove useful.'

Aisly didn't bother pointing out again that the man hadn't any memories. She'd already mentioned it more than once. Perhaps they'd return once he awakened. 'Whoever he turns out to be, he needs rest and I'm in no danger.'

'Nay, not yet, but when he awakens, he could have his strength back,' Cuthbert argued.

She couldn't argue that. 'Then leave him with me bound. He's already injured. If he's bound as well, what harm could he be?'

Cuthbert gave a deep sigh, but he relented. Aisly imagined that he didn't want a wounded warrior lurking around his hall anyway.

* * *

He huddled back into the limbs of the fir tree, hiding himself from the buffeting wind coming in across the water and the people stirring in the small village below. Drawing his knees up to his chest, he wrapped his thin right arm around them and tried not to shiver too hard. His left arm he kept cradled against his ribs. It was the only way he'd found to ease the near constant pain in them.

A jolt of terror bolted through him when the door to the small house opened and a man stepped outside. He despised that cowardly emotion, so he forced himself to watch the man walk down to the dock where his boat was moored, not looking away once. It wasn't until the man pushed away from the dock that Magnus breathed a sigh of relief. Only when the boat disappeared did he take his first step out of the forest in a sennight and make his way down the slope to the edge of the village. The pain on his left side tried to slow him, but he ignored it. There was no telling how long he had, so he must make the most of it.

Still...he hesitated when he reached the door of the house, afraid of what he might find inside. His small hand was shaking when he reached out to push the door open and his heart was pounding in his ears.

Magnus awoke abruptly to the sound of muffled voices. The strange dream along with his pain had kept him from finding a peaceful sleep. He was certain it must be a memory from his childhood, but on his life he couldn't figure it out. As soon as he opened his eyes, it began to dissipate.

It took his eyes a moment to adjust to the low light in the room. A fire flickered somewhere near his feet, but pain throbbed through his temple if he attempted to look at it, so he kept his eyes looking forward. A few moments later he realised that he was looking upward, staring at the underside of a thatched roof. A tapestry hung to his left, separating the area where he slept from the rest of the house. Just past his feet, a hearth glowed with a low burning fire and on the other side of that hearth was a crudely built table pushed up against the wall with cooking implements on top of it. The voices from the front of the house had stopped, but he could hear shuffling sounds.

Before he could even begin to fathom where he was or who could be with him, he became aware of an aching pain in his shoulders. It wasn't the ache of his ribs, which had been hurt in that mysterious battle, but a new ache. A throb that sent pinpricks of pain through his arms when he tried to move them. When they wouldn't move, he looked over to see that his wrists were tied to an unfinished, rudimentary headboard. A wave of panic chilled him to the bone and he pulled in earnest, only to realise that his ankles were somehow tied to the foot of the bed. Anxiety tightened in his body and made his heart pound.

His body twisted and heaved as he tried to jerk himself free, no doubt drawing the attention of his captor, but he didn't care. He needed to get free.

'Foreigner?'

He turned his head at the sound of her voice and just the sight of her was enough to soothe him. It was her. The side of his body where he'd pressed her against him as he walked warmed at the memory. She wore a different dress, this one a green that made him think of her eyes, with a wide apron tied double around her waist. Standing with her arms slightly raised in front of her as if she was afraid she would scare him, she spoke again, but the words were a rush that he couldn't distinguish.

He opened his mouth to demand an explanation for the restraints, but the words wouldn't come right away. Finally, after turning them over a few times, he asked, 'Why am I bound?' He had a suspicion that the words didn't sound as harsh as he intended them, though, because she smiled at him and he couldn't hold on to even a shred of anger when she did that.

'They wouldn't allow you to stay here without restraints. I'm sorry.' She walked closer and kneeled down beside the low bed. 'How are you feeling?'

'Let me go.' He made sure his voice was firm. She flinched back and he regretted it immediately. He tried again, this time keeping his voice even. 'You know I won't hurt you, fair one. Untie me so that I can leave.'

'I know. I don't think you'll hurt me. But it was a condition of them allowing you to stay here.' Her brow furrowed as she leaned forward, her small hands resting on the bed beside him.

'Them?' It was a pointless question. Obviously he was in her village and the leaders didn't trust a stranger, a foreigner as she'd called him. The fact that he was even alive and hadn't been run through beneath the fir where he'd fallen was a testament to their feelings. Though it was possible they were only waiting to verify his identity before taking that step.

'The elders. Cuthbert is our chieftain. After you fell asleep, I couldn't wake you and worried that you wouldn't wake at all. I had no choice but to tell him that I'd found you. He came and a few others carried you here.' Magnus couldn't take his eyes from her face as she spoke. She was so vivid, so vibrant, so alive, that he only wanted to watch her, causing his concentration on her words to falter. It took all the determination he could muster to focus again and make sense of what she said. 'They wanted to take you to the hall, but I didn't think that would be the best place for you. I wanted to watch over you myself, so I asked them to bring you here. They did, but only on the condition that I keep you tied down. I only meant to tie your arms, but you were thrashing in your sleep and I was afraid you'd hurt yourself, so I tied your ankles.'

Confusion must have shown on his face, because she gave him a shy smile and blushed. 'My apologies. I ramble on and on sometimes.'

Blotches of pink swept across her cheeks, drawing his attention to the bit of hair tucked beneath her headrail at her temple. Streaks of russet, or perhaps a darker red, were visible in the low firelight. He wanted to push the atrocity from her head and see it all for himself. An enticing thought that had no right to exist. Pulling himself away from her allure, he shifted and almost grimaced at the pain sparking through his arms from the unnatural position. It had nearly begun to match the throbbing in his skull.

'How is your head?' She reached up towards his temple, her fingers pressing lightly against the edges of a poultice and following the line of a strip of linen that held it in place around his head. Satisfied the binding was tight enough, she pressed her palm to his uninjured temple.

'It aches,' he admitted.

'I've a draught for you if you'd like to drink it. Edyth, the healer who made your poultice, said it's to help with the ache.'

He nodded, a brief move because he was loath to do anything that would make her stop touching him. Her soft palm stroked back through his hair and he had to fight the urge to close his eyes in pleasure. 'You awoke in a sweat last night. I think your fever left. You only feel slightly warm now.'

The words of her unfamiliar language were coming back to him now, but it hardly mattered. He'd listen to her soft voice with its hint of a husky rasp for as long as she wanted to speak to him, whether he understood her words or not. 'Thank you. You saved my life.' Though the villagers might yet see to his death.

'*You* saved *me*.' Their eyes met and the moment stopped. All he could hear was her breath, all he could see was her face and all he could feel were her fingertips as they slid down his face and across his jaw.

'I put your life in danger and for that I apologise. How can I repay you for your care?'

She smiled, the corners of her eyes crinkling and her cheeks turning pink again, as she dropped her hand back to the bed. 'I think you have more recovering to do yet before we should speak of such things.' She didn't step back and her close proximity was starting to affect him. The heat from her body warmed his and her scent filled his breath as he drew it in. She smelled fresh and somehow sweet like flowers. It was a vaguely familiar scent, but his memories were too tangled and confused to draw each of them out separately for examination. Just attempting to extract one from the others caused them all to tumble into a tangled ball of impenetrable threads.

'I shouldn't linger.' No matter how he might want to spend more time with her. He didn't once consider that he might not convince her to untie him. Then he realised what she'd said and the implications of the fact that she'd changed her clothes. 'How long have I been here?'

'Just a night. You arrived yesterday and it's late morning now.'

Almost an entire day and night. Too long. He'd been too weak to hide their tracks. The Danes could follow him straight to her house if they wanted. 'Then I've stayed too long.'

'Nay, you must not leave yet. You're still not well. Your fever may well return and you shouldn't be out there alone.'

Despite his intention to leave her at the first opportunity that presented itself, tenderness for her tugged deep within him. Who was this stranger to stir him the way she did? 'Don't fear for me, fair one. I'm stronger, thanks to you.' He'd touched her the day before. He vividly remembered touching her cheek, the softness of her skin almost like silk beneath his fingertips. A light smattering of freckles swept across her nose and cheekbones and he found himself wanting to trace over them.

Her lips parted, drawing his gaze to them as she took a deep breath. 'You need food and more rest.'

'I'll gladly have more food. Thank you. But I want you to release me.' He gave a tug on his bonds for emphasis.

Her green eyes widened. 'I cannot. If it were up to me, I would. I know you're not a danger, but I can't betray Cuthbert's order.'

Something about that statement resonated with him. Perhaps it was the unwillingness to betray trust, or the structure inherent in an order. Whatever it was, it was familiar in a way that left him little doubt that he'd known them both in his past. He was a warrior, of that he was certain.

'I'll get your food.'

He had little choice but to watch as she moved back and walked past the hearth. As she retrieved a bowl from the table and filled it from the pot bubbling over the fire, he allowed his gaze to wander around her home. The tapestry next to him cut off most of the view, but his eyes had adjusted enough now that some of the front part of the room was visible to him. The side he could see was lined with baskets of various sizes filled with cloth and thread. A table and stools were there, too, currently littered with needles and frames for holding cloth.

'You are a weaver?'

'An embroideress, but I do some weaving as well.' She smiled back at him and pride shone in her eyes. 'I have three apprentices now. Well, two. One is still very young and she only comes in the mornings to help tend my garden.'

'Do you have no servants?'

She shook her head. 'I had one once. She helped with the garden and household chores so that I had more time for work. But after my husband's death, I couldn't afford to keep her.'

Her husband was dead. It was an awful thing, but he couldn't find the grief that revelation should have caused. Quite the opposite, actually. Exhilaration cut through his physical pain and he knew a moment of complete desire for possession. He wanted her for his own.

The feeling was so great that he forced himself to look away and for the first time he was glad that his wrists were bound so that he couldn't act on his nearly uncontrollable urge to touch her. His gaze landed on the blanket folded across his legs. It was faded, its colour negligible and dull, but it was hers. This was her bed. The breadth of his body in the centre of the thin mattress left very little room for her on either side, but it didn't stop his mind from imagining her there, or the way he'd curl around her. The vision was so vivid, the phantom warmth of flesh pressed against his so real, that he knew it was a memory, but the woman's face and body had changed into Aisly's. If he wasn't so certain that she saw him as a stranger, he would've sworn they'd been lovers.

It was a preposterous thought. Of course they'd never been lovers and they'd never be lovers. He should say that he was sorry for the loss of her husband, but it was a bloody lie and he wouldn't lie to her any more than was necessary. So far he'd only lied about his name and he wanted to keep it that way. Instead, he asked, 'Is the tapestry your creation, then?' He tilted his head towards the large tapestry hanging from the ceiling next to him. The embroidery was an intricate floral design of faded pinks, yellows and mossy greens arranged in roundels and arches.

'Aye,' she began without looking up from stirring the pottage, 'my mother started it. You can see how the thread is faded more near the top, but the bottom is mine. It's not as precise as hers. I was learning.'

'It's lovely. You're very skilled.'

She shrugged, but the endearing spots of pink were back to colour her pale cheeks as she stepped away from the hearth. She was very pretty. Just looking at her was mesmerising, but his stomach growled and interrupted the moment. She laughed and he couldn't help but smile and watch her as she moved. Her small frame might have seemed delicate and fragile on some other woman, but not on her. She handled herself confidently, as if she knew just what she was capable of. He wanted to see more of her hair, but he was limited to the little bit around her face that her headscarf revealed to him. It shimmered with copper undertones at her temples.

'Your mother must be proud.'

She frowned, a look of sadness darkening her features. 'I hope she would be.'

He recognised that sadness. Something bitter and hollow swelled within him, some deep longing fated to go unmet. He searched for memories of his own mother, but the effort only caused his head to throb. 'I'm sorry you lost her.'

Giving him a quick but sad smile, she said, 'Both my parents died when I was a child. Eight winters. An ague took them within weeks of the other. I have good memories of her teaching me the skill, but I miss her dreadfully. I miss them both, but mothers are special, aren't they?'

He met her gaze, wanting to comfort her in some way, but unsure how. 'I'm glad you have the tapestry.'

She frowned again and looked over at the bare walls. 'I had more, but they were taken from me. Payment.'

'Payment? For what?'

Shaking her head, she shrugged. 'Payment for something Godric did. It doesn't matter.'

He frowned and opened his mouth to ask more when she continued. 'You should know that a few men went to the stream and found the Dane. They identified him as one in a group of rebels that has been plaguing us since summer.'

'What have the rebels done to plague you?'

'It started small—burned crops, stolen sheep. But at the end of summer two of our young women went missing and the rebel Danes burned our wall. Some say the women were lured away by them, others believe they were murdered, sacrificed in a barbarian ritual. They simply vanished.'

'And what do you think?'

'I don't know. For their sake I hope they found men

to care for them. But it seems unlikely. The Danes are brutes. All of them. The rebels *and* those from the settlement.'

'Do you have no one to appeal to for help? No lord?' It seemed only right that the villagers wouldn't exist on their own in the middle of the wilderness—that they'd have someone to appeal to for help.

'Aye, we have a lord and we did appeal to him. But Lord Oswine wasn't very interested in dealing with any Danes. The Danes at the settlement run the region now. Though the rebels are a separate group and are even supposed enemies of those Danes, I fear there is no safety from any of them. Whatever they want is theirs for the taking. And to complain to them is to invite more trouble.' Her voice and jaw had hardened as she spoke while settling herself on a stool she'd placed next to the bed. She brought a small vial to his lips and he drank the draught down, though his stomach tried to rebel against the bitter liquid.

Once the nausea passed, he tried to place the name, but Oswine was not familiar to him. Not that he'd expected it to be, not when his own name was still an enigma. 'Your lord has not challenged the Danes?' The frustration clouded his mind, but he pushed back the darkness and focused on the bowl before him as she raised a spoonful of stew to his mouth. He felt like a child, but the fact that it was she who wielded the spoon somehow eased the shame of being spoon-fed.

'The Danes at the settlement control him now. He won't do anything to disrupt their hold.'

Finishing that bite, he asked, 'But these Danes that plague you, are they the same ones controlling Oswine?'

'Nay, not precisely. The man at the stream was one

of the rebels. The rebels broke off from the Danes at some point and answer to no one. The man you killed bore the rebels' markings. But it hardly matters. The Danes at the settlement care little for our problems. One is hardly better than the other,' she said, her voice tight with bitterness.

She wasn't his problem, yet he couldn't help thinking that she shouldn't have been out alone when he'd come across her. Not in peaceful times, but especially not with the threat of the rebel Danes. She was a prize any man would find alluring and, with no man to protect her, they could have easily taken her. The thought of her at the hands of that brute he'd killed made his gut clench.

What could he do about it, though? He had to keep moving, to figure out where he belonged and who he was. He undoubtedly had other responsibilities waiting for him somewhere in the world. The thoughts made his head ache, so he forced himself not to think as she brought another spoonful to his lips. Just as he was taking the bite, there was a brisk knock at the door.

Chapter Five

Aisly almost dropped the bowl when the knock sounded.
A knot of dread churned in her belly as she stood and
placed the bowl on the stool. She was expecting Wulfric's
visit any time now. Since Godric's death, his visits had
alarmed her, but she was especially wary after the way
she had challenged him the day before. Not that her words
had helped. He'd still sent the couple to Lord Oswine.
They'd only been allowed to take the few possessions
they'd been able to carry and, with the full force of winter only weeks away, their exile would almost certainly
mean death, unless Lord Oswine was merciful.

Now it wasn't just herself she worried about, but the
foreigner as well. There was no doubt that Wulfric would
have a say in his fate.

She crossed the room and opened the door to see her
brother, Alstan, alone. A wave of relief threatened to
weaken her knees, but she managed to keep her composure. She was surprised to see him. He lived in a small
house at Lord Oswine's manor and shouldn't have heard
about her guest so soon, unless Cuthbert had sent word
yesterday. Lord Oswine wouldn't have wasted any time

sending one of his most trusted men to investigate, particularly since a rebel Dane had been involved. The look on Alstan's face told her that he was very unhappy with her, though that wasn't really an unusual look for him.

'You've come to see the foreigner, I presume. Come in. He's just breaking his fast.' She stood back and cast a quick glance towards the tapestry as Alstan stepped inside.

Alstan's colouring was very similar to her own, with his green eyes, though his hair was a bit darker, only shining copper in sunlight, and his face was more freckled from his days spent in the sun. He stared down the length of his sharp nose, fitting her with a glare so fierce she felt her back straightening for the inevitable confrontation. Since Godric's death a few weeks ago, he'd become almost domineering.

'Aye. You and I will speak afterwards.'

Aisly clenched her teeth and gave a brisk nod. There was no sense in arguing. He'd say what he wanted whether she agreed or not. Instead of replying, she led him over to her bed, pulling the tapestry back slightly to give them more room to stand by the hearth near the foot of the bed. 'Foreigner, this is my brother, Alstan. He's one of Lord Oswine's men.'

'Who are you?' Alstan's deep voice filled her home with authority.

She stifled the urge to remind him that the man had no memory; certainly Cuthbert had told him that. Her guest was still pale, and though his eye was partially covered with the poultice, the skin there was still very swollen and discoloured.

The foreigner spoke up, delivering nearly the same story to him as he had to her. The same story she'd already relayed to Cuthbert the previous day when he'd been unconscious.

'Aisly tells us you fought the rebel Dane with bravery. Why is it that you chose to fight him when you could have continued on your way?'

'I would never leave a maiden to defend herself,' came his immediate reply.

She couldn't help it. Her gaze was drawn to him with those words and she sucked in a breath as she found him watching her. His single unharmed eye was warm and intense, and an odd tenderness softened her heart. Nay, he'd never leave someone weaker to fend for themselves. She wondered what woman had claim to him. For certain there *was* one out there somewhere waiting for him.

But then Alstan's harsh voice cut through the moment. 'How do you know what you would *never* do? You don't even know who you are.'

'Alstan!'

The foreigner didn't even blink, simply narrowing his eye as he answered, 'I know that I would not leave a helpless innocent to face the wrath of a brute.'

Aisly bristled at the word 'helpless' and opened her mouth to defend herself, when Alstan tightened a warning grip on her elbow. She cut her eyes at him but held her tongue. For now.

The foreigner's gaze darted to that point of contact. His brow furrowed as if it displeased him and she couldn't stop a trembling smile from starting as a pleasing warmth wrapped around her.

'And I am indebted to you for that, foreigner.' Alstan's hard face didn't match his words. He seemed angry, not grateful. 'You saved my sister's life. It is the primary reason you still have yours.'

The foreigner gave a curt nod.

Aisly intervened before her brother could continue his pompous display of power. 'Why would you seek to kill him? He's done nothing to us.'

Alstan continued as if she hadn't spoken. 'The man you killed was one of those renegade Danes. A few of us came across a group of them back in early summer and fought them off. He was one who escaped. Did you not recognise him?'

The foreigner's eyes narrowed again. 'Nay.'

'I thought you might...given how you're a Dane yourself.'

'What?' The word tore from her lips before she could get a handle on herself, and she looked to the foreigner for some sort of denial. None was forthcoming. He lay stoically watching her brother, his jaw tight. Tension crackled in the room.

'It's in the way he says his words. He speaks like one of them. His size,' Alstan explained. 'While I admit my debt to him for keeping you safe, I believe it's dangerous for him to stay here.'

'He is not a Dane!' The very word tasted like ash in her mouth. 'Just look at his tunic, the embroidery is that of a mercenary.' She pointed to the foreigner, who hadn't moved a muscle in reaction.

'Aye, he *wears* the tunic of a mercenary, but that man is a Dane.' Alstan spoke with such certainty that Aisly had to cross her arms over her stomach to keep them from shaking. Her one interaction with the Danes, aside from the rebel at the stream, had been the day after Godric's death when they'd come to collect payment and taken nearly everything that she had. She'd been so angry, so afraid, that she couldn't actually remember what words they'd said, much less how they'd spoken the words. They'd been cold, arrogant, entitled monsters. This man was the complete opposite. He was warm, gentle and kind. He was not a Dane.

'How dare you call him a Dane when you've only spent a few moments in his company? He is a mercenary and—'

'Enough.' Alstan raised his hand for silence, keeping his eyes on the foreigner. 'I'm recommending to Cuthbert that you be allowed to leave today, Dane, and then I'll consider my debt to you repaid.'

'Aye,' said the foreigner, his gaze harder than she'd ever seen it.

'That isn't fair, Alstan. That isn't fair at all. He hasn't recovered. Putting him out now *will* be a death sentence.'

Alstan grabbed her elbow again and pulled her towards the door.

'You're being an ogre, Alstan.' Aisly pulled her arm away once they were outside and near the forest. 'Why did you say he's a Dane? Is it because you want them to throw him out?'

'Because he is.' Her brother turned to face her squarely, with his arms crossed over his chest. 'He speaks just like one of them. I've spoken to them when they came to see about taxes.'

He was referring to the autumn a couple of years ago when the leaders of the Danish settlement had visited with Lord Oswine. The same leaders who had killed Godric. Though her life with her husband hadn't been the happiest, she could not forgive them for butchering him. She crossed her arms over her chest to keep from shuddering. If the foreigner was a Dane, she wouldn't feel such tenderness for him. She despised them all. 'He's not dressed like one of them. He has no bands on his arms. I think you're mistaken. Besides, he saved my life.'

'And that is the only reason I'm not advocating his death. He saved your life and I do owe him for that. He can have his life.'

'But he won't have his life if you force him to leave today. Don't you see that, Alstan? Have mercy. He needs to recover first, at least a little.' He didn't respond, but a flicker of doubt shone in his eyes. 'Do you recognise him?'

He shook his head. 'Nay, but with the swollen face, bandage…' he indicated his own hair '…and his hair so short, I can't say for certain.'

'What is the matter with you?' Alstan's behaviour was so odd, so cold and distant.

'Cuthbert sent a warrior with the message to Lord Oswine's. When I heard him speak your name, I thought he must be lying. You would never bring a strange man into your home. Not my sister, I said.' His eyes flashed with anger.

'He's hardly a strange man. You spoke with Cuthbert. He saved me down by the stream and he's obviously injured. I couldn't repay his kindness by leaving him to die. You would have done the exact same thing had you been me.'

'I wouldn't have been so foolish, had I been you.' Running a hand through his hair, he shook his head. 'Why were you even down by the stream, Aisly? You know what happened to those girls. Don't you think those cowards could take you, too?'

She wanted to be angry at his words, but his eyes were so full of worry that it dampened her temper. Alstan had been thirteen winters when their parents had died and she'd only been eight. Alstan had been old enough to apprentice with Lord Oswine's warriors. Old enough to leave her behind and forget about her, but he hadn't. He'd continued to look after her, often bringing her extra food and clothing in addition to what the lady had provided her. He reminded her so much of their father that in some ways he had become that to her. 'I'm sorry. I was preoccupied and drifted closer to the stream than I should have.'

'Why were you out there alone?'

'I was collecting larkspur.' She motioned towards the house, where she'd planted some in small pots inside. 'I had to go find some before the frost comes and kills them. In spring I hope to use them to dye my own thread. I didn't want to bother you. You're busy enough with the warriors, the harvest, and Hilde and the new baby.'

He took in a deep breath as if he was trying to be patient with her, raking a hand over his reddish beard, before saying, 'I would have made time to go with you.'

'Aye, I know, but I'd need to send word to the manor and wait for you to have time. Days would have passed. But I didn't really need you to come with me. I took the sword with me.' She gave him her best beseeching look. It had worked in the past.

'Aisly, I taught you how to wield a sword just in case you ever needed to defend yourself. I didn't teach you so that you could tempt trouble. I never would have taught you had I known that it would lead to you going off alone.'

His worried eyes be damned, Aisly couldn't hold back her anger any more. 'I'm not helpless. I went off alone because I am perfectly capable of handling myself and I know this forest better than any Dane. Aye, I was preoccupied and strayed too close to the stream. It was one mistake that I won't repeat. Haven't you ever made a mistake?'

He glared down at her for a moment before speaking. 'You are too stubborn for your own good. I can't leave you here alone if I can't trust you to take care of yourself.'

'I am not stubborn. I am perfectly reasonable. You are the stubborn one.' She tried to force a calm to her voice, but she feared it wasn't working with her jaw clenched as tight as it was. 'This is my home. This is where I belong.'

'I won't teach you the sword any more and you're lucky I haven't taken it from you. But I will if you continue to prove to me that I can't trust you with it.'

'You are not my father nor are you my husband, Alstan. You have no right to take anything from me.'

'That is true, but you are still my responsibility. Mine and Wulfric's. I'll go to him if I have to.'

She gasped at the betrayal and pressed a hand to the pain in her chest.

He took a deep breath and looked past her shoulder, as if uncomfortable with what he had to say. 'You should consider moving in with us. Hilde would appreciate the help with the children.'

'But I cannot. I have my embroidery.' Alstan and Hilde had just had their third child and their small home had no room to accommodate the space she needed to continue her business. Just last week she'd had so many pieces of vestments that the entire front of her home had been taken up with it. Besides, how could he think that having a few feet of pallet space to herself could ever compare with having an entire home of her own?

'Nay, you're right, there would be no room for that.

You'd have to reduce your work and take only small commissions from the abbess.'

'But I'd never live on that alone. You're not asking me to move in with you, you're asking me to give up my livelihood. Do you realise that?'

He had the decency to look pained and his voice softened. 'Aye, I do realise, but you living on your own as an embroideress is...' He shook his head. 'It's not done, Aisly. You need a husband and children.' He raised his hand in supplication when she would've argued. 'But if your work means that much to you, then you could consider moving to the abbey. Wulfric has spoken to the abbess and I believe she found favour with the idea.'

The idea of Wulfric so easily trying to do away with her made her stomach clench. 'How dare he speak to her about me. I do not want to be a nun.'

This time he raised both hands in supplication. 'It was merely an idea. On my word, no one will force that on you.'

'I don't understand why it's so difficult to believe that I could support myself. I do good work. People know my work. Just last month, Lord Oswine commissioned a cape for his wife and delivered me golden thread to use. Gold, Alstan! Why must I be married or in a convent before I can do that work?'

'Because you do, Aisly. You need someone to protect you.'

She couldn't bear to look at him any more, to think that he could take Wulfric's side. Shaking her head, she turned away. 'Are you taking Beorn and Rowena back with you when you go?'

'The thieves?' He sounded puzzled. 'Aye.'

'Please make certain Lord Oswine hears them out.

Wulfric was not fair to them. Please watch over them.'
Waiting just long enough for his agreement, she blinked
back tears as she hurried back to her house. No one believed that she could live on her own, but she would never
marry again. Godric had had too much control over her,
over her happiness and her despair. She'd never give up
that power again. It wasn't worth it, not when she possessed skills that would allow her to provide for herself.

'You need to be protected, Aisly,' he called after her.
When she didn't bother to turn back, he called out again,
'Fine. Your foreigner can stay the night, but he'll speak
with Cuthbert in the morning. I'll come back for him
then.'

Magnus listened to the bits and pieces of their exchange that drifted in through the open door of the cottage. The way the man had handled her didn't set well
with him, but he wouldn't intervene unless Aisly was actually threatened. Not that he could with the bloody bind-
ings. He gave another harsh tug that shook the bed and
only managed to send pain shooting through his skull.

Aisly raised her voice. He heard enough to figure out
that her brother was trying to convince her to enter a convent or to marry. It was clear that she was against both
of those suggestions. Magnus closed his eyes and summoned up the image of her standing next to the hearth.
She had a slight but well-formed body made for the touch
of a man. Why would she be so against the idea of a husband? Had her last one been so horrible or was she still
mourning him? He found himself imagining himself in
that role. The idea of having the right to touch her any
time he wanted was appealing. Though it was also wrong,

because he had no idea if he was even free to marry. What if there was someone waiting for him to come home?

The thought made him frown. It didn't seem to fit. He'd remember if he was married. He had to find out where he belonged, but it was foolish to go traipsing about the countryside without knowing who might want him dead. That was the only reason that he was accepting his captivity for now. The black spots that had returned to dance before his vision figured in that decision as well. He was weakened and wouldn't get very far with his injury. As the blackness expanded to take him over, sucking him into its warm depths, he admitted the woman's company contributed to that acceptance.

Chapter Six

Something horrible woke her. Opening her eyes to the semi-darkness, Aisly lay quietly on the pallet trying to figure out what had startled her so abruptly out of her sleep. The fire still blazed, so she knew that she'd only just nodded off. Then it came again. A muffled groan that sounded like someone was in terrible pain.

The foreigner.

Pushing her blanket aside, she rose to her feet and ran around the hearth to kneel beside him. From the light of the fire, she could see that his hair was damp with sweat and he twisted and turned in the bed as if something was torturing him. He'd slept throughout the day and in the evening his fever had returned. His skin hadn't been as hot as the day before, but it had been close. She'd fetched another draught, this time asking Edyth to come and look at him. The older woman had merely clucked her tongue and offered a stern look when Aisly had asked her if he'd recover.

Now, looking at the pallor of his skin and hearing the pain of his moans, she worried that the old woman had been right to be pessimistic. At the time, Edyth's doubt had seemed absurd, because Aisly had seen the fire in his eyes when he'd looked at her earlier in the day. He was a fighter.

Hurrying to the bucket that Alstan had filled with fresh stream water before he'd left, Aisly grabbed a wool cloth and fell back to her knees at his bedside. He was talking now in a foreign tongue she didn't understand. Soaking the cloth and wringing it out just a little, she brought it to his head and let the cool water soothe him.

'Please stay calm.' She kept her voice low so she wouldn't startle him, but loud enough to be heard over his own mumblings. 'I'm here, foreigner. I'm here with you.' The steady reassurances fell from her lips as she replenished the cool water on the cloth, until he finally settled down. He kept talking in that strange tongue, the words so low she had to lean forward to hear them. As she watched his lips form them and listened to the rasp of his voice, she found herself wishing she understood them. While before the words had been strong and almost angry, they were softer now. As if he were talking to someone he cared about.

Her gaze travelled over what she could see of his face in the shadows, his strong nose and fine brow. He was such a striking man that she couldn't imagine he didn't have a woman waiting for him somewhere, or perhaps even a wife. The thought made her envious of that phantom woman, whoever she was.

'Do you find favour with what you see?'

She startled and heat rushed into her cheeks. To have been caught so unaware was one thing, but to have him so accurately guess her thoughts was beyond embarrassing. 'I…I wasn't…' Gawking? Oh, she'd been gawking. 'You woke me with your dreams. You seemed to be in pain.'

He let out a breath, a sigh of disappointment. 'My apologies. I'll be out of your way tomorrow.'

'It's no trouble. Don't leave to spare me difficulty.'

He gave a soft laugh at her jest. They both knew it wasn't his choice.

'It's no trouble that I took your bed and woke you from your sleep? That you haven't even been able to do your work because of me? You tell me that is no trouble and I will call you a liar.'

She hadn't thought he'd noticed that her apprentice hadn't come back after he awoke, or that the others hadn't been allowed to even come to her with his presence in her home. She'd assured their mothers that he was harmless, but she couldn't say that she would have allowed her own child near a strange warrior. Because of his presence she *had* been late on the abbess's commission. She'd had her apprentice Bryn deliver the majority of the order, but the rest had yet to be finished.

'It's only a little trouble, then.' She smiled and pulled the cloth from his head to re-wet it. 'But trouble that I don't mind,' she said, bringing it back to his head. Leaving it there, her hand went to his temple and down his jaw to stop in the hollow of his neck. 'The fever has left you again. You feel cool. This is good. If we're very lucky, it won't come back.

'Rest for a few moments and then we'll need to change your bedding. You've soaked it with your sweat and it won't do for you to stay moist all night.' She moved to the chest near the bed and took out linens and one of Godric's shirts and placed it on top. When she turned her attention back to him, she found him watching her, a curious expression on his face.

'Do you find favour with what you see?' She smiled, turning his words back on him.

'Aye,' came his immediate response. 'Very much so.'

The words so casually spoken took her breath away, and when she met his gaze, she was caught in much the same way she had been earlier in the day.

Then he grinned. 'I wonder if you realise that to change the bedding, you have to release me.'

'Aye.'

'And what of your betrayal to Cuthbert?'

'My first duty is to your health and I had planned to secure your vow that you wouldn't run. Do I have it?'

'Why would I stay?' he challenged.

'Because you wouldn't want to have everyone angry with me,' she countered. 'But if that isn't a good enough reason, what about the fact that they have your sword and you won't stand a chance of getting it back unless you meet with them?'

He groaned, but the humour didn't leave his face. 'You force my hand.'

She'd already released the straps from his ankles as he'd slept earlier. Now she walked over and pulled at the stubborn knots of the binding at his wrists. When she released them, she stood back to allow him to sit up. He groaned as he rotated first one shoulder and then the other to work the sore muscle. She absolutely despised that they'd tied him and hurried to sit on the bed just behind his hip. Her hands went to the shoulder nearest her and she rubbed it, trying to help him get the blood flowing to the appendage again. Then she moved to the other. And, while she felt the firmness of the muscle beneath her hands, she kept imagining what he might look like beneath his shirt and tunic. Would he be scarred?

Would his skin be as bronzed from the sun as that of his face and hands? She tried to make herself stop wondering, but she failed.

Finally he moved his shoulders beneath her hands and didn't seem to be in as much pain as before. She allowed her hands to fall to her lap, but she didn't move away. There was something so comfortable and exciting about simply existing close to him. 'How is your head?'

He turned his head a little, just enough to see her over his shoulder, presenting her with a view of the uninjured side of his face. He was breathtaking. 'A bit better.'

The tight way he held his mouth told her he was still in pain but was too much of a warrior to risk admitting it. 'I've another draught for you, but first let's see if I can help you.'

His brow raised and he gave one brief inclination of his head in agreement.

Climbing on to the bed behind him to rest on her knees, she brought her hands up to the back of his neck and hesitated before touching him. Someone had cut his hair so that it stood up in awkward tufts, leaving his neck bare. Aside from his face and to untie his hands, she hadn't touched his bare skin. She couldn't understand why the prospect was so appealing to her. He was handsome, but she would never have a claim to him, so it shouldn't matter.

Forcing herself to get past the ridiculous hesitation, she gently pinched the tendons at the back of his neck. Alstan got headaches from time to time, so she knew that applying steady pressure there often helped to alleviate his pain. The foreigner hung his head a bit to give her better access. Using her thumbs, she made slow circles up and down the back of his head, sliding under the linen bandage. He groaned, a soft hum deep in his throat. The shock of her reaction to the sound he made, and the fact that her touch had drawn it from him, was enough to make her jerk her hands away. This wasn't proper.

He stiffened immediately and looked over his shoulder at her, giving her another view of his flawless profile. She ached to touch his strong jaw and curled her hands into fists to stop the treacherous impulse. This was so ridiculous. She barely knew this man. She clenched her teeth and made herself remember that he was injured and she was recently widowed and had no right to these thoughts.

'Since you're awake, we should change your poultice again. While we have the wrapping off, I could trim your hair a little. I'm uncertain what happened, but it's a bit uneven…' Her voice trailed off when he didn't answer her right away and just continued to stare at her with that intensity that tightened her skin.

'Aye,' he finally whispered.

The foreigner stood and she genuinely wasn't prepared for how tall he was or how he seemed to fill up so much space in the room. Somehow she'd already forgotten how big he was. She rose from the bed just as he turned to face her. His big hand reached up and touched the long braid of hair that had fallen over her shoulder, making her realise that she'd forgotten all about donning her headrail. This was the first time he'd seen her without it.

His fingers slowly stroked the ends, twisting the braid and watching the soft firelight play off the reddish strands. Tendrils of warmth somehow raced up the braid to her head, making it feel as if his fingers were massaging her scalp. 'Such a lovely colour. I've wanted to see you without the covering.' His voice was a harsh rasp that vibrated over her senses.

She swallowed hard. He wasn't looking at her hair any more. It was as if his gaze reached right down into her and found all of her secret longings and knew what they were. 'C-come sit by the fire and I'll change the poultice.'

He allowed the end of her braid to slip through his fingers before moving slowly around the hearth to the bench on the far side. His face flinched in pain as he dropped his large body down on to the wood. It creaked in protest and she knew a moment of fear that it might break under the strain of his weight. The man was solid muscle.

Hurrying to the table beside him, she spread out strips of linen she had already cut. Turning to him, she gently untied the knot and pulled the wrapping away followed by the poultice, tossing them all into the fire. The herbs in the poultice filled the air with a woodsy scent as they burned. The wound was much better. It wasn't seeping any more.

'It's still very swollen. The skin is puckered. Nay, don't touch it,' she admonished, when he reached up.

Dropping his hand back to his thigh, he looked up at her. 'It's still festered?'

'Aye, but it doesn't look worse. The colour is pink, not as angry as before. You'll have a scar to match your others,' she teased.

'Others?' His brow furrowed and he touched his face as if searching for more.

How strange it must be to not know your own body. Gently taking his right hand, she brought it up between them. 'The two on your sword hand. Look.'

Just over his middle knuckles, there were two raised white lines. Scars left from a blade if she had to guess. 'I should know my own scars,' he whispered.

She kept his large hand in the grasp of her much

smaller one, but her other hand she brought to his jaw, drawing his gaze back to her. 'It will come back to you, foreigner. Have your dreams told you anything? Your name, perhaps?'

'Nay.' His gaze left her as he gave a quick shake of his head, perhaps a little too quickly.

'You remember something. Tell me what you dreamed about earlier.'

Breathing in through his nose, his eyelids fluttered closed for a moment before he said, 'I dreamed of battle. There were men and blood. Death. I cannot remember faces or even names, just screams and violence.'

Her heart clenched for him, for how alone and afraid he must feel. 'It's certain that you are a warrior. I'd wager you've seen many battles. Just give it time. You simply need rest and care. You've come to the right place for both.'

That brought his gaze back to her. It skimmed over her face, pausing at her mouth, touching her with the weight of a butterfly's wings. Before she could be caught in his spell, she took a fresh cloth and, moistening it with water, cleaned around the wound as best as she could, making sure to get all the dried blood in his hair. It wasn't until she'd finished that she realised his hair there was a shade lighter than the dark blond everywhere else. A glance at the cloth confirmed it was nearly black. She'd been too worried about hurting him the first time to clean it so thoroughly.

'You've soot in your hair.'

He was silent for a moment before he took a breath and spoke. 'Aye. There was a fire when I awoke. They'd planned to burn me, so I ran.'

'You were wounded in a battle.' It was a logical conclusion given his dream. At first her heart leapt at the realisation. Alstan or someone might have heard of a battle that had recently taken place and they could help him return to his rightful home. But then she remembered Alstan's horrible accusation. Since her brother believed him to be a Dane, he might use that information to unfairly call for his execution. She'd keep that information to herself for now. There was no possible way that this gentle man was a Dane, a monster.

She tried to imagine the battle. Her hand clenched tight around the cloth as she imagined how afraid he must have been awakening to a fire and how horrifying that sort of death must be. Was the rasp in his voice damage from inhaling the smoke? Thank goodness he'd got away. 'I'll wash the rest. It looks as if someone took a blade to it and it's a bit uneven. I could fix that if you want.'

'Thank you, fair one. I owe you a great deal.'

She didn't speak again as she ran the cloth through his hair, washing out as much of the grime as she could before retrieving a clean cloth and beginning again until his hair was finally clean. It wasn't until she'd finished and was running her fingers through his hair in the dim light to try to find tufts that stuck out longer than others that she realised she'd given herself only another reason to touch him again. Biting her lip so that she'd have a distraction, she pulled the tufts taut and sawed through them with the sharp knife she used for cutting cloth, tossing the bits she pulled away into the ash in the hearth.

When she finished, she set the knife down and ran her fingers through the shorter length to make sure she'd removed all the loose hair. It was thick and felt entirely too soft beneath her palms.

'You've a nice touch,' he said once she'd pulled her hands away.

What did one say to that? She actually looked down at her hands to try to figure out how he could think so. Godric had always sneered at how the first two fingers on each hand, more so the right than the left, were a bit roughened from her embroidery work. She wore a piece of leather tied around each one as she worked to help ward off the needle pricks, but for the fine details she found the leather got in the way and took it off. As a result, the skin at the end of those fingers had thickened into rough calluses. She'd actually been glad to see it happen, because the needle pricks didn't hurt any more, but Godric hadn't liked them. The foreigner must not have felt them.

Instead of replying, she knelt before him to help even out his beard. It had suffered the same sloppy treatment as his hair, so that some parts were longer than others. She'd have to scrape away most of it and let it grow out again if he wanted it even. She tried not to notice how his lips were perfectly formed, the bottom slightly fuller than the top one with its gentle arches. She placed her palm against his jaw on the far side and gently scraped the blade down his cheek. She intentionally didn't get close enough to touch his skin with the metal, because she had none of the cream Godric would use when he shaved. It was enough to simply even out the hair.

But as she finished one side and then the other, she was soon left with the hair around his mouth. He smiled when she paused to take in a deep breath and the movement caught her eye. His teeth were strong and even, pale in the firelight, and his lips formed a bow. Her gaze fixated on his full bottom lip. Despite his injuries, it looked as if he hadn't been hit in the mouth. That lip was smooth and appeared very soft. A vision of her leaning forward and placing her lips on his flashed through her mind. The wicked thought didn't surprise her, nor did the answering tug deep in her belly. Blinking to clear it away, she touched his chin and turned his face towards her so that she could better reach him.

'Nay.' His voice was husky as his hands went to her hips. 'You should move closer.'

She gasped at the contact and stiffened as he shifted his position to open his legs wider. He guided her body between them so that she faced him head-on. For a brief instant, she was uncertain if he'd arranged the position for some more nefarious reason. Except he moved his hands back to rest on his thighs and his expression settled into something bland. And then she wasn't sure if she was simply transferring her own wicked feelings on to him. He'd done nothing to make her think that he returned her desire in any way.

Even knowing that didn't stop her wayward thoughts. Only inches separated them. His thighs on either side of her were so close that just a simple movement would have them around her. Heat moved through her body and, while she told herself it was her simple proximity to his body heat, she knew that it was a result of her own seductive thoughts. She kept noticing how much broader his shoulders seemed from this close and how, if he decided to fold his arms around her and bring her against his chest, her face would fit perfectly into the hollow of his neck.

It didn't help that she could *feel* the heat of his gaze on her face. He couldn't have been unaffected by her. When his gaze swept her lips, her cheekbone, even the exposed curve of her neck, it was like a tangible touch on her skin. This had never happened before, not with Godric. She'd never wanted to be touched, to touch, so badly. A glance pulled his gaze to hers and it was so filled with the heat moving between them that it was pulling her forward to its flame before she even realised she was moving. Parting her lips just a little, she pressed them to his. His lips *were* soft.

But then his hands were on her shoulders and he gently pushed her away. Confused, she opened her eyes and he gave one firm shake of his head. 'We can't.'

In that horrifying moment she realised that she had completely misread his attention. Her face flamed in mortification and she moved to rise, but he wouldn't let go of her shoulders. 'Nay, fair one, don't. I don't know who I am.'

'Oh.' It was the only sound she could force out as her heart sank to her stomach.

'I want to. You're so lovely. But it wouldn't be fair.'

His voice was so gentle and his eyes so soft that she wanted to run and hide herself away. She was truly pathetic. Her husband had only just been killed and the last thing she needed was another man in her life trying to tell her what to do and especially not a foreign, possibly Danish man at that. There wasn't space in her life for a man any more, and there never would be. The way her body was responding to him was nothing but wrong. And yet, for some strange reason, she felt close to this foreigner, closer than she'd felt to anyone in a long time. She was just so lonely. That was why.

'I'm sorry,' she whispered and moved back a bit.

He caught her wrist before she could get far. His eyes were so dark she couldn't see the gold in them any more.

'Never apologise for touching me, fair one.' It wasn't an admonishment, precisely. His voice was warm, gentle, and if she didn't know better—he *was* an injured man— it was textured with longing.

She parted her lips to speak but then had no idea what she meant to say. To deny her longing? To say that she shouldn't want him? Her body tingled in ways that made her press her thighs together just to ease it.

'Are you all right?' His concerned gaze met hers and his fingertips glided across her cheekbone as he brushed back a strand of hair that had fallen from her braid.

She nodded and suppressed the way her body wanted to move into his touch. If living with her husband had taught her anything, it was how to move forward as if everything was fine, as if something ugly hadn't just happened. Taking a deep breath and avoiding looking into his eyes, she said, 'Just a little more and we'll be done. Be still.' She gently touched his bottom lip with the pad of her thumb, ignoring the unwanted thrill that darted through her belly, to help pull the skin tight and then pulled the knife's edge downward. Her hand shook a bit and she ground her molars together to force herself to calm down. The area above his lip was next and then she was finished. Sitting back to look at her work, she forced a lightness into her tone. 'It looks better than it did, but a few weeks of growth will help.'

Picking up the cloth used to wash him, she gently ran it over his beard to collect any whiskers she'd left behind. She made sure to keep her touch perfunctory, because she wanted it to be more so badly that she was afraid it would show in her every movement.

'Thank you for this.'

She forced a tight smile and started to collect the knife, but he covered her hand with his to stop her.

'I mean that, fair one. I was too prideful before, but the truth is that I might be dead had you not taken me in.' His eyes were so deep when they met hers that she caught her breath. 'Thank you. I want to repay you. I need to repay you.'

Somehow her hand had turned over in his so that their palms were pressed together and their fingers were weaving together. She was so careful not to touch him, she was almost certain that she hadn't caused that to happen. Had she? If he hadn't wanted to kiss her, then surely he wouldn't be holding her hand now, would he? She shook her head to clear her confusing thoughts as his thumb traced over her index finger, sending pleasant shivers racing up her arm. 'You saved me, too,' she reminded him.

'I led him to you.' His free hand came up to cup her cheek and she actually gasped aloud at the sensations moving through her. Her entire body came alive, tingling and pulsing all over. 'I will repay you,' he said.

She tried to smile, to pretend that her breasts weren't aching for his touch and that her treacherous body wasn't pulsing at just the thought. He was simply being kind and sincere, and she was making this into something it wasn't. 'You don't have anything to repay me with.'

'Not yet,' he agreed. 'But I will. Soon I'll remember who I am and I'll reward you.'

The conversation was pointless. 'If Alstan has his way, you'll be gone in the morning,' she reminded him.

He didn't even blink before he answered. 'I know where you are, fair one. I'll come back for you.'

His jaw was so firm, his eyes so confident, that she

believed him. Nevertheless, she challenged him. 'They won't let you back through the gate.'

His lips twitched in the beginnings of a smile. 'Neither a gate nor a wall can keep me from you.'

Her foolish heart began to beat faster. She wanted to believe it was fear, but she couldn't lie to herself. It beat with excitement. But then she remembered that he'd just stopped their kiss, so he didn't mean it...not in the way her heart had heard it.

'You don't owe me.' She rose and stepped away, immediately missing the touch of his hand on hers. 'Let's get you changed now.'

Chapter Seven

When she stepped around behind him, Magnus took in a deep breath and clenched his jaw against the need that thundered through his body. That need had been reflected back at him through her eyes, but coloured with a shame and uncertainty that made her appear so bloody vulnerable. He wanted to pull her close, to wrap his body around hers and hold her so tight that her worries disappeared, because she'd know then that he'd defeat the fiends foolish enough to threaten her. An irrational desire, because he'd be leaving tomorrow. He'd meant it when he said that he'd return to reward her, but that would be the end of it. It was almost certain that he had a life somewhere and he had to get back to it.

She wasn't a part of that life, and no matter what happened, she never could be. Thanks to his nightmare… the battle…he knew that he was a warrior. He'd known that even before the dream, but hearing those sounds and smelling death had given that term new meaning. His fate was to fight until he eventually died in battle. She deserved more than that.

Her soft voice pulled him out of his thoughts, though

he missed the first of what she said. 'Meat will help you to regain your strength. I'll get some in the morning.'

There had been no meat in the stew she'd fed him earlier, just grain and vegetables. He didn't remember who he was, but he knew that meat would often be hard to come by, especially for a woman alone. 'You don't have to do that.'

'Let's not argue about this.' She fidgeted at the table behind him, so he half-turned to look at her. She stood with her back to him.

'If you have to purchase meat for me, then I'll only be more in your debt.'

She shrugged one small shoulder. 'Then I'll barter for the meat.'

'That's still my debt,' he said.

She finally turned to look at him, her brow furrowing as she asked, 'Would it be so horrible to be in my debt? I won't demand anything you aren't willing to pay.'

There was very little he wouldn't be willing to give her. The thought surprised him, but he couldn't deny its truth. He started to tell her that, but she charged ahead.

'Let's get you out of the tunic.' She didn't look at him as she poured water from a large pitcher into a fresh pot and then sat it in the fire to warm. 'I've found a shirt that should fit you. I looked through my husband's trousers, but you're quite a bit taller. I hope you don't mind, but while you slept, I altered a pair to fit you.' Standing, she walked to the chest by the bed and held up a pair of trousers she'd left there. 'They're not very attractive, but I think they'll do better than the ones you have. Yours are already breaking at the seams.'

They'd clearly been made from two trousers, with two seams on each leg where they'd been stitched. He glanced down at the ones he was wearing to see that she was right. The mercenary's trousers had been snug in the thigh and at some point the seam had given a bit. Guilt surged tight in his chest. He should tell her that he'd taken the clothing, but he couldn't risk that sort of honesty just yet. Not when he had no idea what the morning could bring.

Instead, he simply murmured his thanks as he tugged at the tunic. When she made a move to help, he brushed her off and pulled it off himself. His shirt quickly followed. His body was covered in the same grime as his hair. The water from his walk in the stream hadn't washed it all way.

She sat the clothing in a neat pile before him, but she stopped short when she turned and saw him, her eyes widening slightly.

'What's the matter?'

She shook her head and a patch of colour brightened her cheeks. He knew then that it was him, his body that had stalled her. A rush of arousal moved through him and he gritted his teeth to fight against the erection trying to make itself known in his trousers.

She looked away quickly, as if she knew the battle that raged within him, and dipped a cloth in the water that had been warmed on the fire. Wringing out the excess water so that the fire hissed and popped, she walked behind him again and smoothed the cloth down his back. He had to stifle the groan of pleasure that threatened to escape him. The thin cloth separated them, yet the decadence of her touch seeped into his skin just the same. He hung his head as she cleaned his back with slow, easy drags of the cloth. His skin prickled with the sensation, as warmth settled low in his gut.

Finished, she drew her hand away and paused. He

could feel it there, hovering above his shoulder. 'Do...
do you want me to—'

'Nay.' He cut her short, half-afraid of how he might
react to any suggestion of her touching him further. 'I
can finish.'

'Of course.' Handing over the cloth to him, she busied
herself with changing the bedding.

He kept an eye on her as she worked, removing the
soiled sheet and grabbing a fresh one. She worked ef-
ficiently, confidence evident in her movements. She
smoothed the linen and he imagined it was his chest her
hand moved over. She folded the blanket and he imagined what it would feel like to pull that blanket over the
both of them. Had her husband been half as intrigued
with her as Magnus was?

He jerked his gaze away when she turned back to him.

'I'll leave you to your privacy for a moment so you
can finish changing.'

She had grabbed the blanket and was out the door before he could reply. Not that he would have said anything
to keep her there. His yearning for her was too unwar-
ranted and bewildering.

As soon as the door shut, Aisly fell back against the
wall of her house, pulling the blanket against her to ward
off the cold night air. She closed her eyes against the sight
of the stars twinkling far above her, relieving the sight of
his magnificent torso. The man was beautiful. Breathtaking. Godric had been a warrior, one of Cuthbert's best,
but he hadn't looked like the warrior in her home now.
Godric hadn't been so overwhelming, so much of everything that made a man...well, a man.

Every one of the foreigner's muscles had been so well-developed that there'd been a slight indentation between where one met the next. His skin had been so flawless that for a moment her fingers had tingled as she imagined that he'd feel velvety smooth beneath her touch, except for the parts that were lightly furred with dark blond hair. It had been sprinkled across his chest, but it was the trail leading into his trousers from below his navel that had caught and held her attention. She found herself wondering just what he looked like *there*. She opened her eyes so she wouldn't imagine it and sucked in a deep breath. The crisp night air was cold in her lungs. When she breathed it out, a puff of steam wafted off into the dark.

More than his muscles intrigued her. It was his eyes. The way they sparkled as he spoke to her. The way they followed her and touched her when he wasn't even speaking. Those deep pools of warmth promised so much more than she had any right to expect. It was probably her own loneliness causing her to twist a suggestion of gratitude into something more.

Newly widowed as she was, she had no business thinking about another man. She'd loved Godric when they'd first married, or she'd thought she had at the time. She realised now that perhaps childish infatuation was a more apt description. He had been only two winters older, so she'd grown up knowing of him. They'd seen each other at various times when he came with Cuthbert and Wulfric to visit Lord Oswine. Godric had become one of the village's best warriors. When he'd singled her out for attention, she'd been as flattered as any maiden would have been. When he'd asked her to be his wife, an elaborate affair that had been done in Lord Oswine's hall one night before everyone, she'd been hesitant but had agreed. There had seemed to be no better option and

Lord Oswine had encouraged the match. She'd agreed because she'd been so desperate for a family, to recreate what she'd had before she'd lost her parents.

It hadn't taken her long to realise that her hesitation had been warranted. Marriage to Godric had been difficult. He wasn't tender, not in the ways she heard men could be in the songs some of the women sang when they were washing their linens at the stream, or in the blushing giggles from the women who were already married. Early in their marriage when he'd come to her at night, he'd been hasty and perfunctory. Later, when her body had grown accustomed to his demands, she'd sometimes feel something more, something approaching pleasure that would make her gasp. But Godric had been quick to cover her mouth and remind her that she wasn't a whore. Wives didn't make sounds in bed. Wives didn't move at all when their husbands were on top of them.

He'd been indifferent to her during the daytime hours as well. Since she was his and he had no need to pursue her, he'd spend the majority of his time with the warriors. Aye, much of that time was spent training and working, but even his meals he took at the hall. Or if he came home, he'd go back there afterwards to share mead and stories or whatever men did in the hall after dark. It wasn't until they'd been married for half a year that he'd begun to get angry with her for not yet quickening with child. Men were taunting him and he wasn't happy.

He didn't know that after their third month together, she'd cried in relief when her menses had come. The thought of having a child with such a cold man had been so abhorrent that she'd begun regularly taking a draught Edyth had mixed for her. Despite the fact that a child would've given her the family she wanted, she couldn't bring herself to subject a child to having Godric as a father. He could be so cruel. She shuddered to think of how angry he would have been had he known.

Now she cried for an entirely different reason when her menses came. She'd lost her only chance to have a child and the absence made her ache inside. She'd also lost the only chance to keep her home. She supposed it was a suitable punishment for not wanting a baby with Godric.

And, despite her feelings about sharing his bed, he hadn't deserved to be killed at the Dane settlement. He had gone to approach their leaders about help with the missing maidens. Every one of the warriors who'd gone with him that day had been slaughtered. It had been a massacre and she had felt very real sorrow to hear of Godric's death. He had been a good warrior, a good provider, if not exactly the husband she had wanted.

The fact that she was lusting over a foreigner she barely knew must mean that she was as evil as Godric had claimed in his occasional drunken rants. Dear God, she'd actually attempted to kiss the man. Perhaps she *should* join the abbess in her devotions.

His voice called to her from inside. She took a moment to get her thoughts in order, then hesitantly opened the door and poked her head inside. Of course, he was dressed. He'd behaved honourably. She was the one making unwanted advances.

Closing the door and securing it behind her, she noted he wouldn't look at her as he sat waiting for her to apply a new bandage. Guilt and shame warred for dominance as she retrieved the strips of linen and the bowl with the poultice, setting them on the stone hearth. She couldn't help but notice how he smelled clean as she came to stand just in front of him. She also noticed how he seemed to catch his breath. It was a soft hitch that she mightn't have noticed had she not been so attuned to him. The urge to apologise again came over her, but she managed to squelch it. She'd only make things even more awkward. If Alstan had his way, the foreigner would be gone in the morning and she'd never see him again.

It was best to get him back to bed and pretend that this confusing and disturbing night had never happened. Gently placing the poultice in place, she wrapped the linen around his head a few times to secure it before tying it off.

'Can I trust you to stay until morning? I don't want to tie you up again, but I can't afford to defy their wishes.'

He stood so abruptly the movement pushed her backwards and she wavered until she was able to recover her balance. For one horrible moment, she thought he might run, until she realised he wouldn't get far. The gates were closed and, despite his insistence that they wouldn't hold him, he was in no condition to challenge them. He didn't move further, leaving her opportunity to see that the trousers fit. Godric's undershirt pulled a bit tight in the chest and it was short in the sleeve, leaving a portion of wrist exposed, but it fit well enough.

'Aisly.'

His hand blurred at his side as she closed her eyes against the impossible yearning his voice aroused. Raspy and low, it tugged at some need hidden deep within her. When he didn't continue, she knew that he was waiting for her to look up at him. After an interminable moment while she considered running, she let out a huff of breath and relented, looking up. The fire caught the gold flecks in his irises, making them shimmer. Two lines appeared between his brows.

'I won't lie to you. I've given you my word and I'll keep it.'

She didn't know why she felt the compulsion to correct his version of what had happened. 'You didn't give me your word not to run. You said that I forced your hand and I made the assumption.'

His lips parted in a smile and his thumb pressed into the soft flesh on her chin just below her lips as his fingertips brushed over her jawline and neck. 'Then I give you my word now. It's the least I can do to repay your kindness.' Then his touch was gone, leaving her feeling bereft and even more confused.

She could only nod. There were no words left in her for the night.

'It's right that I speak to them before leaving,' he said, turning away from her. He weaved on his feet a bit, making her jolt forward to help him, but he managed to recover before she reached him. 'The dark spots in my vision,' he explained, 'they seem to come when I move too fast.'

Which was precisely why he wasn't ready to move on tomorrow. He needed more time to rest, but she'd save her argument for Cuthbert in the morning. 'Rest will help.'

He gave a grunt of agreement, but instead of going to the bed, he moved to her abandoned pallet and sat, raising his hand to stop her protest. 'I've taken enough from you. I'll not take your bed any longer.' He was already lying down and pulling the blanket up before she could think of her best argument.

Deciding bed or pallet probably wouldn't matter much in the way of his recovery, she climbed into the freshly made bed and pulled the blanket up over her. Perhaps if she closed her eyes tight enough, she wouldn't remember that the foreigner had lain here so recently. She gave it a try, but it didn't seem to help.

Chapter Eight

Magnus woke up as soon as she left the following morning. The soft knock of the door closing behind her brought him out of a peaceful sleep. Grey morning light found its way through the vent in the thatched roof, making him smile because it meant his sleeping patterns were becoming normal. He was getting better. His head still ached and his wound was swollen, but he'd probably passed through the worst of it with the woman's help.

The vision of her lovely face filled with disappointment when he'd pushed her away came back to him. He'd been shocked at the kiss, but even more shocked at how much he'd wanted it. It would have been nothing to part her lips beneath his and see if she tasted as sweet as he kept imagining. Though he had no idea how many women were in his past, being near her made him remember the warmth of a woman's body, the sensation of all of that soft skin against his and the excitement of finding just the right places to touch. There was no doubt in his mind that he wanted to explore that with Aisly.

Just feeling her touch last night had made him half-rigid with wanting. And then, when he'd taken her hips to pull her closer for his shave, he'd been so hard that the ache in his head had transferred to his manhood. He'd had a very real, throbbing need to pull her closer, to sink his body into hers and show her just how much he appreciated her help. It hadn't helped that when her big green eyes had looked into his, he'd seen his own desire reflected there. He'd forced himself to let go of her so he wouldn't do something they'd regret.

He forced himself to stop thinking about her as he rose to see to his morning ablutions. He'd only just finished when she returned. Other than expressing surprise that he was up, she sat a small bowl of what he suspected was another awful draught down on the table and set about filling a bowl with pottage for him.

Giving her a smile, he took a seat on a stool and began to eat. She smiled back but didn't speak beyond a greeting. It seemed she didn't know how to proceed any more than he did. Her words from the day before had been in his mind since she'd said them, so after a few bites he decided to ask her about them. 'What did you mean about the tapestries your mother made? What happened?'

Surprised, she looked up, the debate to answer clear in her eyes. Finally she looked down, stirring the pottage in her bowl as she answered. 'My husband went to the Danes at the settlement to report the two maidens missing. He was killed. They said he started a fire that burned some of their houses, but I'm uncertain. So they came and demanded payment for the damage.' She met his eyes again and he was shocked to see a thin film of tears. 'The Danes took them.'

It was as if a fist reached in and squeezed his heart and all the air from his chest. The need to touch her, to comfort her, and the equal need to find the tapestries and those responsible for their loss warred within him. 'That's a horrible price to pay.'

'Thank you. It was.' She took another bite before saying, 'They were all I have left of my family. The only reminder of those good days. I always wanted a family to have those days back again, but that won't happen now.'

What had happened that made her think she didn't want another husband? It wasn't any of his business, but he opened his mouth to ask anyway. 'Why won't you have a family?'

'I refuse to live under the tyranny of another husband.'

His mind turned over all the ways her husband could've been a tyrant to her and his vague dislike of the man turned to loathing. Fingers clenching around his bowl, he forced a calm to his voice. 'Was he harsh with you?'

Her gaze faltered. He was asking too much, but something had happened in the past hours with her to make too much seem woefully inadequate.

When she spoke, her voice was so still, so soft, he imagined that she'd never spoken the words aloud before to anyone. 'Sometimes he'd throw things, or he'd destroy my work if he was angry, push me out of the way if I moved too slowly. I think I frustrated him. I wasn't quite as biddable as he'd expected and after the first couple of months he stopped being polite.'

Grinding his teeth together to work back his anger, he took in the gentle slope of her cheek and the smudge of blue under her eyes that said she hadn't been getting enough sleep thanks to him. She was delicate and beautiful and kind, and he wanted to break the man weak enough to think anything else. The warrior part of him was glad the man was dead.

'You didn't deserve that.' That was all he managed to say before an insistent pounding on the door brought Aisly to her feet.

She stared at him for a moment, surprise and gratitude evident in her eyes, before she blinked as if only just now becoming aware of the knocking. Running her palms in a nervous gesture over her apron, she walked over to answer the door. This could be their last moments together. He'd be leaving soon if the fierce stare Alstan gave him from the doorway was any indication. Magnus stood and clenched his jaw in his bid not to waver on his feet as the black spots danced, threatening to overtake his vision, his head pounding.

'You untied him.' Alstan's harsh voice fairly crackled with accusation.

'Aye,' she replied, her voice as carefree as if she'd just offered him a 'good morning'.

Magnus managed not to smile as he paused on his way to the door to give her a final thanks before leaving. Though a thanks seemed inadequate after all that had passed between them, particularly since he might never see her again.

She didn't allow him to speak as she pulled a cloak from the peg next to the door and pulled it around her shoulders. 'I'm going with you.' Her chin was tipped upward in determination.

'That's not wise.'

'Nay,' her brother said from his place in the doorway.

Magnus ignored the man, preferring to admire her sparkling green eyes and the way her face flushed with her vehemence. The woman could have been a warrior queen had she the physique for it. But he frowned as soon as the thought crossed his mind. Had he ever seen a warrior queen? Did such a thing exist? The familiar grey fog rushed in to cloud his mind, making it impossible to follow the thread of that thought.

'Do not frown at me, foreigner. I'm going whether you like it or not.' Tying the cloak under her chin, she pegged her brother with an even fiercer look. 'Let us be on our way. They'll be waiting.'

Alstan frowned and Magnus suspected he would have argued had he not been afraid to appear weak. They both knew she wasn't changing her mind and, short of tying her down, her brother wouldn't win the argument. Instead of replying at all, he turned and led the way to Cuthbert's hall.

Aisly visibly relaxed and gave him a tentative smile as he stepped outside after her. His palms itched to touch her and reassure her that he would be fine. He didn't know that, though, not for certain.

By instinct, his gaze took in the village around him. His best estimate was that there were a little fewer than a hundred buildings, closer if counting the various outbuildings he saw. Aisly's home was one of the larger ones and situated on the western side, one of the furthest from the gates. A quick glance to the wall nearest her home assured him that it was scalable. It had probably originally been built to keep out wolves and boars, not men. Not the Danes who plagued them.

Hastening his pace, Magnus drew up next to her. If these were the last moments he'd get to spend with her, he wanted to make sure she knew enough to protect herself. 'The walls are too low to keep out men who want to get in. Do you have weapons? A plan to protect yourself?'

'What?' She skittered to the side away from him but immediately straightened her pace and looked to the ground as her exclamation caught her brother's attention. Only when the man had turned forward again did she ask, 'What are you talking about? The wall has served us well.'

Magnus had no idea how that was true given it would take only a sturdy pair of shoulders to lift him up and over it or a well-thrown and cleverly knotted grappling hook. As if the thought had conjured it, he could feel the sensation of the rope slipping through his palms. What did it mean that he so quickly found their weaknesses? Was it simply the knowledge of a seasoned warrior or an enemy looking for vulnerabilities? He shook off the disturbing thought.

'Your home is one of the closest to the wall. If an enemy comes over, you'll have precious little time to run. Your home has wooden floors. Is there a dugout beneath?'

She still looked at him as if he'd lost his mind, but she nodded. 'Aye, like most of the others. I store root vegetables there.'

'Good. Make sure the panel is covered with rushes at all times and keep a knife down there. You can hide there if you have to.' It wasn't much, but it was all the help he could offer her for now. He reaffirmed his vow to figure out some way to repay her, even if it could only be done after he figured out who he was…if he lived that long.

When she agreed, he turned his attention back to the village. People were just beginning to move about, eyeing him with either interest or outright hostility as they passed. He focused on each face, hoping something in one of them would cause a flicker of recognition to light within him. None of them did. Of course not.

Alstan turned a corner around a large stone forge, giving Magnus his first look at the hall. It had to be where their leader lived, situated as it was near the middle of the village. Flexing his shoulders, he ran a hand over the back of his neck, where the skin had started to feel too tight. Every instinct he possessed told him not to walk into that building. He had no idea what could be waiting for him there, but even as he thought it, he knew he had no choice. Two warriors stood just outside the door, swords at their sides and their eyes levelled on him. Alstan turned when he reached them, lending weight to their sentry as his eyes dared Magnus to run.

Magnus gave another glance around. Villagers were already starting to gather, lured from their early-morning chores by the prospect of excitement. Even if he were capable of running, he wouldn't get far without his sword. It was best to walk in and face them head-on.

'I won't let them harm you.' Aisly walked beside him, giving him a soft smile as she looked up at him.

There was no doubt in his mind that she would do everything she could to uphold that vow. He couldn't say that he wanted her to leave with him; he had no way to care for her. He couldn't pull her into his arms to just once feel her body against his; her brother would intervene. He could only return her smile and silently vow to reward her for her generosity. He'd come back for that.

'Foreigner.' Alstan's voice drew their attention.

Magnus levelled a glare at the man before Alstan turned and led them inside the hall. They entered on the long side of the building, which meant the large, single room was spread out to either side and a long, rectangular hearth sat in the middle. The fire burned low, as the house's occupants had apparently finished their morning meal. Four tall posts bisected the room, supporting the high, vaulted ceiling. He couldn't help the niggling thought that the house seemed small for a hall, though the bloody grey fog kept him from remembering other halls he'd seen. The walls were covered in tapestries depicting hunting scenes and Magnus wondered if Aisly had embroidered them. He didn't get much of a chance to ponder the issue, though, because he pulled abreast of Alstan, who nodded to two men seated across the hearth. Aisly stopped as well and Magnus shifted slightly so that he was half in front of her.

'I am Cuthbert, chieftain of Heiraford, and this is my brother, Arte.' The man with a shock of white hair sat straight and indicated the round man sitting next to him. 'We've a few questions for you and how you came to be near our village.'

Magnus relayed as many of the details of his journey to their village as he dared. It was a delicate situation, not knowing who he was or who they were to him. It was impossible to know which detail might reveal too much. He left out the fact that he'd awakened by a fire about to be burned after battle, not knowing if that was significant or not. He paused in his story and almost smiled when Aisly didn't bother to correct him and reveal his secret. The woman deserved whatever reward she requested of him.

When he finished, they had a few questions about the confrontation with the rebel Dane at the stream. He was proud of her when she raised her voice and firmly answered the questions directed towards her. His palms itched to touch her, to rub a hand down her back and reassure her, but he held himself away. Though he'd clearly been incapacitated while in her home, he didn't want to give anyone cause to doubt her.

When they'd finished their interrogation about his meagre past, Cuthbert lowered his head to consult with his brother. Alstan gave Magnus a suspicious look, gave a glance to make sure there were two warriors nearby, in case he tried to run, and made his way around the hearth to offer his own opinion. Their voices were too low for Magnus to make out more than a murmur.

Aisly surprised him by placing a hand on his arm and rising up on her tiptoes to whisper as close to his ear as she could reach, 'Don't fret, foreigner. Alstan will make sure they let you go.'

That wasn't precisely what concerned him. He believed that her brother would honour his word to let him leave. However, he knew that wouldn't stop anyone who might want him dead or who considered him a threat from following. A quick glance around confirmed that the few warriors who loitered in the room were staring him down. He didn't want to alarm the woman, so he gave her a nod over his shoulder. Her face lit up when he winked at her.

She seemed too young and spirited to be a widow. Their eyes met and there was that tug again. Low, deep and exciting, right in the gut. Perhaps, once he figured out his place, he could come back to her and convince her that wherever his home was it could be hers, too.

It was a foolish thought for many reasons. If he was a warrior, he couldn't offer her what she wanted. His home could be days away, across seas—he saw a deep blue ocean spread out before him, the sun glinting off the small whitecaps of the waves.

'Foreigner?'

The voice repeated itself at least twice before Magnus could jerk himself away from the strange imagery. He stumbled back into Aisly, who put her arms around him.

'Do you see what you've done?' She raised her soft

voice to be heard by Alstan over the whispers of the warriors at their back.

'Aisly—' The warning came from Alstan, but she didn't heed it. Of course she didn't, not his warrior queen.

'He's not yet ready to be up and about. A blade nearly split open his skull and you have him standing here as if he's well.'

'That's enough, Aisly. He needs to be questioned.' Her brother turned back to Cuthbert, who stood up to speak.

'Where were you planning on going now, foreigner?'

Magnus stood as straight as if no injury had befallen him, refusing to appear any weaker before these men who were judging him. Aisly dropped her arms but kept a hand on his back. Had he ever felt a touch so clearly? Shaking himself from the thought, he said, 'I'd planned to retrace my path. See if I can find where the rebels who trailed me are camped. I'll capture them one by one until I find one who knows me.'

'D-do you think that's wise?' Aisly tensed and spoke so low that only he had likely heard her.

He spared her a glance. The concern in her voice was almost his undoing. 'They're the only clue I have to figuring out who I am.'

She frowned and her teeth tugged on her bottom lip, but she didn't argue.

'You have nowhere to go, foreigner, and soon the frost will come. Stay and recover,' Cuthbert said.

Alstan glowered but didn't offer a dissent.

Magnus didn't know how he felt about staying. The trail back to the men who'd tried to kill him got colder every day. 'I fear that more of the rebel Danes might follow me here and it's best I lead them away from your village.'

Cuthbert nodded and cast a wary glance towards Alstan, as if he knew that the younger man wouldn't agree with his words. 'I fear the rebels plague us whether you are here or not. They've plagued us since late spring.'

'Aye, I've been told of your troubles. I was sorry to hear them. Once I find where they're hiding, I'll take care of that problem for you.'

Cuthbert waved his words away. 'We'd like you to stay through winter. I'm not convinced the rebels have given up their attacks just yet and we've lost a few warriors to the Danes at the settlement. Aisly's husband was amongst them.' The older man paused to gesture to her. 'You've likely had more dealings with them than the rest of us. When your thoughts settle and your memories return, you could be a great help to us. Staying would give you a place to regain your health during the cold months, before continuing on your way come spring.'

His first instinct was to reject the invitation, but he couldn't deny the sound reasoning in the chieftain's offer. Staying would give him time to regain his health, which in turn would make his triumph against the rebels more likely. The drawback was that he risked losing the cowards the longer he waited to look for them. Staying would also give him more time with Aisly. He'd barely begun to ponder that before Alstan's voice cut through his thoughts.

'Nay, Cuthbert. You should not invite this man into your village.'

'Alstan.' Cuthbert raised a steady hand in supplication. 'I understand your concern.'

'*My* concern? He's one of them. The man is clearly a Dane. It's everyone's concern,' Alstan argued.

Behind him, Aisly's breath hitched, the sound wrenching his heart. He couldn't tell her that he wasn't. He didn't know if it was true.

'A Dane, you say?' This was said in a deep voice from the doorway.

Magnus turned to see an older man standing there. He was clearly of high rank, like Cuthbert and his brother. His tunic was a supple green with embroidered hem. Though Magnus was almost a head taller, the man had bulk that made him the biggest man Magnus had observed in the village. He stood with a sneer, his nose pointed towards them and his beady eyes sweeping over them like a snake's, sliding up and down Magnus's height and finding him lacking. The sneer stayed in place as he transferred that disrespectful gaze to Aisly. She tensed and it took all Magnus could do to stop himself from moving between them.

Her hand dropped from his back and she drew herself up straighter. But something about the movement had drawn the snake's attention. His gaze narrowed in on the place where her hand had been, drawn by some scent of impropriety only he could smell. The sneer widened as he let his eyes settle on Aisly before walking towards the hearth and addressing Cuthbert. 'Many apologies for my tardiness. A quarrel detained me, but it's settled now.'

Cuthbert nodded. 'This is the foreigner that our fair Aisly has been caring for. Foreigner, this is Wulfric, a trusted advisor.'

Magnus clenched his molars as he was forced to acknowledge the newcomer. He disliked him instantly. Distrust and selfishness practically leached from the man's skin.

'What is this I hear about a Dane?' Wulfric asked, looking to Alstan, who had voiced the accusation.

Alstan nodded. 'His voice, the way he speaks, his size, they all lead me to think he's one of them.' He spat out 'one of them' like it had tried to bite him.

'Are you?' Wulfric fitted Magnus with another stare.

'I have no memories.' Magnus didn't elaborate.

Wulfric grinned again, his hand going to the forked beard that rested on his chest. 'I don't trust a man with no beard.'

'I don't trust that he has no memories,' Alstan added. 'He could be lying. He could be a spy.'

'Enough!' Cuthbert's voice cut through the house. 'Mercenary or Dane, it matters not. He killed the rebel Dane. He is not one of them. Even if he is a spy, there is nothing he can learn here that the Danes at the settlement don't already know. He can stay through the winter.'

'He'll not stay in my house,' Wulfric said, his voice quiet but firm.

Aisly gasped behind him, and he wasn't sure why.

'Of course not,' Cuthbert hurried to reassure him. 'It wouldn't be seemly for him to stay with Aisly. He'll stay in the hall with my warriors.'

Magnus narrowed his eyes as he took another look at Wulfric. The man must be a relative to her if he owned her house. Or perhaps he was a relative of her late husband. Either way, that put him entirely too close to her. Could no one else see the depravity this man wore with pride? Magnus glanced to Alstan, wondering how her own brother could allow the man near her, but Alstan still glared at him. At *him*, the one who had saved Aisly, while the man who silently threatened her stood unmolested.

He ran a hand through his hair, stopping when he came to the linen binding he'd forgotten about, and unintentionally stepped back to be closer to her. Perhaps this was how he could repay her. He could save her from that snake. But his protection could only last through winter. When spring came, what would happen then?

Arte finally broke his silence. 'Putting him with the other warriors is bound to cause tension.'

'Ah.' Cuthbert nodded. 'You are wise, my friend. After the massacre, I can't expect them to accept a possible Dane. He can stay in Leofwyn's hut.'

'Who is Leofwyn?' he asked Aisly as the men continued their discussion.

'She was the eldest woman in the village until she passed away in the summer. Her home is one of the older, smaller ones, closer to the stream, away from the centre of the village. Far away from me,' Aisly said.

They all agreed that Leofwyn's hut would be the most suitable, but Aisly objected.

The men paused in their discussion to look at her.

'He should stay nearer so that I can look in on him. I'm not sure you've bothered to notice, but he is still injured.' She pointed towards his bandage just in case they'd missed it.

'I'm fine.' He gave her a solemn look. Did the woman not realise the danger she was in from Wulfric? It wouldn't do to challenge him openly, even if indirectly.

'You are not fine,' she argued.

'Aisly's right,' Wulfric intervened, making the hair on the back of Magnus's neck stand upright. The way the man said her name so casually rattled him. 'He should stay closer. Let him have Beorn's hut. He and his wife won't be returning to us.' The sneer returned as the man settled his gaze on Aisly to say those last words. It was a private message meant to unsettle. Something threatening passed between them.

Magnus had to fight the impulse to put his fist in the snake's face. The conversation continued around him, but all he could see was Wulfric watching her.

'What say you, foreigner? Will you stay with us through winter?' Cuthbert finally asked, drawing his attention to the three men at the front of the room.

There was only one option.

'I'll stay through winter, or until I'm recovered enough to remember my place. If I have responsibilities, I'll need to see to them.' He glanced to Aisly, but she seemed upset, her gaze on the floor at her feet.

'Fair enough,' Cuthbert agreed. 'Are you feeling well enough to go to the hut now?'

'Nay, he's not well,' Aisly answered before Magnus had a chance, jerking her chin up to face the men. 'He's still a bit fevered and I've a draught for him to drink.'

Those draughts would be the death of him.

'I'm well enough,' he said, drawing a disapproving frown from her. Wulfric was already looking for anything he could use against her. Magnus would not give the man any fodder for his mysterious scheme. Though as quick as the man had been to agree to these new living arrangements, Magnus had to wonder if he might wake up with a sword in him later that night, which reminded him. 'Where is my sword?'

'It's here.' Arte smiled in appeasement and gestured to one in a row of chests lining the back wall. 'You'll have to earn our trust before we give it back, but it's here.'

Magnus took in a deep breath through his nose. He didn't like being left without a weapon. This could all be a ploy and he'd be killed in his sleep, but he didn't have a choice.

As if he'd passed some rite, the warriors who'd been

milling about during the interrogation came forward and introduced themselves. He kept his eye on Aisly, who had gone over to talk to her brother. Once they'd all come forward, Cuthbert called an end to the meeting and Aisly returned to his side. He had to physically stop himself from putting a hand on her to keep her close. Wulfric had rattled him badly.

'Come.' She smiled up at him, seeming to have recovered herself. 'Let's get you to your new home.'

Chapter Nine

Aisly walked beside the foreigner on the way to his new home, aware that something had subtly changed. More people were out now that it was later in the morning. They'd all apparently been delayed in making their way to the fields, because there were far too many of them milling about. Unlike when she and the foreigner had passed through the village on their way to see Cuthbert, most of them were merely curious rather than hostile as they watched him. Word had undoubtedly spread about what had taken place inside. It was impossible to keep secrets in the village. She didn't miss much about living in the manor. Life there had been good, but lonely. As a ward, she'd been treated with the detachment reserved for servants and hadn't the freedom she did here. But loss of privacy was the one thing she missed about living in the manor. Here people seemed to have nothing better to do than eavesdrop.

It wasn't until they'd been stopped by yet another man speaking to the foreigner that she realised what was bothering her. It seemed he was being cautiously welcomed and she was grateful for that, but she didn't like what it implied. He wasn't *hers* any more. Though he hadn't been hers at all anyway. He wouldn't stay in the village past winter and he might even leave sooner if his memory returned. But there had been a strange comfort to having him in her home.

Now that he was out in the village, with his own temporary home no less, he was theirs. What sort of person did that make her that she would begrudge him their acceptance?

A lonely one.

The confession was bitter, but it was the truth. She'd been lonely for as long as she could remember. Certainly at least since her parents' deaths. Alstan had gone to live with the warriors and she had become a servant living in Lady Oswine's chamber. She hadn't had a particularly difficult life. She'd even been encouraged to continue learning the embroidery her mother had taught her. But she'd never had someone who was hers.

Godric had been handsome, and charismatic, and all the things a young warrior was supposed to be, but he'd never really been hers. Their marriage had never developed into that feeling of family that she craved. There had never been that sense of belonging, not deep in her bones where she wanted to feel it.

Loneliness was a thorny emotion. It was no doubt making her attribute her longing for someone to the stranger, a man she had known for only a short while. Her connection to him was tenuous and completely attributable to her need to have someone, anyone apparently, to call her own. It was that realisation that made her hang back as they approached the small cottage that was to be his home for the winter.

He wasn't hers. She wasn't his. The very idea that her

thoughts were starting to turn this way made her glad that he was moving out. Clearly she couldn't trust herself with him.

Cuthbert and Arte had led the walk to the cottage and it was the chieftain who stepped forward to open the door, speaking to the foreigner as he did so. The foreigner nodded but glanced back at her when Cuthbert walked inside. His brow furrowed as if he noticed her reticence and disapproved. Thankfully he didn't comment and he followed Cuthbert inside.

Aisly wavered. It was only right that she follow them inside and help him get settled. Most of the supplies Beorn and his wife hadn't been able to carry with them had been given to Wulfric as payment for the debt. Who knew what Wulfric had done with it all? The only certainty was that he wouldn't offer it to the foreigner. Yet something kept her from following him into the cottage. A protective instinct, she supposed.

Just when she was telling herself that she was being ridiculous and stepped forward to follow, someone cut off her path. She almost stumbled when Arte's wife, Lora, and daughter, Wyn, stepped forward from the crowd that had gathered with blankets and supplies for the foreigner's new home. They both mumbled apologies, but Wyn was paying no attention to her. She was too busy giving the foreigner a shy smile as she walked past him and into the hut, carrying an iron pot for his cooking. Before Aisly could stop herself, she rushed forward. 'He doesn't need that. I can cook for him.'

The girl, who was just a few years younger than Aisly, turned at her words and then cast an uncertain glance to her mother. Realising she sounded like a jealous shrew, Aisly stopped and became aware of her face flaming.

Turning her attention to Arte's wife, she said, 'It's very kind of you to bring it, Lora, but I don't mind providing his meals while he's here. It's the least I can do.'

The older woman gave her a grandmotherly smile and patted her shoulder. 'That's very thoughtful of you, dearest, and while I'm certain he'll be most grateful, we have it to spare.'

Aisly nodded. Of course, it was only right that they set him up with the supplies he'd need. She couldn't stop herself from glancing at the man in question. He was watching her with a slight smile. When their eyes met, a blaze of warmth moved through her and his smile widened. It was as if he knew exactly what she was thinking, that she was feeling possessive. She didn't know how she felt about the fact that he could read her so easily.

'Aye, I'd be very grateful for your meals.' He didn't say 'fair one' and she found that she missed it. His eyes said it, though, as they touched her just as gently as his fingertips had the previous night. She only barely managed to contain herself so that no one knew how her rabbit heart fluttered in her chest. He looked back at something Cuthbert was saying about the harvest, releasing her gaze and leaving her free to glance about to make sure no one else had noticed. Everything the man did and said was almost too much for her.

Her gaze ended up settling on Wyn, who was partially hidden in shadow inside the small hut. She'd found a home for the pot on the stones of the hearth. The pretty girl stood there staring at the foreigner, the admiration on her face clear for anyone to see. That bitter pang of unreasonable jealousy came back, but Aisly squashed it down. There was no reason she should be jealous. She couldn't blame the girl for her admiration. He was handsome to look upon and, thanks to the Danes, there was a distinct lack of warriors in the village. Wyn was pretty and unmarried; she had every reason to look upon him with admiration.

But when the foreigner finished his conversation, he paused, giving Wyn a smile that had the girl blushing. 'Many thanks.' He inclined his head.

Wyn smiled and made to leave, slowing to brush past him in the narrow doorway. Aisly didn't miss how the girl's hand trailed across his arm or the way he turned his head just slightly to watch the girl walk away. Jealousy twisted inside her even though it had no right to exist. Forcing herself to breathe, she turned away and made her way through the crowd, stopping occasionally to greet someone or answer questions about the incident. She hadn't realised how curious they all would be about what had happened since she'd been isolated with him. By the time she made it home, she had come to terms with the idea that her time with him was over. Distance between them was a good thing.

Nay, it was more than good. It was necessary.

Over the course of the next several days, Aisly's life returned to normal. The foreigner came to share the morning meal and she'd change his bandage. He'd be gone before her apprentices arrived, spending the day resting. As his condition began to improve, he'd spend the day with Cuthbert in the hall or visiting the fields. She frequently saw him with either Cuthbert or Arte and he seemed to be interested in the workings of the village. But there was always a warrior nearby. Watching and waiting, proving he wasn't completely trusted yet.

Cuthbert's wife had commissioned a few pieces of

embroidery for her winter mantel, and every time Aisly made a trip to the hall, she looked for him. Often she found him in discussion over a cup of ale, but if she didn't see him, she'd take the long way through the village just to look for him. A few times she saw him in the fields as the men harvested wheat. Once, she'd passed by the blacksmith's to see him out front in deep discussion about the best technique to properly sharpen a blade.

If he saw her, he'd immediately give her that smile that caused her belly to flutter. But it was his eyes that made her catch her breath. They touched her no matter the physical distance between them. Like a caress, she could feel their weight wherever his gaze brushed her.

Shaking herself from her pointless thoughts, Aisly quickly folded the last tunic and placed it on the pile with the others. The abbess had been understanding about the delay, given her unexpected guest, but Aisly was anxious to get the vestments returned to her so that she could collect her payment. The coins weren't much, but every bit helped. She could feel Wulfric watching her, circling like a vulture waiting to make his move.

A chill swept down her spine as she remembered his words in the hall.

He'll not stay in my house.

Her father-in-law had never referred to her home as his before. He'd implied it plenty when he'd asked if she'd considered moving into Alstan's small home, but this was the first time since Godric's death that he'd stated it. Wulfric's youngest son would be marrying soon and, though he'd yet to say it, she knew that he wanted the home for his son. Not her. She'd failed to bear Godric a child, so Wulfric and his wife had no use for her.

Lord Oswine must have the marriage papers she and

Godric had signed. She'd asked Alstan to look for them. They'd protect her claim, her business, her livelihood.

The firm knock on the door startled her, causing her hands to tremble and nearly capsize the stack of vestments on the worktable. She turned just as the door flung open, hand over her heart. It had been unlocked, but it was rare that someone enter without waiting for her invitation. Except Wulfric considered it his house, so he wouldn't care.

The man's face split into a grin as he shut the door behind him, undoubtedly happy to see that her apprentices were gone for the day. Pinning her with his gaze, he stalked closer to her. 'How are you, my dear?'

Something had changed since the last time he'd visited her. He looked bloated with a secret that was begging to be released. What had he come up with now? She had to tread carefully, lest he figure out a way to get her banished from the village as well.

'Good day, Wulfric. How are you?'

He came to stop next to her, leaning an elbow on her worktable while a finger traced the embroidery along the hem of a tunic. She had to resist the urge to swat his hand away, as if a touch from him could sully them. 'You do good work. It's admirable how much you're improving.'

'Thank you. You're very kind.' She swallowed and forced her tongue to spit out the nicety.

He nodded. 'We haven't had a chance to discuss what happened in the hall.' His gaze flicked up to her face, gauging her reaction.

'Oh, I've been busy getting these finished for the abbess. She's due any moment now to pick them up.' It didn't hurt to let him know that they wouldn't be alone for long. 'I appreciate your help with the foreigner. It was kind of you to offer him a place to stay the winter.'

His eyes narrowed in displeasure and he ran a hand along the left side of his beard, a habit he had when he was irritated. 'It's not your place to be appreciative.' But he gave a tug and allowed his hand to drop, impatient to move on to his nefarious reason for this visit. 'I was referring to what happened with Beorn. I know you were friendly with him and his wife.'

Ah, he'd come to gloat over that victory.

What could she say that wouldn't anger him? She wanted to tell him how wrong he'd been to banish them, but it wouldn't change his mind. It wouldn't change anything. It would only give him more reason to dislike her.

'A most unfortunate situation.' She kept her voice low and her eyes even lower.

He gave a non-committal tut at the back of his throat and she could feel his gaze on the top of her head. Sizing up her sincerity, she imagined. 'Aye, it was. I so dislike having to use a heavy hand as I did. It's much better for everyone when people simply do as they should. Don't you agree?'

She nodded, certain they were now talking about her, and she squeezed her eyes shut briefly before opening them again. It wasn't wise to let him out of her sight for long.

The room went silent, tension stretching out as she waited for him to pounce. There was a reason for this visit. She didn't have to wait long, because he wasn't a patient man. Soon enough, a huff of air escaped from his nose. 'Have you determined if you are with Godric's child yet?'

Her heart fluttered before pounding against the wall

of her chest. She couldn't trust her voice and shook her head instead.

'Look at me, girl.' His voice was stern, all trace of civility gone from it.

Fearing what he might do, she raised her head but knew that she couldn't hide the hatred in her eyes. It shone there for him to see, whether she wanted it to or not. Before she could stop herself, the words formed of their own volition. 'You should not have banished Rowena. She was with child and could die out there this winter.'

His reaction surprised her. He actually smiled so wide she saw most of his teeth. He should sharpen them like she'd heard some of the Danes did. Little points on the end would at least warn people of the sort of man they were dealing with.

'There she is. There's the girl I know.'

Aisly kept her tongue firmly clamped between her teeth to avoid responding to that.

'I had an interesting talk with Rowena before she left.' He paused to give her time to absorb that, a self-satisfied smile in place.

'What did you do to her?' she whispered.

He shook his head, brushing off her question. 'It's what she did…what she told me.'

That statement truly frightened her, because she had no idea what he meant. Rowena had nothing to tell him that would interest Aisly. Or at least nothing that Aisly knew about.

'Ah, I see that I have your attention now.' He stood up straighter, brushing off his tunic, taking his time, making her wait for the verbal blow that was sure to follow. 'Beorn has lived in this village since his birth. His father and mother died within a week of each other. The ague, much like your parents. His sisters married and left. He was always a bit slow, not fit for any work except for the field. Bound to be poor. But he met Rowena when she came here with her sister, just before you married my son.'

For the life of her, Aisly couldn't figure out where he was going with this. She sensed a trap closing in.

'He didn't have the coin to marry her, but do you suppose that stopped their baser natures? Nay. I found them rutting one day in the fields. I ran them off, but I'm not daft enough to believe that stopped them.' He sneered. 'That was a full year before they married, my dear. A full year of rutting that produced no child.'

Now she knew what he was getting at. Her heart continued its frenetic beat, though she managed to keep her face calm.

'I find it convenient that she found herself with child so soon after marriage.'

'It was a rather happy occurrence. As I remember, she was overjoyed,' Aisly offered.

Wulfric laughed and shook his head. 'A happy occurrence is how most view it. I, however, know that it was more than just coincidence. She confessed to me, Aisly.' His face reddened and a vein throbbed in his temple as he leaned towards her. She took a step backwards to keep distance between them. 'She told me of a potion you gave her that kept her from getting with child. She stopped taking it upon her marriage. Do you deny that?'

Aisly shook her head, uncertain how to respond. Rowena was a simple girl, one of the first who had approached Aisly when she'd moved to the village. Though they hadn't had much in common, the girl had been kind and they'd struck up a friendship. When Rowena had asked her about delaying motherhood, she'd shared with her the draught Edyth had prepared for her. It had been only a few times.

'Do you deny that you took the same potion to refuse my son a child?' Spittle sprayed out of his mouth to land on his forked beard. 'You couldn't possibly be with child now. Not after taking that.'

'I don't—'

But he didn't allow her to finish, just kept on talking as if she hadn't spoken. 'I want to know if you brought it here from the manor, or if Edyth prepared it for you.'

'Leave Edyth out of this. She has nothing to do with us.'

That horrible sneer twisted his lips again. 'Oh, I'll be paying her a visit. I hear she's quite friendly with you, too.'

Too? Suddenly everything became clear to her. As if a bucket of cold water had been dumped over her, she was simultaneously cold and hot with anger. The realisation of what he'd done was too much. She couldn't hold back her words any more. 'You made Rowena and Beorn leave because they were my friends, didn't you? You targeted them because I'd been friendly to them.'

He didn't deny it as he crossed his arms over his chest. 'You won't triumph in this, girl. Once I determine you aren't with child, I'll make you leave, too. You w—'

A knock at the door interrupted his threats. When she looked up to see the foreigner's broad shoulders filling her doorway, Aisly knew a relief so profound that she could have cried with it.

Chapter Ten

$Magnus$ drank in the sight of her lovely face, pale and drawn tight with fear. She was so slight next to Wulfric's bulkier form; it seemed almost grotesque that the man was trying to intimidate her. He'd heard nearly every vile word the older man had said to her.

Magnus had been around back, halfway between her home and his, trying to figure out a reason to go see her. She'd been obviously avoiding him all week. Even when they talked at breakfast, her words were restrictive and bland, not like the days when he'd slept in her home, not like that morning when she'd confessed about her husband. He'd spent only a precious few conscious hours in her company but found that he missed the sparkle in her eye and the direct way she had of speaking. He wanted to learn more of her secrets. He had intended to talk to her, to figure out why she'd put this chasm between them. That was, until he'd seen Wulfric go inside. Knowing that he was invading her privacy, but unwilling to stop himself, he'd crept up and listened through the wall.

He'd heard most of it. Every vile, despicable thing that had come out of Wulfric's mouth had only served to make Magnus's aversion to him grow. The moment the older man's tone had changed and become more aggressive, Magnus hadn't been able to allow the confrontation to go on any longer. It wasn't wise to challenge someone so important to the village and someone so important to his own immediate future, but he wouldn't allow Aisly to be bullied.

He stood almost a head taller than Wulfric, causing the man to have to look up at him. Magnus felt some vicious pleasure in that, even though he spared the coward only a passing glance. Though his fists clenched at his sides, Magnus forced his voice and face to appear calm as he addressed Aisly. 'I've come as you asked, so that you could change my bandage.'

Her brow furrowed for only the quick blink of a moment before she controlled her features and went along with his lie. 'Aye, you're just in time. I have the poultice just over here.' She stepped away from Wulfric and her worktable, retreating further into the house to the table where she kept her cooking utensils.

Once she was far enough away from him, Magnus turned his attention to Wulfric, who was staring at him. The man's expression wasn't angry or menacing now, merely calculating. It was as if he could see the undercurrent of whatever it was that constantly seemed to move between Magnus and Aisly. It was an invisible string that inexplicably tied them together. Now that he knew Wulfric was a threat to her and still had no idea as to his own identity, the danger of that string was very real. The fact that Wulfric saw that it was there terrified him.

'Good day.' Magnus forced a blandness to his voice, as if he hadn't just heard everything.

'Foreigner.' There was a hint of a bitter inflection in the word. 'Cuthbert says your health is improving.'

'Aye, much improved. I'm back to wielding my sword with precision and strength.' Now that the swelling had gone down, Aisly had adjusted the bandage so it didn't cover his eye. He still had spells of dizziness and headaches, but he was markedly improved from when he'd arrived. Enough so that he'd begun to practise in shortened intervals with Cuthbert's few warriors. Though his proclamation to Wulfric was as much a warning as a description of his health, he hadn't yet been allowed to keep the sword. They packed it away in the hall after each practice.

If the man heard it as a threat, he didn't comment on it and instead turned to Aisly. Magnus tensed and stepped into the room under the guise of walking to the stool he generally occupied while she changed his bandage. For her part she didn't look up, just continued cutting strips of linen with a blade.

'Good day to you, Aisly. I'd advise you to think over my words to you.' With that cryptic warning, Wulfric left the cottage, pulling the door with a thump behind him.

Magnus wasted no time in pulling the wooden latch on the door closed just in case Wulfric decided to come back. Then he turned to Aisly. She had stopped cutting and stood clutching the edge of the table, her shoulders shaking. He didn't even stop to think before he crossed the room and pulled her back against him, his arms going tight around her waist. Her scent assailed him—sunshine, linen, feminine perspiration. Somehow they all blended to create a fragrance that he wanted to bury his face in, breathing it in until it became a part of him.

Her trembling increased and she turned, her small arms going around his waist. Tears rolled unchecked down her cheeks before she buried her face in his tunic. One arm stayed so tight around her waist he feared hurting her, while his other hand cupped the back of her head. When the bloody headrail hindered his ability to touch her, he slid his hand beneath, his fingers curling into her hair. He wanted to tell her not to cry, to reassure her that everything was all right, but to lie to her wouldn't help. He didn't know that everything would be all right. He could promise to watch over her, to not allow that ass to hurt her, but the promise would only last until he left. What would become of her once he left her to the clutches of that vile man?

'I heard the horrible things he said to you.' His voice was muffled against her headrail. She was so soft and warm in his arms, and the curves of her body fitted so tightly against him that he had to fight back the surge of his immediate desire. All the blood in his body rushed downward and he was certain she could hear the pounding of his heart beneath her ear. He made himself think of how fierce Wulfric had looked standing next to her to get himself under control. 'Tell me what this is about, fair one.'

'He despises me and wants me out of Godric's house.' Her arms tightened, bringing her even closer. Her breasts were fitted against his chest now so that he knew their size. He could even imagine how soft they'd be as he touched them, just filling up his palm.

What a bloody lecher he was, feeling this way when she was falling apart. He cleared his throat and pulled away under the guise of leading her to the bed to sit. He couldn't quite release his hold on her and kept an arm around her slim shoulders. His hand went to her cheek before he could think better of it. The desire to touch her was so strong that it seemed second nature.

Lifting her face so that she looked at him with watery green eyes, he asked, 'Why does he want you gone?'

She sniffled, rubbing her eyes with a sleeve, but not pulling away from his touch, he noted with satisfaction. 'He never wanted Godric to marry me. I was a servant in Lord Oswine's household. Wulfric wanted someone better for his son, perhaps a chieftain's daughter from another village. He ultimately agreed because I was Lord Oswine's ward and he generously provided coin to Godric on our marriage. In exchange I was to retain rights to Godric's property upon his death.' She shook her head. 'No one thought his death would be so soon, or that we'd have no children to show for the marriage.'

Magnus couldn't resist running his thumb over the trail of one lonely tear, overtaking it and brushing it away. 'And you're certain...there is no child?' He didn't mean to, but he glanced down at her belly, hidden in the skirt of the green woollen dress he liked.

She shook her head and drew in a shaky breath. 'Nay... It's not possible... It has been months and months since Godric and I...' Her voice trailed off and her face reddened as she appeared to realise what she was discussing with him.

He didn't even try to deny the selfish satisfaction he felt at those words. The thought of another man, especially a coward like Godric, having the right to touch her was abhorrent. 'Do you have the agreement you mentioned? That should solve the issue. If Lord Oswine had made that concession, then there must be witnesses or a record.'

She nodded. 'I already spoke to Alstan about it and

he's checking with Lord Oswine. I can't rest until I hear from him.' She paused and looked down at her fingers twisting the fabric of her dress.

'You'll hear soon. I'm confident of it.'

She looked up and the pain in her gaze twisted his heart. 'I still worry. You see, his real anger stems from the fact that I didn't have Godric's child. Godric was his most favoured, his most prized. Wulfric's angry about his death and feels I stole some part of his precious son from him.'

'You can't help that you didn't bear a child, Aisly.' But the stricken flash of guilt that crossed her face told him otherwise.

Her face fell and more tears came. 'I did…I did as he claimed.' Magnus put his arms around her and pulled her against his chest. 'Godric wasn't a good man and I couldn't bear the thought of any child being at his mercy.' Whatever else she said was unintelligible as she buried her face in his neck.

His hands ran up and down her back, soothing her, savouring how good and right she felt against him. Before he knew it, he was brushing his lips against her head, along her hairline. Her skin was so soft, so smooth and warm beneath his lips that he wanted more. Anger, desire and the need to protect her battled for right of place within him. That such a gentle and loving creature as she could be subjected to a brute infuriated him. Godric must have been horrible if she'd feared having his child. He despised that he hadn't been able to protect her from that.

After a moment, she sucked in a deep breath and pulled back, wiping at her tears with both hands. 'Perhaps I shouldn't have… Perhaps Wulfric has every right to be upset. I deprived him of his son's heir. I won't ever have a child now, so I'm being punished as well.'

'Nay, don't say that. You're kind and courageous. When anyone else would have left me to die, you risked yourself and the ire of your village to help me. You're so brave, fair one. A warrior couldn't be more courageous.' Though it physically tore something in his chest to say it, he said, 'I can't imagine such a warrior not wanting you for his own.'

She was already shaking her head before he finished, looking up at him with those luminous green eyes. 'I won't marry again. I won't subject myself to that again. Godric was perfectly agreeable until we'd married and then he was so commanding. I couldn't have friends. Oh, aye, I know all of the women in this village, but I don't have a close friendship with any of them. I knew Rowena, but she barely talked to me except in secret when Godric wasn't around. He controlled the coin I earned and even made me turn down a commission once…I think just to show me that he could have that power over me.' She gave her head another vigorous shake. 'I won't subject myself to that. I know that I can earn my own way.'

'Not all men would treat you harshly. Some men would count themselves lucky to have you as a wife and do anything to keep you happy.'

Giving him a wry smile, she asked, 'And how would you know? You can't even remember your own name.'

He tried not to flinch at her words. His name was the only thing he did know and yet he couldn't share it with her. Not until he was completely certain that his name wasn't known here as the name of an enemy. 'I know, because I am one of those men.'

His words created a deep chasm between them. It

opened up and pulled in all of the sounds, the smells, the very atmosphere in the room until there was nothing left but air thick with tension. Then it expanded, engulfing them and narrowing, sucking them down into its depths. Somehow without even moving, he found himself even closer to her. His thigh pressed against the length of her much smaller one, her torso snug against his. His arm was still around her waist, fingers pressed into the warmth just below the curve of her breast. If he moved his thumb, he could touch the underside of that plump, soft mound. Suddenly he felt like the worst sort of betrayer, using her pain and unhappiness to touch her. Aye, he wanted to comfort her, but he wanted the pleasure that comfort brought to him almost as much.

Magnus dropped his hand from her and closed his eyes for a moment to swallow down the fierce desire licking its way up his spine. He hoped she would move away, but she didn't. She just sat there, staring up at him in shock. Focusing on her eyes was impossible because he couldn't stop his gaze from dipping down to her lips. They were so soft, so pink and ripe that he couldn't help but imagine fitting his lips to them and slipping his tongue between them.

When the tip of her tongue came out to moisten her bottom lip, he was sure he must have groaned aloud. His manhood surged to life, lengthening and throbbing with need for her. The need to suck on that tantalising bit of wet flesh and lay her back on the bed was so strong that he feared he might take action before he could come to his senses. As he moved to take himself away from her, her tiny hand came out to rest on his thigh. His gaze pinned it in place. Her fingers were so close to where he wanted them, his entire body began to throb and hum in anticipation. Just a few more inches and she would know what a lecher he really was. His erection was obvious. How could she not see how he wanted her? But a glance confirmed she was too caught up in staring at his face to notice anything else.

'I believe that you'd make a good husband. But…' Her voice trailed off and she pulled her bottom lip between her teeth.

'Aye, we both know I can't stay here. I don't belong here.' He finished the thought for her.

She nodded, her eyes still wet and shiny from her tears.

He sucked in a shaky breath. It would be impossible to leave her knowing that she was vulnerable and there was no way he could keep her safe. Then his mind cleared. In an instant he realised how he could help her. The fact that it'd give them both what they wanted notwithstanding. 'How long do you have after your husband's death to birth his child?'

She frowned, two tiny lines appearing between her brows as she looked up at him. 'Late summer, perhaps a little longer,' she finally said. 'Lord Oswine's daughter was widowed a few years ago when her husband was hunting wolves. She bore his child nearly a year later and obtained a claim to his manor. But it hardly matters. It'll be apparent soon enough that I'm not with child.'

'I could—' He broke off abruptly and raked his fingers through the short hair at the back of his head, giving it a tug. Bracing himself for her disgust, he continued, 'I could give you a child.'

Her brow furrowed even more. Not disgust, perhaps, but horror.

He rushed on to explain. 'A life for a life. This will

be the only way to fully repay you for what you've done for me. I'll give you my seed and we can create a life together.'

She snapped out of her stupor and jerked away from him, rising to her feet to put distance between them. 'Nay…nay, it isn't right. It isn't… It isn't…seemly.' Her face flamed as she gave him her back.

Magnus stood, clenching his fists at his sides to keep from reaching out for her. It was clear that he'd over-stepped his bounds. Of course he'd overstepped. A vision of what she'd look like spread out beneath him, wait-ing for him, forced him to close his eyes to get his body under control. 'It wasn't my intention to offend you. My apologies.'

Getting her with child had simply been the best solu-tion. She'd keep her home and livelihood. Magnus had no hesitation about her being a good mother. She'd shown herself to be caring and compassionate. Any child of hers would be well cared for. But her reaction was reasonable and he didn't know what else he had expected. He was only glad that his tunic now covered the erection that still had the audacity to strain against his trousers.

'You didn't offend me. Shocked, perhaps, but I'm not offended.'

He took a deep breath, getting a noseful of her scent to which his body responded with another surge of blood to his groin. He gritted his teeth to fight against himself as he stepped closer. No matter how he fought it, his hand went to her hair, sweeping it and the headrail to the side, revealing the creamy skin of her neck and her profile as she turned her head towards him. His thumb settled on the nape of her neck, making gentle circles that somehow sent frissons up his arm. 'I only meant to help you. To offer some protection for you after I'm gone. I can protect you from him while I'm here—and know that I will not allow him to harm you while I can physically stop him— but I'll have to leave when winter passes. I must belong somewhere. But I want to leave knowing you'll be safe.'

She turned then, but he didn't let go of her hair and the resulting position left them in a near embrace as his arm hooked around her shoulder. 'What of the child?' she whispered. 'Would you leave your child so easily?'

'I've no doubt that you'll be a fine mother, fair one. But, nay, I wouldn't abandon you. I'll find my place eventually and...'

When his voice trailed away as he considered, she picked up where he'd left off. 'You'd expect me and the child to join you?'

Aye, that idea held appeal. His entire body warmed to it, before he got a hold of himself. He was a warrior. Warriors had families, aye, but they left them behind. She deserved better than to be left behind. 'I wouldn't expect anything from you. You've given me enough. I'll keep you in food, coin, whatever you need.' There was no doubt in his mind that he could provide for her. 'I'm a warrior.' He raised his sword hand to remind her of the scars she'd found on it, then gestured to his still-healing head wound. There were other scars he'd found on his torso as well. All battle scars made with a blade, a fist or some other weapon. Those, coupled with his memory of waking up almost burned to death after that battle, told him all he needed to know about the likelihood of his being able to have a family life. 'I don't think I'm meant to have a family. But I can give you one, Aisly, if you let me.'

She sucked in a deep breath, her bottom lip trembling.

'You don't have to answer me now.' He should let her go, take his hands from her and walk away, but they had a mind of their own. His sword hand cupped her jaw, his thumb tracing over that bottom lip, as he tightened his grip in her hair to bring her closer. 'Just think about it. I know it's not much that I offer you, but it's yours if you want it. I owe you everything.' Finally he allowed his lips to touch hers. Just a simple brush against her mouth, a barely there touch that made desire punch like a fist to his gut as it washed over him, demanding that he take more.

She gasped, a soft sound from her throat that told him of the pleasure she felt. Magnus forced himself to let go of her and step away. She seemed dazed and he cursed himself for pushing too hard too fast. Before he did something else equally thoughtless, he turned and left her home.

Aisly couldn't breathe, much less think clearly, until long after the foreigner had left her alone. She stood there for a long time. Her lips still tingled from his, her breasts were tight and achy, and the place between her thighs throbbed with need. His offer hadn't shocked her nearly so much as her immediate *need* to accept. The need was what had coursed through her body, pleading with her to say 'aye' to him. The need was what had frightened her so much that she'd had to put distance between them to even have a hope of thinking through what he'd said. A child shouldn't be decided on a whim and certainly not when she wasn't certain the urge to agree hadn't stemmed solely from her desire for him.

These things needed to be decided with clear minds and bodies that weren't throbbing.

Tightening her arms across her chest, she endeavoured to get her trembling under control. The abbess was due any moment and it would be unseemly to welcome the woman in her current state. Realising that her face still flamed, she hurried to the bucket of fresh water and splashed some on her face. It didn't stop the searing hot visions that played through her head. All of them involved the foreigner touching her with his hands, his mouth…every part of his body actually. They shocked her, but they did nothing to make her body stop responding as if he was there actually doing those things to her.

Chapter Eleven

Aisly grabbed a handful of rushes and cut through the thin stalks with her knife. They were damp from the sprinkle of rain they'd had that morning, but a few minutes by the fire would dry them for tonight's feast. The pleasing, sweet scent of the grass wafted up to her nose and made her smile. That scent never failed to make her remember all the times she'd done this very same task as a child alongside her mother. There was a song her mother had sang as they worked and she thought of it now.

Sunlight lit her hair with fire and kissed her cheeks with gold,
So that in the winter she could shine and warm away the cold...

Her mother had contrived it entirely to make Aisly feel better about her flaming hair and the flecks of colour on her cheeks. She couldn't help but smile as the song ran about in her head, though it made her sad as well as happy. She'd always imagined she'd sing it to her own child, but it seemed that would never happen now.

Unless she allowed the foreigner to give her a child.

Her hand trembled. Slick with the mist of the morning rain, the knife slipped from her grip, falling into the centre of the clump of rushes. Inexplicably her breath came in short pants, while her heart raced in her chest.

Was it really possible to have everything she'd ever wanted so easily? Her home? A child? Her independence? She closed her eyes and imagined the child that she and the foreigner might create. A boy, big and handsome like his father, or a girl with Aisly's own flaming hair, but with flecks of gold in her eyes like her father.

Those visions had haunted her over the past several days since he'd made the offer, and they always led to thoughts of the actual act of making that child.

I'll give you my seed... Even days later those words caused her face to flame and heated her blood in a way she couldn't have described had she tried. What would it feel like to have that magnificent body—

'Have you finished, Aisly?'

Aisly opened her eyes and scrambled to find the knife she had dropped, before looking up to see Wyn approaching. The girl's eyes were vivid with the excitement of being outside the village for the last time that season and her face practically glowed with a youthful joy Aisly almost envied. She'd had that naiveté once and it hadn't served her well.

'Aye, almost.' Aisly redoubled her efforts and sawed through the last few handfuls in the cluster. Depositing them on top of her almost overflowing basket, she stood and wiped away the bits of grass and sticks that clung to her skirt. Adjusting her heavy woollen shawl around her shoulders, she grabbed her basket's handle and made her way down the slope with Wyn to the path by the stream.

Warriors had been out all day making sure the area was clear of any rebel Danes so that the women could safely gather all that was needed for the feast. Tonight was a full moon and the start of winter. Over the next several days animals would be taken to other villages to be sold and some would be slaughtered so the meat could be preserved to eat through winter. Soon it would be too cold for them to stay outside and there was hardly enough room for them all inside. It was Cuthbert's tradition to invite all the villagers to a feast on this night.

Since coming to the village upon her marriage, Aisly had enjoyed the feast and she looked forward to it every year. There were usually plenty of stories, songs and ale passed around the large fire they'd build outside to cook the meat. There was already a tinge of the woodsmoke in the air, though it was only midday.

Wyn looked particularly thoughtful as Aisly stepped up beside her as they made their way towards the village. It took only three steps before the girl's impulsive mouth overtook the silence. 'Tell me of the foreigner, Aisly. I still can't get over how he saved you. He's so courageous.'

Aisly managed not to falter in her step, though the question took her by surprise. She was valiantly trying *not* to think of him. 'Wh-what do you wish to know?'

Wyn shrugged, her cheeks reddening as she brushed a tendril of midnight hair from her face. 'Is he kind?'

Not all men would treat you harshly. Some men would count themselves lucky to have you as a wife and do anything to keep you happy.

'Aye, he's kind.' The kindest man she knew.

'I've gone to the hall a few times to see my father and *he* was there. His words sound strange, but I find I want to listen to him, even when he says them wrong.'

Aisly glanced over to see a dreamy expression on the girl's face. She could sympathise, as she was certain that she'd worn that same smile in regards to him. He seemed to have that effect on the fairer sex.

'And he's so strong and tall. I'm sure I've never seen a man quite so large,' Wyn continued.

A shiver of pleasure ran through the girl's words just as surely as one ran through Aisly's body. Aye, he was big, so big that he should be frightening, but he'd been nothing but gentle with her. When he cupped her face, she could feel the strength he kept restrained in his hand, but she'd never had any fear that he'd turn that strength on her. Her palm tingled as she remembered the solid strength of his tree trunk of a thigh beneath it. Would he be large…everywhere?

'Do you… Do you suppose his—'

'Wyn!' Aisly's reproach caught the girl unaware. 'That isn't something we should discuss.'

'Oh?' Wyn frowned. 'I only wondered if his memories had begun to return to him.' The girl gave her a bewildered look and Aisly chastised herself for attributing her own inappropriate thoughts on to Wyn.

'I'm sorry…I…' There was no explanation except the truth of her thoughts and she couldn't tell her those. Instead of explaining, she shook her head and said, 'I don't think so, but I haven't spoken with him in a few days.' He'd stayed away after his illicit offer. Aisly assumed he was either taking his meals in the hall or preparing them himself. She'd caught his gaze on her a time or two as she passed through the village, but he hadn't approached her. She would've been hurt had she the slightest notion of what to say to him.

Wyn smiled, her expression a bit smug. 'He took the evening meal with us yesterday.'

'Oh.' Aisly kept her tone light and interested, while inside her heart fell a little. Wyn was a perfectly pleasant girl. It was natural that she'd draw his interest.

'Aye. Father likes him, I can tell. They spoke the entire meal. He seems to know a lot about fighting and training warriors.' She sighed. The sigh of a young woman in the first stages of love. 'He's so handsome. I think I may try to convince him to stay, even after winter.'

'I don't think that's possible. He's not from here, Wyn. He'll need to go back to his people.'

Wyn shrugged. 'Perhaps, but we could be his people now. If he's truly a mercenary as you claimed, then he probably has no home.'

Aisly nodded, but inside she didn't really believe it was true. Everything Wyn had said about him was accurate. He was virile, handsome, strong, brave. He belonged somewhere and it wasn't here. Somewhere there were people waiting for him. That ache of quiet longing—the one that said he would never truly be hers no matter how hard she wanted him—was back to tug at her heart.

As they'd walked, the women who had accompanied them to fill their baskets with rushes for the hall that night fell into step behind them. Yet two of the young women stood ahead of them on the rise where the path veered from the stream and into the woods. Aisly called to them, but they only giggled, covering their mouths to block the sound, and waved her over.

Aisly walked over, the women following behind her. Curiously she skimmed the stream several yards below the embankment to see what held their attention. She had to wait only a moment before the foreigner broke the surface of the water, his strong arms taking him across the deep pool of water and to the opposite shore. When he put his feet down and rose, they were all treated to a view of his pale buttocks. It was an exquisite view. The water lapped around him, clinging to the well-formed curves. Aisly followed the developed muscle up to the two dimples pressed into the flesh just above each cheek. Then kept moving upward, caught by the lean line of pronounced muscle up his back. He pushed water back from his face and his hair, causing droplets to run down his wide shoulders and pool in those fascinating dimples.

A flame of warmth flickered to life inside her and bloomed throughout her middle. It was strange how just looking at him could light her up inside. Stranger still how she could so vividly imagine how those muscles would feel beneath her hands. Smooth, but solid, like the finest velvet over stone. Her fingertips tingled as they remembered washing his back, reminding her how warm he'd been. She wanted to wrap herself in him.

The women giggled, simultaneously breaking her spell and alerting him to their presence. He turned his head to see them there. His ears reddened, betraying his embarrassment, as his hands went down to cover his essentials. What a shame it was that he had emerged from the water turned away from them. He called out in mock outrage that sent the women into peals of laughter.

'Go.' Aisly shooed them away. A few seemed genuinely reluctant to leave, including Wyn, but they finally turned to continue their trip home with renewed enthusiasm. Aisly couldn't resist a glance back at him, or more accurately the well-developed cheeks of his bottom. He still stood with his back to her, but he caught her admiring gaze over his shoulder. His eyes narrowed, but they weren't warning her away. They were assessing, gauging her thoughts and pulling them out into the open, knowing she wanted him.

Heat passed between them even across the distance. She whirled away before she could do something foolish, something like joining him in his bathing.

'How can that be true? You were there, Alstan, you saw Lord Oswine sign it.' Her voice rose in frustration as she again questioned how her marriage contract could have gone missing.

Alstan glanced around and gently grabbed her arm to lead her away from the crowd. Night had long since fallen and most had already stuffed their bellies with roasted meat and ale. The large fire still roared outside and people milled about it deep in conversation. Inside the hall, a storyteller's dramatic voice could be heard recounting the exploits of a legendary warrior.

Alstan dropped his hold when they walked around the corner of the hall, putting some distance between themselves and the crowd. The moon was full and high, and had claimed its freedom from a mass of clouds, so that she was able to see her brother's features. He wasn't happy about what he'd found.

'I don't know. There's record of the marriage. It's recorded in the ledger, but there's no contract and there's no record that there ever was. I've spoken with Lord Oswine and he promises to look into it…but…' His voice trailed off and he looked away from her, hands on his hips.

'But? Alstan, what are you saying?' If there was no record that the house was hers, then she might as well leave now instead of waiting for Wulfric to toss her out.

Shaking his head, he said, 'It doesn't feel right. I'm not

certain, but it seems that it was intentionally misplaced. Or perhaps it was destroyed.' He said that last so low that she had to lean forward to hear it.

She plopped her heels back into the dirt and teetered a bit, her shoulders catching her weight against the side of the hall. She stayed that way. Dejected and defeated, leaning on the building because she was too weak to hold herself up. Her anger and frustration fled, because despite her initial alarm, she realised that she'd been expecting this. Wulfric always got what he wanted. She might now appeal to Cuthbert, who was kind and just, but even he couldn't force Wulfric to allow her to stay in her home. Not if it wasn't hers.

She wasn't surprised at all. It was only at that moment that she realised how much she'd been considering the foreigner's proposition. Her fingers even went to her mouth, touching her lips, which tingled from the memory of the phantom touch of his.

She had to accept. It was the only choice that made sense. If they were successful, she'd keep her home and not have to marry. But even more, she'd have a child. She had to bite back the smile of relief that threatened to overtake her. Her arms crossed over her belly as she imagined herself growing large with the foreigner's baby. Perhaps it should have felt wrong—she'd been trying to convince herself of that fact ever since he suggested it. But the very idea filled her with such a sense of hope and tenderness that she was nearly overwhelmed with it.

Alstan spoke, but she had to blink away her thoughts before she could make sense of what he said. 'I'll look into this. I vow to you that I'll figure out what happened. But whatever happens, I want you to know that you'll always be welcome in my home. You won't be alone.'

She couldn't hold back her tears and threw herself into his arms. He could make her so angry sometimes that she wanted to stone him, but he always took care of her. 'I know that I am, Alstan. There's still hope of a child, though.' She bit her tongue after the falsehood and hoped it wasn't too sinful.

He pulled back, hands on her shoulders. 'Do you think it's possible?'

She nodded but refused to say anything. It hurt to keep anything from him, but this…she could not share it.

He gave a hint of a smile and hugged her again. 'I know a child is what you want, so I pray that it's true.'

There was one other issue she needed to discuss with him before she went to find the foreigner. 'What of Rowena and Beorn? What did Lord Oswine decide? Did you make sure he was merciful, as I asked?'

Alstan nodded. 'I convinced him Beorn's transgression was too small to warrant his concern. I've dealt with them both.'

'What did you do?'

'Two years of servitude.' At her expression of dismay, he held up a hand. 'It seems harsh, but it's the same work he was doing here. Wulfric did have evidence, so I had to do something. They have lodgings and won't suffer.'

Aisly nodded. In the face of what could have been, this wasn't so bad. 'Thank you. I knew I could count on you to make it right.'

'You can always count on me, Aisly.' He tugged the end of her braid and gave her a grin as he bid her good-night.

Immediately she turned to look for the foreigner. She'd seen him earlier in the evening. He'd been the object of adoration of a few of the young women as he'd stood talking with them and their families. He'd caught her eye even then and some unspoken tide had passed between them. Hurrying around the building, she searched for the foreigner's face in the crowd. She was suddenly anxious to accept his proposition before that option, too, was taken away from her. Not seeing him there, she glanced inside the hall but didn't find his handsome face amongst those listening to the storyteller. Turning back to the crowd outside, she fought against the disappointment threatening to take root and hurried around the fire. After a few moments of searching through the people, she thought that perhaps he'd gone home, but she couldn't risk knocking on his door so late at night. What if someone saw her?

Magnus had kept an eye on her all night. It wasn't that she needed to be watched, it was that he couldn't look away from her. She was constantly lingering in the periphery of his thoughts, but ever since the day he'd made her that offer, she'd somehow pushed her way in even more. Every time he'd seen her since, he'd meant to approach her, to take back the offer because even not knowing who he was, he knew that it had been too much, too far. He had nothing to offer her beyond fathering a child. Yet every time the opportunity had presented itself, he'd held back.

He wanted her to accept him.

Whether it was because he wanted her or because he wanted the primal satisfaction of watching her grow round with his seed, he didn't know. They tumbled and twisted in his mind until they became one and the same.

Other men watched her as well. She didn't notice them, but he did. They watched her when she wasn't looking, or as she passed them and walked away. They couldn't openly show their interest because she was so recently a widow and he'd learned that she wouldn't be allowed to marry until summer. He wanted to tear their eyes from their heads, or at least put his arm around her and claim her as his own. He wasn't certain if it was a primitive instinct that made him so fierce, or if it was some leftover trace of his previous existence.

Perhaps he didn't want to know who he was. Perhaps he could start anew. With her.

His heart picked up speed when he saw her searching around the large roasting fire. She was looking for him.

'Fair one.' His voice reached her before she saw him. It was husky with longing. He'd been rigid with wanting her since she'd seen him at the stream earlier. If it had been just her, he'd have turned so that she could see what she did to him so easily.

That was another reason he'd stayed away. If she didn't want him, he didn't want to put pressure on her. Only, the look in her eyes at the stream had been easy to decipher.

Aisly looked for him, turning her head until she spotted him emerging from the shadow of a house just outside the light cast by the fire. His eyes ate her up as they passed over her, making her lips part in pleasure.

The tiny gasp was welcome, as was the way her eyes warmed when they touched him. The desire was clear on her face for everyone to see. A quick glance found that no one was paying them any attention. Still, he stepped back into the shadows away from prying eyes, silently beckoning her to follow him. His heart gave a jolt when she did.

'Were you looking for me?'

'Aye.' But she didn't say anything else and her eyes

roved his chest. She was remembering the encounter at the stream.

He stood straighter for her scrutiny.

Aye, look at me and imagine yourself beneath me.

She bit her lip and looked down, as if she knew his thoughts. After a moment, she found her courage and boldly met his gaze again. 'Why do you look at me like that?'

'Like what?' He cocked his head to the side, though he knew what she meant. He just wondered if she realised that she looked at him the same way.

'As if... As if I'm someone special to you.'

'Because you are someone special to me.'

Her cheeks turned rosy and she glowed with pleasure. 'You barely know me.'

He laughed. 'I barely know myself, but I *know* you. You're compassionate, fiercely independent, courageous, kind...beautiful.'

She looked away, unable to meet his gaze as he recited the praise. 'Why do you say such things?'

'They're true.'

'It'll only make things more difficult when...'

Ah, so she was thinking of the inevitable, too. He would leave her sooner than they both wanted. Somehow the knowledge only made the need to be with her now even stronger.

'I see they've given you back your sword.'

'Aye.' His hand automatically went to the scabbard's strap that crossed his chest. 'Cuthbert gave it to me earlier today. It seems I've earned his trust.'

She nodded, but her thoughts weren't on the sword. He held his breath as he waited for her to speak.

'I've thought about your offer.' Her voice dropped

to a whisper and his heartbeat hung suspended while he waited.

When she seemed reluctant to continue, he gave a nod of encouragement, all the while telling himself that whatever she decided wouldn't be the end of him. Though either way he knew he was lost.

'Aye. Tonight.' She was too embarrassed to wait for his response. She simply turned and ran in the direction of her home, droplets of rain dogging her steps.

The rain that had threatened the entire day finally began to fall. Slowly at first, but the sky opened up before she'd passed from his sight. Magnus stayed where he was, allowing the cold water to cool his overheated body. He wouldn't follow right away, because he wouldn't dare to draw attention to the fact that he was doing so. Also, he was fairly certain that his ability to walk properly had been compromised.

As the sprinkles settled into a steady drizzle, it soaked through his tunic and shirt. Scraping a hand over his face, he sucked in a breath and vowed to not attack her. No matter how he wanted her, he had to go slowly, but first he needed to make sure this was what she wanted.

People scurried about, gathering the last of the roasted meat and putting it away. Some clogged the doors of the hall, hoping to get inside where the feast still continued. Others ran for their homes to avoid the downpour that was sure to come soon. Magnus was impervious to it all. His thoughts were centred solely on the woman waiting for him.

Finally, when he'd beaten back his desire to a manageable level, he allowed his steps to take him to her. He took the long way, meandering so no one could guess his intention. His heart beat in his ears with every step, matching the answering throb in his trousers.

Before it seemed possible, he was raising his hand to knock on her door, but she must have been listening for him, because the door opened before he brought his fist down. She smiled a shy smile and the fierce edge of his arousal changed to something infinitely more tender. She stepped back to allow him inside and closed the door behind them. The sound of the latch fitting into place threatened to stoke the savage flame to life again, but he fought it back down, holding it in his tenuous grip.

Not yet. Not until—

Her soft hand pressed against his forearm as she came up behind him. The cold wet sleeve did nothing to dampen the heat of her touch. His eyes closed and his jaw clenched as he fought the battle within him.

Chapter Twelve

Aisly shivered from the cold she'd let inside when she'd opened the door, but it was chased by the secret thrill she felt from the intensity of the foreigner's gaze. Even with Godric—nay, she wouldn't allow thoughts of him this night. She'd never felt so wanted. The wanting was so poignant that it was almost like need. Perhaps if she'd been less inclined to restraint, she'd allow herself to believe it was need.

But that was foolishness, as this was simply an arrangement. He was paying her back for saving him.

Still. The need to touch him was overpowering now that she felt she had some right to him. Pressing her palm to his forearm, she felt him tremble and knew an answering weakness in her knees. Clearing her throat, she said, 'Come. Take off your tunic and I'll dry it by the fire.'

She preceded him into the room, uncertain of how to continue. She'd changed into her nightdress when she'd arrived home, but beyond that and unbraiding her hair, she'd been at a loss as to what he might expect. When a moment passed and there was no movement from him, she turned and lost her breath at the intensity of his expression.

'I need to hear you say that you're certain, that you've thought about this.' The husk of his voice raked across her skin, drawing it tight with yearning. The wet wool of his tunic and the linen of his shirt underneath was plastered to his chest, emphasising the broad expanse of muscle. His hands were closed into loose fists at his sides, she imagined to keep himself from reaching out to her, though that was probably wishful thinking. He couldn't possibly feel the way she felt.

'Aye.' It was a breathy whisper and she was surprised she'd managed that with the way he looked at her. Swallowing, she tried again with more confidence. 'I've given it a great deal of thought. This is what I want.'

He shrugged out of the scabbard, leaning his sword against the wall before moving towards her. His steps were solid, somehow final, on the bare wood floor as he crossed the room and came to a stop in front of her, way closer than he ever had before. There was an intimacy in the proximity, a knowing that he had the right to her now. Slowly his arms came up around her, drawing her into their circle without ever really touching her. His fingers tugged on her loosened hair, burying themselves in its length. He smelled like rain mixed with clean male sweat, a scent that her body evidently found so pleasing it ached for him. A pulse beat between her thighs and her breasts swelled with longing. Something that shouldn't have been possible without him even touching her.

'I'll want to look at you...touch you.' His breath teased the hair at her temple as he spoke and his low voice rumbled through her. 'I want your pleasure.'

A shudder moved through her as languid heat settled between her legs. Her nipples tightened, pebbling as they begged for his touch first. She wasn't entirely sure what he meant, but she sensed this would be different than anything she'd ever known. She wanted whatever he wanted as long as it meant he'd keep touching her with those gentle hands, looking at her with those intense eyes and speaking to her in that voice that moved through her. Giving a jerky nod that she hoped he interpreted as consent, she pressed her hands to his arms, moving them up until they rested on his broad shoulders.

His lips brushed her temple, a slow drag that raised goose bumps along her skin. Fingers tightening in her hair, he tilted her head back, forcing her to meet his gaze. His eyes burned hot with arousal, so dark the gold was completely obliterated as they moved down to rest on her mouth. Her lips tingled in anticipation of his touch. Slowly, so slowly she was afraid something might stop him before he reached her, he leaned down.

He stopped so close that his breath caressed her lips and she knew he'd taste of ale. She wanted the touch of his mouth. 'Foreigner.' The whispered plea finally coaxed him lower to tease at her mouth. He brushed her lips once, twice—on the third pass some wicked instinct made her open to him so that his tongue could fill her and brush against hers.

He groaned and his hands flattened against her back, pulling her body flush against him. He was hard against her belly, long and thick, making her body clench in response while at the same time a dart of fear made itself known. It seemed that he *was* big everywhere. But she couldn't give that fear time to flare, because his hands were roaming up and down her back, veering lower on every pass. Finally he filled his hands with her bottom and lingered there, gently squeezing before moving back up again. Her body answered that with a flood of damp heat between her thighs, while her blood thickened and warmed.

Just when she was catching on to the rhythm of his tongue, he pulled back. A soft grunt erupted from his throat as he stepped back, his hands moving over her waist and up her front to rest on her breasts for the briefest of touches before moving back down to her hips. Somehow her nipples tightened even more and stood firm, begging for his hands to come back to them.

When her puzzled gaze met his, he explained, 'I fear hurting you. I promised myself I would move slowly, but I can't keep my hands from you.' The concern on his face won over any threat of fear.

'I'm hardly delicate,' she assured him.

'But you are precious.' His large hand moved up to brush back her hair as he cupped her cheek. His fingertips brushed the sensitive skin of her neck and she shivered with the delicious pleasure of that simple touch.

No one had ever called her precious before. And yet...the way he looked at her made her *feel* precious. He looked at her like he'd never seen anything that could compare, like he never wanted to look away.

'I want to...' She hesitated. Perhaps it wasn't right to want the pleasure he promised, but he made her feel as if nothing she said could be wrong. 'I'd like to see you.' Her gaze dipped to his chest, not daring to stray lower, not yet.

Already his hands were going to the neck of his tunic, pulling it up and over his head to fling it away. His undershirt was quick to follow and there he stood, naked from the waist up. She'd seen that magnificent expanse of muscle before, but never while knowing that it was hers...if only for the night.

'You can touch me.' He stood still as he waited.

She wanted to touch him. Her palms tingled just imagining the feel of all that hard, solid strength beneath them, but she couldn't get over the idea that it was wrong. She was shaking her head when he stepped forward. She instinctively stepped back, but he only smiled and followed her, taking hold of her hips and pulling her to him.

He misconstrued her hesitance and whispered, 'I'll be careful with you, fair one. I'll not hurt you.'

If she didn't know anything else, she knew that with certainty. Her hand automatically went to his chest to keep herself balanced, but his left hand covered it and moved it across the dips and bulges of his chest. 'Feel me.'

Her fingers couldn't resist their own exploration of him. He was so powerful, so wrapped in muscle that she could hardly believe he was real and hers...at least for the night. Her hands moved over his shoulders and down his chest, which was covered in a light furring of hair, to the ridged muscle of his flat stomach. His shoulders were so wide and his waist so narrow, she couldn't help but admire him. Just below his navel, dark blond hair created a path that led down into his trousers. She'd somehow managed to keep from looking at that very obvious sign of his arousal, but she did now and felt her mouth go dry. The bulge seemed quite as large as it had felt. It wasn't surprising considering the size of everything else about him, but still. She licked her lips and allowed her hand to go further down, cupping him, though he had entirely too much to contain in her hand.

His fingertips skimmed up the sides of her body to her breasts. She hadn't expected such a direct approach. His thumbs circled around her rigid nipples before his fingertips scraped across them through the thin material of her nightgown. She might have gasped before she managed to close her mouth, containing the sounds to tiny exhales through her nose. His gaze wasn't on her breasts as he worked. It was on her face, taking in every nuance of her reaction.

She felt so exposed to him, but he didn't seem to mind her reaction. In fact, it seemed he was looking to cause it. When she breathed heavier, he'd repeat whatever it was he'd just done. When he pinched her nipple, the resulting dart of pleasure was so unexpected she startled and he merely grinned in approval.

'You seem to have done this before.' He seemed to know her body as well as he knew his sword. He'd obviously known women.

His grin widened. 'Some things are instinct. Your face tells me all that I need to know.'

She couldn't explain what made her voice her next question. Perhaps it was her own desire as much as his. 'Would you like to see me?'

His eyes widened before seeming to darken even more. 'Very much so.'

It gave her the daring to shimmy from his hold and grasp the skirt of her nightdress. She hesitated only a moment before raising it, gaining courage by the way he followed the hem up her legs with his eyes. Though she lost her nerve as she reached her hips and faltered, holding the bunched-up skirt there.

He didn't allow her to falter for long. His warm palms moved beneath the fabric, cupping her hips and making her gasp aloud from the contact. She'd never known her skin was so sensitive as it prickled beneath him. The linen tugged from her hands as he pushed it upward. Before she realised it, he was pulling it off over her head.

He wasn't smiling any more as he allowed it to slip from his fingers to the floor, his gaze on her body. His hand moved up slowly, as if giving her time to object, but she didn't want to do anything to dissuade him, so she stood still and allowed his hand to cup her breast. The rough skin of his palm abraded her sensitive nipple, sending a jolt of pleasure straight down to her centre. He stepped forward again, so that barely any space was left between them.

She'd worried that he might find her too small, but he didn't seem to mind as he cupped her other breast. His thumbs made gently circles around the nipples, mimicking his motion from earlier, before flicking across the sensitive tips. Only, this time the sensation was so much sharper now that his calloused fingertips abraded her bare skin.

'You're beautiful.'

He pulled his gaze from her breasts to her eyes. She hadn't been quite sure what to expect from this exchange. At its surface it was him giving her what she needed—his seed—in exchange for saving his life. Yet it felt like so much more than that. They could have finished by now.

Nay, this wasn't a simple transaction. This was something more. She wasn't quite sure what to say that it was, but it was more.

His hands dropped from her breasts, fingertips grazing across her stomach and hips before landing on the fastenings to his trousers. She took a deep breath as she watched him work them, anticipation coiled tight within her. He paused after he finished. She knew he looked back at her, but she couldn't tear her gaze from the massive bulge. He pushed his trousers down just a little so they dipped past his hips and his manhood sprang loose.

It jutted up proudly from the thick dark blond curls at its base, curving upward towards his navel. He was long and impossibly thick. She was quite certain that if she grasped him, her fingers wouldn't meet her thumb.

'I don't...' She licked her lips to give herself time to find the right words. 'I don't know if this will work. I'm not certain we're properly matched.'

He exhaled on a laugh, making the thing bounce with the movement. 'I'll fit.'

'How do you know?' She looked up at him, suspicion niggling at a corner of her mind. 'Have you memory of doing this before?'

That made him frown and his brow furrowed as if trying to remember. 'Nay,' he admitted. 'But I'm a man and you're a woman. We're supposed to fit.'

She wasn't so certain. It seemed entirely possible that some women and some men just wouldn't fit properly. Yet before she could tell him so, his hands slipped around her and pulled her against him. One arm went around her shoulders to hold her close, while the other moved down over her hip. His fingers brushing against the curls at the apex of her thighs.

She gasped and pulled away as much as he'd let her. 'What are you doing?' She had a suspicion that her body was entirely too ready to try him. It wouldn't be seemly if he felt her and realised just how much.

He didn't answer immediately and instead pushed his fingers through her curls, between her closed thighs. 'Open your legs for me, fair one.' A gentle push of his knee encouraged her feet to step apart.

His longest finger found its way between her lips, spearing them apart to find the liquid proof of her arousal.

Aisly closed her eyes to hide her shame, just waiting for him to mock her. He didn't say a word, though. He only made a guttural sound deep in his throat that was suspiciously like approval as he rubbed his fingertip round and round, raking over her tender and aching flesh. Before she realised it, she was clinging to that arm with both hands, her face pressed to his biceps as she gasped silently against his warm skin.

The word 'please' tumbled from her lips in a repeated whisper. She just wanted to be filled, an ache expanding within. Somehow he knew. His thick finger found her and pressed inside, retreated and pressed inside again. It wasn't enough, not nearly enough. Her greedy body only ached for more to fill her. It wasn't until he pushed a second one in, slowly working its way inside her, that she realised what he was doing. He was showing her how she would accept him. He was making a way for himself.

His right hand tangled in her hair and pulled her face back so that he could look at her. She had no hope of opening her eyes, though, not while the fingers of his left hand kept moving in and out in that maddening rhythm that made her hips move right along with him. But she felt his mouth against her cheek as he spoke.

'Do you feel how your body is made for mine? We'll fit, I swear it.' He pressed his erection against her hip, grinding it against her. His groan brushed against her cheek and she clenched around his fingers. 'I'll go slowly,' he said and withdrew his fingers, only to pick her up and lay her on the bed.

She could barely open her eyes from the consuming pleasure to watch him sit back on the edge of the bed to undress, but she did because she didn't want to miss any of his magnificent body. His boots fell to the floor, followed by the trousers, just before he was turning into her arms. His massive thigh tucked itself between her legs, pressing against her folds in a way that would have been vulgar had the pressure not have felt so good. Just the one was so wide and muscular, a tingle of excitement moved down her spine. One arm wrapped itself in her hair, while the other pressed to the mattress to hold most of his weight from her, as his mouth crashed down to hers.

His tongue filled her mouth, but this time she was expecting it and opened beneath him. It didn't stay there nearly long enough, before he was dragging hot, open-mouthed kisses down her neck. The subtle scrape of his teeth made her bite her lip to keep from crying out. Then his hot, glorious mouth found her breast and it opened over the tip, drawing her nipple deep inside. The pleasure was so profound, so primal that she couldn't stop the sounds, so she closed her mouth, making a series of stifled groans instead. She hardly realised she was grinding her hips against the hard muscle of his thigh until his thumb worked its way between them and found her there. It circled around and around her aroused flesh until she only knew that she ached more than she ever had in her life.

Just when she thought it might be possible to die of longing, he rose up, supported by his knees and the forearm that was wrapped in her hair pressed against the mattress. His hold on her hair should've been too tight, too controlling, but she liked it. She liked that he handled her as if he knew exactly what to do. With a start, she realised she trusted him completely. His hold wasn't to control her...it was to reassure her. He grasped his shaft, pulling back the foreskin to reveal a rather large glistening head, but she got only a quick glimpse. As his other knee gently spread her thighs wider so that he could settle between them, her earlier fear returned.

He must have sensed a change, because he met her gaze, then looked back to where she was splayed out beneath him. 'You're the most beautiful thing I've ever seen.' He let go of his shaft to gently run his fingertips between her open folds.

He really did seem to think she was precious. The action, so simple yet so eloquent, calmed her fears a little. At least until he lined up the head of his erection with her opening and gently pressed forward. At first the sensation was indescribable, an exquisite pressure that countered the ache within her perfectly. But then it was too much, she was stretched too taut and her body rebelled. She was too small. He was too big. Too tight. She involuntarily bucked her hips, but he held fast with his hand on her hip and didn't allow her to move away.

'Does it hurt?' he asked. His eyes were so gentle despite the firm hold he had on her, and the obvious desire in their depths that she felt immediately comforted. If she said aye, he'd stop.

'It's too much,' she whispered.

'Then I won't go further yet.' He released her hip and brought his thumb to his mouth. She was almost jealous as he brought it between his lips and sucked the tip, wanting more than anything to have his mouth on her breast again. It was glistening when he pulled it out and returned it to that place just above where his body was joined to hers. As he worked over that nub of swollen flesh, that all-consuming ache began to return, throbbing harder with every beat of her heart. He must have read her thoughts, because his mouth returned to her breast, sucking a nipple into the hot, wet heat of his mouth. She bit her lip to stay silent as her hips pushed against him. Just that quickly she went from afraid he would push forward to afraid that he wouldn't. Mercifully he sank in a bit more, drawing a reluctant gasp from her. His own groan against her breast drowned out the sound and his thumb abandoned her as his hand grabbed her hip to hold her steady. Only then did he slide in, filling her so completely that their hips were pressed flush together. She was so full of him, so completely possessed by him, that she wasn't certain how anything could feel any better.

At least, not until he moved. His hips pushed against her in a slow grind. Not a thrust really, just a gentle rocking that had her clenching around him for more. He released her nipple, but his clever tongue stroked over the puckered flesh, a vison so sinful she imagined it would stay in her head for the rest of her days. Then he looked at her and the intensity and concentration of that look made her tighten around him. 'You've taken all of me. How does it feel?'

He ground against her again, so hard and thick that he should've been uncomfortable, but she only wanted more. Her voice sounded breathy and not her own. 'It's never felt like this before.'

He grinned and gave a little push of his hips. Waves of pleasure moved through her. It must have shown on her face, because he got bolder and withdrew nearly all the way. She was certain she'd never be whole again. Only, he pushed back in again, making her whole only to take it away again. The drag of his hard shaft against her overly sensitive body was nearly more than she could stand. 'By the gods, Aisly, you feel so good. So tight.' He fell forward and gasped the words against her neck.

Some thrill moved through her at his words of acceptance. This was better than good. It felt incredible. Her arm held him clasped to her, afraid that he might stop if she didn't, while her other hand clutched at his nape. Her legs flailed a bit. Every time she got purchase with her heel on the bed, he'd move in that delicious way he had and dislodge her.

His arm took pity on her and hooked itself beneath her knee, solving her dilemma and holding her open so they both gasped at the new level of pleasure as he sank even deeper. She managed to stop the sound halfway through and he noticed. Drawing up a bit to look at her, he stopped that wonderful rhythm, making her hips buck beneath him because she wanted it back. Her body clenched desperately around his shaft. 'Why did you do that?' he asked.

'What?' Though to be fair, it was more a sound than a word she made.

'Why do you stifle your sounds?'

She shook her head, too far gone in pleasure to even be capable of deciphering his meaning. He meant to get an answer, though, and grinned as he pinched her nipple between his thumb and forefinger. It might have hurt had it not already been swollen and anxious for his attention. She couldn't stop her cry as pleasure darted through her body straight to where his shaft was nestled deep within her. He did it again and she nearly shattered inside.

'I don't know.' She did know. Only whores made sounds, but she didn't care to enter into that conversation just yet, not when there was still pleasure to be had.

'I want to hear your pleasure. Don't hide it from me.' The way he looked down at her, that smile that curved his lips and the adoring way his eyes caressed her face, made her not care what was right any more. She just wanted to please him and would do whatever it took.

She nodded and reached for him. Her arms going around his shoulders as he fell over her, hips pumping against her, hard and deep. Prickles of light danced behind her eyelids. She almost managed to quell the gasps, but he was relentless and she couldn't stop them any more.

'Aye, that's it.' His jagged voice prickled across the skin of her neck. The firm slide of him thick and hard inside her felt so incredibly good that more cries fell from her lips. He grinned against her ear. 'Good girl.' His voice was strained as he set a harsh and fast rhythm she couldn't hope to keep up with, so she held on and cried out as deep, wrenching spasms rippled through her body, causing her to clench around his shaft.

He redoubled his efforts, holding her tight until his hips faltered and he found his own release within her. His grunts of pleasure echoed her own.

Chapter Thirteen

Magnus fell on to her, crushing her, so weak he didn't think he'd ever be able to move again. He just wanted to lie there between her thighs, half-rigid within her, her scent all over him, her soft body beneath him, her arms clutching him tight. This was what he wanted, he realised as a sudden clarity came over him.

Aisly was what he wanted. Aisly and everything life could be with her. The thought was wrong in so many ways. His life was not here, and his life—the life of a warrior—was not meant to include someone like her.

Her breath came in soft pants against his ear. He hesitated, because he didn't want to see regret or anything resembling it in her eyes, but after a few moments, he couldn't resist rising up a little to look down into her lovely face. The tiny flecks of colour on her cheeks stood out against the paleness of her skin, making him realise that he hadn't kissed them all yet. But her hand on his cheek drew his eyes up to hers.

'You've done that before.' She smiled.

He settled a forearm on the mattress above her head. Knowing how to touch her had been instinctual. He had to admit that must mean he'd done it many times before, just the way he'd been able to find faults in the security of her village. It came from years of training, practice. But the way his heart raced as he looked down at her, and the way he couldn't get enough of her, had nothing to do with his past experience. It had everything to do with her.

'Aye, but never like that.'

'How would you know? You can't remember.'

'Because I've never done that with you.'

She blushed and her face returned to that same glowing pink that had overcome her when she'd found her release. He'd already been half-rigid, but that made him harden with wanting her again. Gently, he pulled out of her and leaned to his side. She moved over, but the bed was so narrow that his shoulders took up most of it. After some shuffling, she ended up half-draped over him, her knee resting between his thighs and her hand on his chest. His arm went around her, keeping her close. She rested her head on his shoulder, but it took a little longer for her to relax against him. When she finally did, her hand on his stomach, her breath soft on his chest, he felt like he'd won a victory. For a moment, everything seemed right.

'Aisly?'

'Hmm...' Her eyes were closed and he couldn't resist stroking her cheek as he pushed a piece of her hair back off her face.

He licked his lips, unwilling to bring up discussion of her husband, but at the same time yearning to know about her. It bothered him the way she'd been so unwilling to respond to him. It wasn't that she hadn't wanted to. There had been very real fear in her eyes. Taking a deep breath, he decided to just ask. 'Why were you so unwilling to let me hear you?'

She stiffened and he stroked his hand down her arm to her small hand, settling his own on top of it. To his relief, she didn't try to pull away and relaxed into him again. 'I didn't think you'd want to.'

He lay still for a moment as he contemplated what that meant. As far as he could tell, she'd only been with her husband. His arm clenched her to him a little bit tighter. 'Did he tell you to be quiet?'

It wasn't necessary to say his name. They both knew. She nodded, her hair sliding against his chest, and her hand turned over underneath his so they were palm to palm. When she spoke, her voice was so soft he had to strain to hear it. 'He said that only whores make sounds. Only whores move during it. Only whores enjoy it. I suppose that's what I am now.'

'Nay!' He shifted so that he was on his side facing her, but he kept his arm around her and their legs tangled together. It was impossible to get closer and still see her face. 'Your body was made to enjoy the touch of mine. Did he never touch you to ease his way?'

She shook her head and her wide green eyes were almost his undoing. 'He wasn't gentle…not like you. It was a duty to him.'

The thought of her at that man's mercy was a knife to his heart. 'Did he hurt you?'

She leaned forward and dropped her forehead to his shoulder. His chest tightened in gratification that she was seeking comfort from him, while at the same time he suspected she hid in needless embarrassment. He ran his hand up and down her back while still keeping her close.

'Sometimes. Not intentionally, perhaps, but…'

But how could it be avoided if she wasn't ready when he took her? He closed his eyes and fought the rage that clawed within him. 'You're perfect, fair one. I'm sorry that happened to you.' It was all he could think to say to adequately express the depth of his feelings.

She shook her head. 'I don't think I was a very good wife.'

'He wasn't a very good husband.' She was so small against him, and when he'd pushed inside her, she'd been so tight he would've injured her if he'd gone too fast. Only a coward would've been anything but gentle with her.

Surprising him, she met his gaze and agreed with him. 'You're right, he wasn't.' The way she looked at him then, eyes soft and full of something better left un-examined, made him think she was imagining him as her husband. He liked it.

Then she sat back a little, resting on her elbow. 'I...I don't expect you to stay...if you want to leave.'

'What if I don't want to leave yet?'

The way her eyes lit up, despite the way she tried to hide it, made him harden instantly. She must see it, but he was reluctant to push her if she didn't want more. Instead, he took her hand and put it on his stomach. He grinned when her fingertips moved lower of their own volition. She stopped just short of touching him, but she was right there. 'Thought I might stay awhile. I'm uncertain how these things work, but it seems reasonable to expect better results if we try often.'

Her eyes widened.

'Unless you don't want to... Did I hurt you?'

Her shy gaze flitted away just to come right back to him. 'Nay. It was...better than I'd imagined. I just...I don't know what happens now. Where do we go from here?'

His heart shuddered to a stop, before resuming its already frantic pace. 'I'll come to you when it's safe.'

Anticipation brightened her eyes for a moment before she tamped it down. 'I know that Edyth believes that making a child is a task that should be undertaken daily. We don't have much time.' She glanced away and her cheeks turned pink again. 'Your seed will have to take root this month or the next at the latest.'

His shaft jerked in response to the very idea of being inside her every one of those nights. 'Every night, then.' Grabbing her hips to drag her astride him, he pulled her forward so that his throbbing shaft was nestled against her centre. 'Can you do it again tonight?'

When her eyes widened, they'd darkened so the light green was a mere sliver. Her breathing changed to shallow gasps. 'Aye.'

He loved the way she wanted this as much as he did and couldn't resist grinding up against her to watch her mouth fall open in a groan. She wasn't trying to hide it any more.

'We can try two or three times a night, just to be safe,' she said, rising up to get her balance with her knees on either side of him.

As he watched himself disappear inside her, he realised that a few weeks would never be enough. Regardless if his seed took root, he wanted more time.

It turned out every night wasn't enough. Magnus craved her during the day as well. He was mad. It was the only explanation for why he'd attacked her the moment they were far enough away from her village that no one would see them. It was the only explanation for why he'd thought it might be a good idea to allow her to sit astride him and milk him of his seed in the broad light of day. Neither of them had attempted to keep themselves quiet. His throat was still raw from calling out his release.

Clutching her to his chest, he managed to drag his eyes open to scan the area. Aside from the trees that bore silent witness to their mating, there were no signs of life. No one had seen them. By the gods, he hoped no one had heard them. His gaze dropped to the empty basket that had been tossed to the side and he was assailed by a wave of guilt. She'd asked him to come with her so that she'd be safe gathering plants for Edyth. It'd be the last she'd get before the frost set in, which would happen any day now.

'I'm sorry, fair one.' His lips pressed into her hair, making him remember how he'd torn her headrail away to get to the silky mass of reddish-brown tresses. Somewhere off to the right, it fluttered in the cool breeze. 'I can't control myself with you.'

She laughed and looked up at him from where she straddled his lap, placing a kiss on his bearded chin. 'Why do you think I asked you to come with me? Edyth has all the herbs she'll need to last through winter.'

He groaned at the further confirmation that she was as lost as he was. 'That explains yesterday.' It'd been less than a week and they were already becoming reckless. He'd taken her the previous morning after they'd finished their meal. They'd only just finished moments before Cuthbert had knocked on the door, requesting a new tapestry for his hall, and this was followed soon by the arrival of her apprentices. It could've been disastrous.

She giggled and cuddled against him. He'd noticed she did that more lateiy. Laughed. She touched him and found comfort in those touches. Every night she'd fallen asleep in his arms, seeking him out as she slept, and he'd bemoaned having to leave her alone to go back to his temporary home. He wanted to know what it was like to wake up with her. But the same instinct that told him how to touch her and how to fight was telling him now that they weren't meant to last.

He didn't belong here. There was an unknown life out there waiting for him, looming over them.

Drawing her face up to his, he kissed her gently. She kissed him back before moving away to arrange her skirts and he fastened his trousers. But instead of letting her get away, he pulled her back on to his lap and buried his face in her sweet-smelling hair.

'When will you know about a babe?'

'I'm due for my—' She broke off, embarrassed. 'Any day now, but Edyth says sometimes that can happen even with a babe in the womb. It'll take months to know for certain.'

He nodded and took a deep breath, hating what he had to say. He'd put it off for days now and couldn't put it off any longer. He probably should've left as soon as his sword had been returned to him. 'I'm leaving tonight.'

'Why?' From the way her face paled, he knew she thought the worst.

'Only for a few days.' He ran a hand over her hair, tucking a strand back behind her ear. 'I need to find out who I am. The only clue I have is how I woke up and the rebel Dane who followed me. I need to go back and see if I can find them.'

'Go back! Why would you go back to the men who tried to kill you?'

'Because they knew me.' He'd yet to tell her his name and how he'd figured it out. The guilt still grated at him, but he absolutely could not tell anyone until he knew for sure what he'd be revealing. What if they knew the name Magnus as belonging to an enemy? 'They're the only clue I have to my identity.'

'You haven't remembered anything?' She took his hand and brought it to her lips. She did it so absently as she pondered his declaration that he wondered if she was even aware of it. His thumb traced over her kiss-swollen bottom lip and then the pink skin beneath where his beard had rubbed against her. By the gods, it should be obvious to everyone what they were doing.

'Not much. I have visions of battle. There are faces, but I don't know who they are.' He'd yet to have another like that strange dream of his childhood.

'Faces?'

Her face fell, and he couldn't help but smile at her misplaced jealousy. 'Men, fair one. Friends...enemies... I don't know which.'

His words didn't seem to help as she brought her hands up to her face. 'What if there is a woman? You may have children with her. What have I done? I've stolen from her and you—'

'Nay. Aisly, look at me.' He took her hands and pulled them down to see her face. 'Your village felt wrong. I know that I don't belong there. Your food, your ale, your language, it all feels wrong. But you...you feel right. This...' he pulled her close and pressed his lips to hers '...this is right.'

'You say that as if this is more than getting me with child.'

His heart pounded so hard he was certain she must feel it beating against her breast. He knew he shouldn't say more because it was so out of reach, but he couldn't hold back any more. 'It could easily become more than that for me.' It already had.

She sucked in a breath as her gaze flew to his.

'I don't want to go away after winter and never see you again.'

'You could stay.' Her eyes widened with cautious hope.

He took in a deep breath. 'I belong somewhere, Aisly. Somewhere out there I have responsibilities, people waiting for me.'

She paused and took a breath before gently posing the question. 'What if you don't? What if those men with you were all you had?'

Magnus had tried to match up the faces of the men who'd died next to him with those in his dreams, but with no success. He'd been barely coherent when he awoke on the pile of bodies to commit any of their faces to memory. He was almost certain that he'd lost some friends to that battle, but it wasn't likely that was everyone. 'I don't think there's a woman, but I must have family, people somewhere. Besides that, I'm a warrior. You deserve more stability than I could offer you.'

She nodded, acceptance and understanding in her eyes. She'd thought about that. She wanted a family and he could give her a child, but he couldn't give her that promise of a home that she wanted.

As the days had passed and he'd learned more about her people, he'd realised that he was not one of them. Wulfric, like her brother, had taken to referring to him as 'the Dane', not 'foreigner' as the others called him. Magnus was hard pressed to refute him. The phrase 'by the gods' came with more frequency to his lips. It wasn't the phrase of a Saxon. Aye, there were other people who were bound to believe in other gods, but they were in faraway places. The Danes were here, he was here. It made sense.

'Have you considered the fact that your brother is right? That I'm a Dane?' He'd never voiced the thought to her, but he couldn't hold back.

She stiffened immediately and shook her head. 'It's not true. Alstan was merely being bitter.'

Magnus had refrained from speaking in the tongue that came natural to him—the one he used in his dreams—because he hadn't been sure he wouldn't be signing his death sentence. But now that he saw her looking at him with such trust, such tenderness, it seemed almost deceitful. What if he'd spoken it and Alstan had recognised it? What if he'd offered up his name and Alstan had known him? What if Magnus had stolen her heart only to foster her hatred if it was revealed that he was the enemy?

He had to figure out his identity as soon as possible. She deserved that.

'It could be true.'

'It's not true.' Her eyes widened in desperation. 'I care about you too much for that to be true. They are horrible men and you're not one of them.'

He moved a hand up and down her arm to calm her.

She took a deep breath and continued, 'I understand your need to figure out your past, but you're not well.'

He smiled and tightened his arms around her, whispering against her temple, 'I think we both know I'm healthy enough.'

Her eyes softened, but she didn't smile. 'For that, aye, but you'll be gone for days.'

He'd already planned it out, so he was ready to put her fears to rest. 'I'm much better thanks to you and Edyth. I don't need her poultices any more. My dizziness is gone and the headaches are less frequent. I'll take plenty of food to see me through. It'll only be a few days.'

'I'll worry,' she whispered, lowering her face.

He pulled her tight against his chest and brushed kisses along the gentle curve of her cheekbone. 'I'll come back to you, fair one. I promise.' Her small hand ran over his chest and settled on his heartbeat. This strange connection had been between them from the very beginning. The past few days had only fanned that flame into a full-blown fire. 'I need you to promise me something.'

She looked up at him again with a question in her eyes.

'I'll come say goodbye first, but I'm going to leave tonight. I need you to not say anything.'

'Why would you leave without telling anyone?'

'Cuthbert has made vague references to sending men with me to backtrack my path. It's a solid idea, but I can't do it with his men. They mean well, but I've never fought with them and I can't trust their instincts.'

'That means it'll be more dangerous for you.'

He gave one firm shake of his head. 'Nay, it's safer. Alone I can travel faster, quieter. If I do find the rebel Danes, I can watch them and try to learn without confrontation.'

She nodded. 'I won't mention you leaving, but won't Cuthbert be upset when you come back?'

'Perhaps, but I'd rather face his wrath than go with warriors I don't trust.' Besides, Cuthbert had proven to be an honest man. He'd listen to whatever Magnus had to say before giving way to anger and Magnus was certain that he could make the man understand his reasons for leaving.

She nodded again but was clearly uncertain as she nibbled her bottom lip. He hoped he'd done the right thing for her. His hand moved over her hip to rest against her belly, where their child could even now be growing. A wave of tenderness for her washed over him. No matter what happened or who he turned out to be, he'd make sure she was taken care of.

It took Magnus the better part of three days to find the rebel Danes.

Any trail he had left behind as he'd run for his life those weeks ago had long since vanished. It'd come as no surprise that many of the landmarks he'd thought that he'd remember had disappeared with it. The ancient tree with gnarled roots half in the stream—a marker he was certain he'd recognised—could have been any one of several. The sharp bend in the stream that made it nearly turn back on itself had been found, but then he'd found another just like it.

He'd almost turned around and headed back to Aisly when the tinge of woodsmoke tickled his nose. Following the smell, he made his way through the forest, until he saw the flickering of a fire through the trees. It was well ahead of him and he probably wouldn't have seen it if not for the gathering twilight. Now that he was closer, he smelled roasting meat and his belly grumbled. It reminded him he had only the coarse bread he'd brought with him and that his supply was dwindling. A sword and knife weren't adequate tools for getting food, unless he planned to use them to take it from someone.

Getting as close as he dared, he settled belly down on the ground and waited. It wasn't long until he counted five men in the camp. It looked to be temporary with no permanent structures. They didn't seem particularly guarded or anxious about anyone finding them. They simply sat around the fire, talking and passing around a jug of what he assumed to be ale, while watching the rabbits roast over the fire.

These men were Danes. Arte and Cuthbert had described to him the group that plagued the village. They were big like Magnus himself and with various shades of light-coloured hair, some tinged with red. The way they wore their hair got his attention more than its colour. Three of them wore it long on top but short on the sides and back. His own hair had been like that before he'd cut it off. He'd seen none of the Saxon men grooming their hair that way.

At first it was difficult to hear them, but as night settled in and the wind shifted, he was able to make out bits and pieces of their conversation. The first thing he noticed was that he understood them perfectly. There was no waiting for his mind to translate their words and stumble over them. They just came to him and he found himself mumbling the phrases he heard just to test them out on his tongue. He'd been too afraid of being overheard by someone back at the village that he hadn't dared to speak the language of his thoughts.

With hearing only every third or fourth word, it was difficult to follow their conversation, so he strained forward. When two of them rose to take a spit off the fire and argue over who got to eat first, he took the opportunity to crawl forward, certain that any noise he made would go unheard. Once they'd divided up their meat and settled down to eat, they resumed their conversation. They spoke of women and battle, sights and travels. He heard one of them called Henrik. He was clearly their leader, because they all went silent when he spoke.

It didn't sound familiar, though, which relieved him a bit because he didn't want to be one of them.

He wanted Aisly.

But the next name he heard chilled him to the bone. Magnus. Whether they were referring to him or not, he couldn't tell and listened closer.

'Magnus hasn't returned home yet,' Henrik stated.

'Neither has Gautr,' another one remarked.

'Perhaps they've killed each other.' A third one said this, eliciting a round of laughter from the group.

Then Henrik shook his head. 'Nay, he killed Gautr. Gautr never was much of a swordsman, despite being quick on his feet. Magnus killed him and is hiding. He wants us to think he's dead.'

The third one disagreed. 'His skull was split with your sword. He's dead. The animals have long since torn the flesh from his body.'

Henrik nodded, but he didn't appear convinced. 'If he's not, he will be soon.' He glanced up to the black sky—not a star could be seen and even the moon was covered. The clouds had been dark and flat all day, making Magnus fear rain or snow with how cold it was becoming. 'After we get back from the north, we'll root him out. Heir will send word if he returns to Thornby. I won't rest this winter until I know he's dead.'

One of the men who'd been silent finally spoke up. 'Jarl Eirik will have received notice that Magnus is missing. If we come back south before winter is over, the Jarl could be looking for us.'

'Let him look. He hasn't found us yet.' Henrik smirked. This prompted a bit of nervous laughter from the group. Throwing the bones of his meal on to the fire, Henrik grabbed his fur and pulled it around his shoulders. 'Rest well tonight. We have long days ahead of us, but when we come back, we'll find him.'

Magnus waited until they all slept before daring to creep backwards. He half-considered approaching them quietly and attempting to kill them all. But there were five of them and he wasn't completely recovered. Aside from that, he still didn't know who they were or why they were a threat to him. The name Jarl Eirik had pulled loose one memory from the tangle in his mind. A fair-haired man wearing a cape affixed with golden filigree broaches. He was clearly wealthy and important. It must be the Jarl. There were no other memories, though. Nothing that gave Magnus any idea of who he was to the Jarl or why he'd be missed.

Once he'd moved far enough away to keep watch without being seen, he settled down to rest. It was cold and the fur cape that had belonged to Aisly's husband was all he had to keep warm. It wasn't enough, but it kept the worst of the chill away. He didn't sleep much, because he couldn't stop his mind from churning through the tangled mess of his memories trying to figure them out.

By morning his head was pounding, but he followed the rebels long enough to determine they were moving further north away from the village. Once he made certain they were no immediate danger to the villagers, he turned and made his way back to Aisly.

Chapter Fourteen

When a few days turned into the better part of a sennight, Aisly became so worried she couldn't sit still. Then the snow started falling and her concern became almost unbearable. She hadn't realised how much the foreigner had come to mean to her until he wasn't there any more. Their arrangement had become so much more than she'd dared to even think it could be. She missed everything about him. His teasing smiles, his deep voice, the way he'd look at her as if he was the only one who could truly *see* her. The way he'd hold her in the night.

It felt as if he was hers and she liked that. Even more, she liked feeling as if she was his. But those feelings frightened her as much as they comforted her. He didn't belong here. No matter how often she'd lain awake imagining a future with him right here in this house, it could never come true. Being a warrior was in his blood. Godric had been a warrior, but also a farmer, and a husband, albeit a bad one. The foreigner was different. Instead of acting as village defender, he pursued the fight. Wherever his homeland was, he'd left it to be a warrior. He wouldn't be content living here in her small village tending crops.

She repeated that to herself so often it should've been ingrained in her being. Perhaps partially it was. She hadn't any trouble imagining him in his prior life leading a faction of warriors and she admired that about him. His ability to take control, to command respect. Though her admiration was foolhardy, because those were the exact reasons she needed to keep him at arm's length. He wouldn't ever be able to give her that family life she craved in her heart.

Regardless of what she suspected to be true, the more nights passed, the less she was able to sleep for thinking of him. So she was awake when the harsh knock sounded on her door in the middle of the night. Jumping in surprise, she rose from her bed and walked on silent feet to the door. The knock came again, only this time she heard his voice calling her name. She ran the rest of the way and threw open the latch to see him there. Snow clung to the fur of his cloak and stuck to his beard and lashes.

She was so happy to see him, she didn't care about the cold or the possibility of someone seeing them as she flung herself into his arms. He opened the fur to wrap it around her and pull her tight against him, all the while pushing her back inside the house and closing the door behind them.

'You said a few days and I was so worried because I thought something had happened.' She didn't let him go to look up at him. Instead, she nuzzled her face against his chest and listened to the soothing beat of his heart, relief making her legs weak. He was home.

'I know, fair one. I'm here.' His voice rumbled through her chest, filling in the hollows he'd left with his absence.

Only once her own heartbeat had begun to slow could she pull back. Even then her hands went to his face, his shoulders, his hands to unwrap the cloth that had kept them warm as she checked him for signs of injury.

He grinned. 'I'm unharmed.'

Fingers clenched in his short hair, she pulled him down to her, her mouth seeking the reassurance of his. He answered her immediately. His lips were cold at first contact, but they warmed quickly as the kiss deepened and her tongue brushed his. One touch and she was lost. The anxiety of his absence turned to a gripping need in her that she couldn't control, much less deny. Her hands shoved at the fur, pushing it back from his face and off his shoulders. He helped her by shrugging out of it, but his hands came up to cup her cheeks as he broke the kiss.

'I missed you.' A smile gently turned his lips, but it didn't seem to reach his eyes.

She had the awful suspicion that something was terribly wrong. Before he'd left, he'd met her gaze with nothing but tenderness. And now, though the tenderness was still there, it had been joined with apprehension. She didn't like that he'd be worried with her. She didn't like the fact that their relationship was so tenuous, but now something must have caused it to be even more so. She was a fool. Of course it was tenuous. It would be ending soon.

'Are you all right? Did you fight someone?' He'd said he was unharmed and he looked good. There were no new bruises on his face and the ones he had were faded. He'd lost his bandage, though he didn't really need it any more as the wound had closed. He was so striking that her heart fluttered to look upon him, but it was the depth of his eyes that held her attention.

He shook his head without breaking eye contact. 'Nay,

I found a small group of Danes. I believe they were the rebels plaguing your village and they knew me.'

'Did you…?' Suddenly she didn't want to know what he'd found out. She didn't want anything to intrude upon the tiny bit of happiness they'd found together, but she had to ask because the threat of the unknown was always lurking over them. 'Did you know them?'

'Nay.'

He took in a hesitant breath, as if he wanted to say more and was trying to figure out how to say it. She couldn't hear it, though. Not now. Not when she was just so happy to have him back. Before he could ruin that with anything that might have happened, she brought his mouth back to hers and redoubled her efforts to get him undressed, starting with his tunic. Her fingers went to the hem.

'Aisly,' he groaned against her lips.

'Please…I've missed you so much.' She brought his hands to her waist, craving his touch.

That seemed to break down his hesitance. He gripped her gown, fisting it in his hands and bringing her fully against his front. 'I've thought of nothing but getting back to you.' He pulled back just enough to say the words in a hoarse whisper against her lips before crushing her mouth with his again.

As she responded to his urgency, heat flooded her middle, settling to an insistent ache between her thighs. She'd missed him so much, she wanted him there again. She wanted to be as close to him as it was possible to get. Tugging at his tunic, she brought it up between them until he pulled it off over his head. He didn't hesitate to grip her gown and pull it up and over her head in one move.

Her body tightened from the cold and the way his gaze heated her skin as he looked her over.

But he was just as hungry as she was by now and he tugged his shirt off before picking her up and walking towards the bed. Her legs found their way around his hips. He was so large it felt a bit awkward, but it didn't matter if it got her closer to him. She loved the scrape of his light furring of chest hair against her nipples, so she found herself rubbing against him. His hands moved down from her waist to her bottom and squeezed her against him, bringing the full swell of his erection to rub against her centre through the fabric of his trousers. She cried out at the familiar sensation as her body clenched, aching for him to fill her.

He laid her on the bed, coming down with her. 'I need you now.'

She murmured her agreement against his mouth, but it came out as incoherent babble. He seemed to know she felt the same, as his hand moved to touch her between her legs. She was so ready he was able to easily push a finger inside her. She gasped at the sensation, breaking their kiss.

He buried his face against her neck, biting and teasing the tender skin he found there. His hands fumbled with his fastenings, making her start with excitement every time his knuckles brushed against her smooth inner thigh. She needed him so badly, her entire body ached with it. Then he was there. The hard flesh of his manhood nudging against her sensitive flesh, finding her opening and notching there. Crying out at the exquisite torture, she reached down and met his fingers as he took himself in hand to guide his shaft into her. Their eyes met as their fingers lined him up.

When he flexed his hips and pushed the head inside, he took her hand in his and brought her fingers to his lips. Placing a gentle kiss to them, he placed her hand on the mattress above her head and laced his fingers with hers. Then he pushed forward a bit more, before pulling back and repeating the motion, slowly making a way for himself. Finally he sank as deep as he could go, pulling a groan from each of them, before he paused, resting on top of her.

Her entire body throbbed and her channel clenched around him, begging for more, but she closed her eyes and savoured the consolation of having his weight above her and inside her at the same time. He felt so right. *This* felt so right. He exhaled sharply as he pressed his forehead to hers and thrust once, hard. Darts of pleasure wove through her body from where they were joined. But it was more than physical pleasure. It was solace and passion all rolled into one. She'd never known such a feeling of well-being. Her entire body glowed with the warmth.

'Tell me you're ready, fair one.' His ragged voice made her tremble.

'Aye,' she reassured him and arched beneath him, trying to get closer. It was all the encouragement he needed, because he thrust again, setting a rhythm that quickly turned frantic, which she had no trouble keeping up with.

Very soon her body clenched and contracted around his length. His grunts of pleasure against her neck coupled with the uncoordinated jerks of his hips told her he'd found his release within her.

Afterwards she held him against her, unwilling to let go. Kissing her brow, he pulled away just enough to work off his boots and push his trousers down. She wrapped an arm around his waist from behind, placing kisses along his shoulder, because she couldn't seem to stop touching him. He only smiled and managed to not stand up before ridding himself of the clothes and lying down with her. She curled against his chest, her legs tangled with his, and his arms went around her. She wanted to stay that way for ever, with his heart beating beneath her ear.

Magnus pulled the blanket up over them and held her tucked beneath his chin, wondering how he'd managed to feel this way about a stranger in such a short amount of time. The more he thought of a life without her, the more he wanted to fight against that sort of life. He wanted her. Even the idea of returning to his own hut before morning was distasteful. She belonged with him. The idea had taken root in his bones and he couldn't dislodge it no matter how often he reminded himself that he didn't belong with her. He wasn't one of them.

'Didn't Cuthbert want to see you?' she asked after both their heartbeats had slowed to normal.

'He doesn't know I'm here.' He ran his palms over the silken skin of her back, savouring her softness. She fit against him as if she'd been made for him.

'But the men at the gate must have told him.' She pushed up a little, her eyes wide in surprise.

He couldn't help but smile as he pushed her dark hair back from her face. It seemed to reflect the firelight with pieces of it shimmering red. 'Don't worry. No one knows I'm back. They won't come looking for me here.'

'How did you get in if not through the gate?' Some of her alarm had faded, so the tension went out of her arms, leaving her resting on his chest as she looked at him.

'I told you the walls here are not good. They're too rough and short. It wasn't difficult to find notches to climb it. I needed to see you first, so I waited until the village was quiet before coming in.'

'Oh, I suppose I didn't believe you when you said the gate wouldn't stop you.' She frowned and a crease appeared between her brows. 'Perhaps we need you here.'

His smile faded. There was no question that he could be useful here. The only question was: where did he belong? He wanted a life with her, but no matter how right she felt, it didn't feel right to turn his back on who he really was. It didn't feel right to turn his back on her, either. It just seemed that having her and having himself were mutually exclusive.

'I want to tell you my name.' He hadn't planned to tell her, but he couldn't hold back any more. Though it was unlikely she'd recognise it, since no one in her village had known him, but it was possible.

She tried to stifle it, but a smile teased the corners of her mouth. She drew in her plump bottom lip and held it between her teeth. 'I want to know your name,' she finally said, her words a little breathless.

He pushed back her hair and allowed the pad of his thumb to trace over her cheekbone.

'Did the rebels say your name? Do you know it?'

Why had he said anything? He couldn't tell her, not when he wasn't sure what his name meant. Now he had to lie to her and he despised that. 'They said a name. I'm uncertain if it's mine.' He dipped his head down and closed his eyes, hating that he couldn't tell her.

'Will you tell Cuthbert?'

He shook his head.

'Why?'

'Because I still don't know who I am… What if I'm an enemy?'

'That's not true.' She gave an emphatic shake of her head. 'You're not our enemy. I won't believe that's possible.'

'I might be, Aisly. We have to acknowledge that.'

'It's impossible. You're too kind, too good.' Pulling out of his arms, she rolled on to her side away from him.

For one very brief moment, he considered that it might be kinder to leave her now and pretend that it wouldn't break him. Just as quickly, he pushed that aside and pulled her back into his arms, fitting her back along his front. As his hand ran over her belly, he remembered how this had all started. They were supposed to be creating a child, not simply indulging themselves in pleasure. But not once tonight had he even considered that he was touching her for that reason. It had all been about her and their need for each other.

He wondered if that was why she was so sensitive to the issue of him being an enemy. Would she regret allowing him to father her baby? 'Are you with child?'

She hesitated only a moment before shaking her head. 'I'm not sure. I bled while you were away, so perhaps not.'

Relief and disappointment warred for dominance. In the end, disappointment won out, because he was selfish and wanted to bind her to him in any way he could. He moved his hand up to cup her breast and her nipple beaded in response beneath his palm. She didn't stiffen or pull away and he couldn't convince himself to not touch her.

'I'm sorry,' he whispered against her ear.

Slowly her hand came up to cover his on her breast. 'We can keep trying.'

'Are you certain that's what you want? We have to consider the fact that I could be—'

'Aye, you're right. I know.' She turned in his arms to look at him. 'But it's unlikely. Besides...' Her bottom lip trembled as she took in a shaky breath, but her gaze held his. 'I tell myself that I should keep you at a distance because I know that you'll leave. I know that you have a life somewhere and there's no room for me in it. I understand that. But I just want to hold on to what we have right now...even knowing how it'll end.'

Some sense of self-preservation tightened in his chest, urging him to go now. They both knew it would end, but he had the feeling it would end worse than either of them could fathom. And still his arms tightened around her. As he gazed into her pale green eyes, he knew that he would take as much time as they could get until that end came.

He stared down at the broken creature with sunken cheeks, lined skin and hair so stringy and faded she bore no resemblance to the woman he remembered. He disgraced himself by gasping at the change and her eyes opened. They were the only part of her to retain a recognisable shadow of the woman she had been—a clear blue that always warmed when she saw him, as they did now.

'Magnus.' Her hand reached out and touched his face. The act nearly caused the ache in his throat to overwhelm him. 'I knew you'd come back.'

'I'd never leave you.' His voice came out too scratchy as he hurried to assure her.

But his words didn't reassure her at all. To his surprise, her eyes filled with tears and her voice was sad when she said, 'Aye, I knew you wouldn't. Not while I'm living.'

He frowned at the strange words and what they foretold.

'It is your birthright to be a great warrior. I want you to leave here and make that happen.'

'Nay! I'll not leave you.'

She ignored him and pointed to the far corner of the chamber. 'Move the chest there and dig below. You'll find a small satchel of coins.' When he protested, she looked to the door, reminding them both that their time was limited.

He knew he was dreaming then, because with no effort on his part the satchel appeared in his hand, but he couldn't muster the will to rouse himself. Heart in his throat, he leaned forward to better hear her words.

'Travel northward along the coast and you'll find his hall. Tell him that you are Magnus's son and he'll take you in. I should have let you go before, but I was selfish and wanted you for myself. Please forgive me, Magnus. If he refuses you, then offer him the coin. But only if he refuses.'

Magnus jerked awake, his entire body trembling. The fire was a mere orange glow in the hearth, barely enough to see the outline of Aisly leaning over him. She stroked his face and ran a hand down his chest. 'I'm here. You were dreaming.'

He sucked in a deep breath and closed his eyes as he allowed her touch to soothe him, just as it had when he'd been injured in this same bed. Except this time, the smooth skin of her naked body pressed against his. His eyes flew open as they sought out the vent to check how long he'd been asleep. He'd taken her again and must have fallen asleep afterwards.

'It's not morning yet. I think we'd only just drifted off.'

There was no light filtering in from outside. He let out a breath, relief and frustration mingled together. Relief that they wouldn't be found. Frustration that he'd never have the right to keep her in his bed until morning. 'Come here,' he said, his voice rough from sleep. Gripping her waist, he tugged until she complied and laid down next to him, where he curled himself around her, tucking her under his chin and taking solace in her presence.

'What did you dream about?' she whispered against his chest.

The dream had been a memory. It hadn't pulled any significant threads loose, but there'd been a familiarity about the scene. He hadn't seen it in the dream, but he knew there was a wolf's head and pelt on the wall of that chamber. Its wooden eyes had tormented him as a child. He breathed in the scent of her hair and stroked the silken skin of her back. 'My mother. I don't remember, but I think she must've died when I was a child.'

'Oh.' That simple sound was filled with pain and empathy.

'She was kind. I remember that.' The pain he must've felt when he lost her echoed through him now. 'It was important to her that I be a warrior. It's all she ever wanted for me.' Though he couldn't remember why or why there'd been such a sense of urgency in the dream. There'd been some dark presence looming over them.

She waited, but when he didn't continue, she said, 'I dreamed about my parents for years afterwards. Sometimes I still do. They're all good dreams, but I always wake up sad. So lonely.'

Was that the pain he felt now? Loneliness? 'I don't want you to be lonely.'

Her smile was in her voice. 'How can I be when you hold me so tight?'

But they both knew that would end soon. 'You make me think of being more than a warrior.'

She stilled against him, her fingers curling against his chest before flattening out over his heart. 'But that's who you are.'

He nodded. Aye, it's who he was and he didn't know if he could change it. 'Sometimes I close my eyes and imagine us, our children around the hearth as we eat our meal. You with your needle and embroidery sitting by the fire…and it's all I want.'

'I remember doing that as a child. My mother near the hearth working on her tapestry. My father telling us stories.' She took a deep, trembling breath. 'It's what I want, too…with you.'

They didn't speak about it any more. It was too painful with the future so uncertain.

Chapter Fifteen

Magnus spent the next three days ensconced in Cuthbert's hall. The man had been understandably angry that Magnus had gone ahead in his search for his identity without Cuthbert's men. Magnus had anticipated that and the resulting near-interrogation. It had all been handled respectfully—the questions, the endless retelling of what he'd heard and seen, though he'd left out the part of him understanding their language—but there was no denying the suspicion in Cuthbert's eyes now. Magnus would have felt the same. So when it was suggested that he move into the hall due to the cold weather, Magnus accepted it as his punishment. He knew that he'd earn their trust again soon.

It was harder to accept being kept from Aisly. With so many people around at all times, it wasn't easy for him to talk to her alone during the day and impossible for him to sneak out at night to visit her. After the sennight he'd spent away, it was akin to torture. They'd had only the few stolen hours that night he'd returned and it wasn't nearly enough to quench his thirst for her. He'd left early that morning, scaling the wall again and disappearing into the forest, to make an appearance at the front gate later in the morning, never suspecting that circumstances would keep him from her.

A fist pounding the table before him brought his attention back to the group. Drops of spittle flew from Wulfric's mouth as he pounded one last time. 'We have to go after them. We cannot sit and wait for them to come back and attack us.'

Someone immediately dissented.

It was the same conversation the group, comprised of Cuthbert, Arte, Wulfric, a few other elders and warriors, had every morning now. Cuthbert consistently argued that they didn't have enough men to track the rebels and leave the village protected, while Wulfric argued for aggression. Aside from offering what he knew about the small group of rebels heading north, Magnus had kept silent. It wouldn't help in any way for him to weigh in this early, not when he'd compromised their trust.

Not when none of them wanted to hear the truth. They didn't have enough warriors to aggressively challenge the rebels, but their fortifications weren't good enough to withstand a well-executed assault. There was no guarantee that the five rebels he had seen worked alone. Magnus hadn't found their permanent home or camp. He'd found only the five travelling north. It was possible there were others nearby, or even that the five were returning to their home in the north and would be back with more men.

The fate of the village was grim and it wouldn't improve as long as the disagreements amongst the leaders continued. Magnus had tried to support the need to work on fortifications, but no one had wanted to hear that they were compromised. In truth, it hardly mattered now that the frost had settled in. A frozen ground made the work challenging.

The moment Aisly walked into the hall, his gaze settled on her standing in the doorway. She sought him out, too, her gaze passing over the people until she found him. The moment their eyes met, he felt a rush of excitement deep in his belly, followed by a tug of warmth that spread from his chest across his whole body. A primal urge to hold her and feel the weight of her slight body against his surged through him.

Cuthbert's and Arte's wives greeted her and she was forced to look away. The older women led her over to some tapestries hanging on the far side of the hall, where they paused to examine some frayed edges. Magnus watched her walk away—the sway of her hips had him imagining the many other ways they could be passing the time in her bed. Their days apart had felt like an eternity.

Catching him watching her, Cuthbert cleared his throat and gave him a wry grin. Magnus hadn't been aware his interest had been so obvious and shot a glance to Wulfric. The man continued to talk to a warrior at his side about the need to fight, so he hadn't noticed.

'You seem to fancy our fair Aisly.' Cuthbert leaned over and spoke in a low voice.

Magnus hesitated to make his interest in her known. If it turned out he was a Dane who was important to a man like Jarl Eirik, and the people of the village chose to turn their backs on him, he didn't want her unduly associated with him. 'She's lovely and I'm very thankful to her for her care.'

Cuthbert's grin only widened. 'Aye, she is that. As you know, she's newly widowed, but in the summer you might stand a chance of winning her.'

Magnus was in no way prepared to discuss his intentions towards her with the older man, so he thought it best to steer the conversation in a different direction. 'Aye, I'm told her husband was killed by the Danes at the settlement.' He'd been very careful about bringing up the subject, though he'd been anxious to learn the details. Aisly hadn't wanted to talk about Godric, and the incident was too recent and raw for the warriors to discuss.

The smile dropped from Cuthbert's face and the elder nodded as he brought his ale up for a drink.

'Can you tell me what happened?' Magnus pressed.

'The bloody Danes didn't want to help us after our women were kidnapped by the rebels, Godric became enraged and they killed him. Simple as that. They killed all the warriors that day.'

It was the same version of the story he'd heard from other warriors. Though Aisly hadn't said anything overtly, he had the feeling she might have more insight if only she'd open up to him.

'Was Godric only there to confront them about the women?' Magnus kept his voice low so that it wouldn't carry across the narrow table to Wulfric.

Cuthbert nodded and appeared almost offended Magnus would even ask. 'He was devoted to us.'

Of that, Magnus had no doubt, but he'd begun to suspect that Godric might have had ulterior motives. He couldn't help himself from looking back to where Aisly spoke with the older women. Her soft voice drifted over to him and he found himself straining to hear her words.

'If that's the way your thoughts are going, you should know that she's barren.' Cuthbert's voice interrupted him. 'Godric was frustrated with her and had begun to think about divorce.'

'Godric didn't see her true value.'

The older man's smile returned. 'She is a skilled embroideress. The abbess will value her.'

That wasn't the value he was alluding to, but Magnus nodded just the same. It was a shame they didn't see her compassion and spirit as value. 'How do you mean?'

'Wulfric's been kind to allow her to stay on in her grief, but the convent will be a better place for her. Come the warmer weather, he'll ask her to make that decision.' Cuthbert paused before adding with a knowing grin, 'Unless you'd like to declare for her.'

Perhaps concerned with their private discussion, Wulfric raised his voice to gain their attention. 'How many warriors would you spare for an excursion?'

Cuthbert set his cup down with a thump. 'No warriors will go.'

This set off another debate and Magnus had had enough. Grabbing his empty cup, he got to his feet and made his way to the table holding the ale, thankful it was near where Aisly was bending to examine a tapestry. The other two women had moved ahead to discuss the merits of replacing versus repairing the next tapestry on the wall, leaving her alone. He made a fist to keep his fingers from reaching out to touch her, but he couldn't resist allowing his thigh to brush against her as he passed. She gasped and he smiled as he stopped at the table and poured himself more ale.

He wouldn't let her know what Cuthbert had said, but he was suddenly very fearful for her future. As of now he had nothing to offer her but the hut the villagers had been kind enough to allow him to use for the winter. When spring came, he wouldn't even have that. What would happen if Wulfric's charity ran out before spring?

'I've missed you,' she whispered, surprising him by coming up beside him at the table.

'I've been watched.'

She nodded in understanding as she grabbed an empty cup and poured a little ale for herself. 'I know. I only wish there wasn't a need for deception.'

'Do you?' His gaze caressed the curve of her cheekbone much the same way his lips longed to do.

'Aye.' She smiled but didn't meet his eyes as she brought her cup to her lips and took a drink. She kept her lips behind the cup as she said, 'Do you not see how the women look at you? Wyn drools every time she sees you. I want them to know you're mine.' She blushed as she said that, as if she'd revealed too much.

He tried not to smile, but he'd already started before he could contain it. Glancing to the opposite side of the room, he confirmed that Wyn kept sneaking glances at him as she worked on weaving rushes into a rug. The girl was pleasing enough in her looks and demeanour, but she wasn't Aisly. 'Am I yours?' he teased.

He wanted to be alone with her so that he could reassure her that he was hers in any way she'd have him. He wanted to bury himself in her and hear her cry out his name. His *true* name. Just imagining it spilling from her lips as she came apart on his shaft had him rigid.

'I want you to be.' Anyone could have looked at her and seen the longing on her face. It tore at his heart and made him want to pull her against him and hold her so tight she'd never doubt again.

'I am, fair one. I'm yours.' He met her gaze for one deliberate moment so that he could make sure she understood before he glanced away to the two older women nearby. He vowed then to find some way to go to her tonight.

'Come home with me now.'

His gaze rushed back to hers.

'I've finished the tapestry, so I'll need someone to bring it back. And I need to take this one to mend. You can carry it.' When he hesitated, she pressed. 'They'll be watching you tonight, as long as you're staying in the hall. There won't be any other way until you regain their trust.'

What she said was true, but it was dangerous. Yet the need to have her to himself was so strong he couldn't wait any longer, and he agreed.

I love you. The secret thought nearly tumbled from her lips before she could close them.

He gave her a particularly arrogant grin as he tucked himself back into his trousers, almost as if he'd heard it. Once they'd reached her home, they hadn't even made it to the bed. He'd taken her against the worktable so hard the memory of it beating against the wall still echoed in her mind.

Her skirt was still up around her waist and she sat on the table, but she was too weak to find her feet and regain her modesty. When he was done, he stepped between her knees and his arms went around her, pulling her close for another kiss. He gave her another grin. 'Your lips are swollen. They'll know what we were doing.' His thumb ran over her lips and across her chin. The sensitive skin there was no doubt reddened from his beard.

She needed to pull herself away, to figure out how to compose herself so that when they returned to the hall she could pretend nothing had happened. But she couldn't stop touching him, her fingers in the short hair at the back of his head. She was fast running out of ways to pretend that nothing was happening between them. 'They don't suspect, do they?'

He shook his head, but his eyes were clouded with worry as they met hers. 'Nay, but they might if we allow this to keep happening. We have to wait until I stop sleeping in the hall to do this again. Night is our only ally.'

She didn't bother to say that this was their last month to try for a child. If he didn't get her with child this time, then it'd likely be too late for her to claim a baby as Godric's heir. She didn't say that, because she wasn't doing it solely for that reason any more. She wanted him. She wanted him in all the ways she could have him. She wanted his child and she wanted him to *be* the child's father. Perhaps it was foolish, because he didn't even know who he was, but she simply wanted the foreigner. The man she had come to love.

'I don't want to have to wait for night any more. I want to be able to touch you and smile at you and talk to you without having to worry about them.' She knew she sounded needy and she took a breath to make herself stop.

He didn't seem to mind, though. His hands came up to tilt her face up to his. 'I want that, too.' His smile was enough to steal her hard-won breath. 'But until I know who I am…' His voice trailed off, because there was no point in stating the obvious. He wouldn't stay.

She didn't make him say it. She nodded and resolved to pull herself together. 'We should get this tapestry to the hall.'

He bent down to place a kiss atop the mound between her thighs. She gasped at the simple, tender gesture. He wasn't smiling when he straightened. There was a solemnity in his expression as he helped her down from the table. She wasn't sure what it meant, but he placed another kiss on her lips before moving to pick up the rolled-up tapestry she'd finished for Cuthbert's wall.

Making sure her skirts were straight, she watched him toss it over his shoulder. He allowed her to lead the way back through the village. She was certain it must be easy for everyone to see what they'd done. But as they walked, no one approached them to berate them for their immorality. No one even noticed them as the villagers went about their daily chores and the few who did tipped their heads in greeting.

Aisly took a deep breath to calm herself. Everything was fine and no one suspected a thing. Glancing over at him, he gave her a half-smile that was far more intimate than friendly. The gold flecks in his eyes caught the meagre rays of the afternoon sun and made a pleasant warmth surge up through her chest and spread over her entire body.

I love you.

She didn't dare say it. She could barely acknowledge she felt it. There would be plenty of time throughout the winter to better figure out her feelings towards him. There were still too many unanswered questions, but a tiny ray of hope opened up within her as she thought of a future with him. He must have seen something in her eyes—his own darkened almost imperceptibly. She smiled back at him.

'Magnus!'

The single word rang out. It was so out of place she would have sworn she'd imagined it if only the foreigner hadn't turned his head to look for its source. The man who spoke it sat on the back of a giant horse, having just rounded the corner of Cuthbert's hall. The man was broad and strong, his well-kept hair and beard fairer than her foreigner's. He wore a short chain mail tunic over his finely made wool clothing. As he dismounted she could see that he wore leather breeches and a thick crimson cloak that trailed down behind him.

He was a Dane like those who'd ridden into the village after Godric's death. A handful of other Danes followed, their horses filing in behind his. There was something familiar about him. A sickening suspicion tightened like a knot in her belly.

Chapter Sixteen

'Magnus!'

He'd never expected to hear his name, especially spoken by a voice that was so familiar. The man dismounting was nearly as tall as Magnus and better dressed than anyone in the village. He knew instinctively that this was one of the Danes the villagers had spoken of, though not one of the rebels. This man was from the settlement.

As the man walked closer, Magnus could tell that he was a few years younger than himself, though more warrior than boy. His blond hair was shaved on the sides and the rest pulled back in a knot above his nape. He walked with the swagger of a man who'd been battle-tested and come out the victor more than once. He was a warrior in his prime with his wide shoulders and the confidence he carried with him. The man's face was as vaguely familiar as his voice. Then the darkness of his memories let out one ray of light and Magnus saw this man fighting beside him. The warrior's sword arm was raised high as he gave a shout of victory.

'Vidar!' The name spilled from his lips before he could stop it and he was moving forward to embrace the man in greeting, thumping his back with his fist, as he'd done countless times before.

'Magnus. I never thought to see you alive again. You disappeared after the battle and we thought you must be dead.' Vidar's brow furrowed as he cast a puzzled glance at the rolled-up tapestry Magnus had dropped to the ground, wondering why he was here in the village performing household chores.

'I nearly was. I have no memory of the battle, but I awoke on a pile of dead warriors being readied for burning. For that matter, I have no memories at all. I was close to death until Aisly—'

Aisly. He glanced over his shoulder to see that her face was contorted in pain and disbelief. His heart twisted at the anguish she must be feeling and he wanted to reach out to her, but already the mask of anger was beginning to take the place of the agony.

Cuthbert's voice drew his attention back to the others. He'd come outside flanked by warriors on either side. Magnus looked to the Danes who were dismounting. He paused on each of their faces, waiting to see if a memory surfaced, and just like waves clearing back sand from the clams nestled beneath the grains, those memories emerged one by one. The blackness still filled his mind, but it was softening to grey.

'What are you doing here, Dane?' Cuthbert addressed Vidar.

Magnus realised how volatile the situation could become if he didn't take control. Aisly had turned and run, no doubt headed home to hide herself away from him. A part of himself had been torn away and gone with her as she'd fled. He pledged to find her soon, after he headed off the confrontation, and explain.

Explain what? That he was a Dane? That he was someone she hated? A knot of dread settled heavy in the pit
of his stomach as he thought of her almost certain rejec-
tion. He wasn't who she wanted him to be.

Vidar's sharp gaze swung to him and then back to
Cuthbert, who stood stoically appraising them all. Magnus appreciated the older man's ability to stay calm in
the face of his enemies. 'I told you we'd be back to collect payment after we found the rebels,' Vidar answered
him in the Saxons' tongue.

Shrugging off the impending sense of dread, Magnus stepped forward and put a hand on Vidar's shoulder.
'Vidar, we need to speak privately.'

'You know these men, foreigner?' Cuthbert asked.

'Aye, I know them. I must...' *I must be one of them.*
He didn't say it. It was true, but even recognising these
men, he didn't understand exactly how he fit or what his
place was with them.

'This is Magnus Magnussen, our leader. Have you
dared to keep him here against his will?' At his raised
voice, a few of the Danes reached for their swords, but
Magnus raised his hands to halt them.

'Halt! We'll not fight today.'

The Danes halted, but they didn't relax their postures.

Magnus was still trying to come to terms with the idea
that he was their leader. Wouldn't he remember if such
were the case? Cuthbert stared at him as if trying to see
him with new eyes. There was no recognition there, so
Magnus was certain the older man had never met him
before as a Dane leader. Though he'd cut his hair and his
beard, he wouldn't have changed that much in appearance from the Dane he had been.

'You've tricked us.' Cuthbert declared and ran a hand

over his white beard. It was the first sign of agitation the man had shown. 'For what purpose?' His keen eyes went to the spot behind Magnus that Aisly had so recently occupied and a dart of fear shot through Magnus's heart. They'd think that somehow she was a part of this.

'Nay, there was no trick, Cuthbert. It is just as I've told you. I was gravely wounded in battle.' Magnus brought his hand up to his head where his wound was still visible. Aisly had assured him there would be a vicious scar. 'Aisly found me and brought me here to the village. I still don't have all my memories returned, but I remember Vidar and the men.'

Cuthbert opened his mouth and closed it again as if he didn't quite know what to say. He looked torn between confusion and disbelief as he ran a hand over his beard again. 'It's difficult to believe, forei—' He cut off the word but didn't seem to be able to bring himself to say 'Magnus'.

'You must believe that I had no ulterior motive here, Cuthbert. I thank you and your village for accepting me when I was near death.' He turned his attention back to Vidar, who still seemed torn with his own disbelief and suspicion that Magnus might have been kept against his will. 'We owe these people our gratitude, Vidar.'

Vidar paused before nodding. His expression didn't change from angry suspicion, but he said, 'We'll postpone the payment until after winter.'

Cuthbert huffed in anger. 'Payment for what, Dane? The rebels are still out there.'

'Nay, we've rooted them out. Found their encampment just to the south,' Vidar explained. A few of the Danes at his back added in their confirmation. 'They won't bother you any more.'

'Impossible,' Cuthbert challenged and pointed a finger at Magnus. 'Your own leader found them just days ago to the north.'

'When did you find the encampment?' Magnus asked.

'A sennight past or more.' Vidar tilted his head as he thought back. 'Nine days.'

Nine days was enough time for them to have found the encampment and sent the few he'd seen fleeing north. 'I found five of them fleeing to the north.'

Vidar nodded. 'We must have struck while they were gone and they fled. None escaped our attack.'

'Are there others to the north they went to join with?'

'Not that we're aware of,' Vidar answered.

The rebels had said they'd come back, though. They wouldn't come back without reinforcements.

Cuthbert interrupted his thoughts to ask Vidar, 'Did you find any women with them? The two that were taken from us?'

'There were no women, only warriors,' Vidar answered.

'Liar.' A new voice entered the group. Wulfric had just walked around the opposite corner of the hall, probably summoned by one of the onlookers. 'You just want them for yourselves.'

'There isn't a need to lie. We have all the women we want. We don't need to steal them.' Vidar's voice was hard.

Wulfric walked out to stand beside Cuthbert. 'How do we even know you found an encampment? You've brought no proof and could be lying simply to secure payment.'

Vidar appeared bored, his expression unchanged, as he reached into the pack on his horse and drew out a necklace. It was a string of hide with small stones strung on to it. There were around a score of them. Though when he held it up, Magnus could see the small stones, in shades from white to yellow marred with brown mud, were teeth. The mud was dried blood. Across the front of the teeth were horizontal lines filled with a black substance. It matched the design he'd seen carved into the rebel Dane's teeth at the stream.

'Here is your proof. One from every warrior slain.' Vidar tossed it to Wulfric, who caught it against his chest before holding it aloft to examine it.

'There will be no payment yet.' Magnus raised his voice to be heard over both groups of warriors who were getting anxious. 'We'll go now. There's much to be discussed.' Specifically the fact that his memories were still hazy or absent altogether and he refused to punish the people who had helped him.

He was surprised that Wulfric only stared and didn't accuse him of spying as Cuthbert had. The man's eyes were calculating, though, leaving Magnus to worry how Wulfric might use this against Aisly. He had to go talk to her.

'I'll send reward for your help,' Magnus assured Cuthbert.

The older man only shook his head. 'We only want to be left in peace, Dane.'

'Come.' Vidar took his shoulder.

'Nay.' Shaking his head, Magnus took a few steps backwards and his foot came up against the forgotten tapestry. Aisly had worked hard on it, it didn't deserve to lie in the dirt. Picking it up, he handed it over to Cuthbert, who took it as if he expected a serpent to slither out of it. 'We'll go soon,' he said to Vidar. 'I have to say goodbye first.'

And it was goodbye. As he turned to retrace their footsteps to her home, there was no doubt in his mind that she wouldn't want him any more.

That tall blond Dane was the one who'd come to her home after Godric's murder. He was handsome in a way that blended warrior with boy. She remembered that at first she'd been struck by how his eyes reminded her of the larkspur flowers, but they'd only been coldly assessing as he'd taken everything that had been valuable to her.

And her foreigner knew him. He *knew* him.

He'd called him by name—Vidar—and embraced him with the same hands that had just held her. The warmth of her foreigner's fingers still lingered on her hips and she could still hear the echo of his groan against her ear as he'd filled her with his seed.

Tears blinded her as she stumbled back to her home using the heel of her hand to swipe them away. What a fool she had been all along. Alstan had tried to tell her and she'd refused to listen.

Her foreigner was a Dane.

He'd already forgotten about her. Except he hadn't. Before she ran, he'd glanced over his shoulder and for just an instance their eyes met. Guilt crossed his face, jagged and raw and plain for her to see. It was his confession. He hadn't lost his memory at all. He spoke to the Danes as if he knew them. He spoke their tongue as if he'd been born to it.

Her foreigner was a Dane. His name was Magnus and he was one of them.

His name was Magnus. The word pounded its way through her skull, matching the vigorous throb of her heartbeat.

Magnus. Magnus. Magnus.

It wasn't the name of the man she loved. That man had disappeared right before her eyes. He had become one of the men responsible for Godric's death. *The* man responsible for Godric's death if her brother could be believed. He'd told her that the leader of the settlement was a Dane named Magnus. It didn't seem possible that it'd be this gentle man she knew, and yet…

A hollow opened up in her. It drew in the love, the comfort, the tiny rays of hope, every beautiful thing that he'd made her feel until there was nothing left but a great big hole that hurt so badly she wasn't sure she'd survive. It seared right through her middle, shredding everything she'd hoped to give him.

She'd fallen in love with her enemy, with the man who'd killed her husband.

She pushed open her door and was faced with the awful, empty space that was her home. He was still here. At the workbench. At the hearth. In her bed. He was everywhere and nowhere. Slamming the door behind her, she moved towards the fire, seeking some warmth to heat the cold inside her.

It seemed only moments passed before there was a light knock on the door. A part of her wanted it to be her foreigner, but a stronger part simply wanted him to go. The sooner he left, the quicker she could start to pretend that nothing special had happened between them. That his touches hadn't meant anything, that lying beside him at night hadn't felt about as close to heaven as she'd get while breathing and that everything that had happened between them had really been about conceiving a child to secure her future.

The hollow rap against the wood sounded again. This time a bit firmer and more insistent. Perhaps it wasn't him. It was entirely possible he'd ridden away with the Danes and wouldn't look back. Her heartbeat sped as she imagined that scenario and the very real possibility that it would mean she'd never see him again.

She didn't want that. She didn't know what she wanted, but she didn't want that. Turning, she started for the door, only to watch it open.

The foreigner walked inside and his eyes reflected relief when he saw her. With a firm shove, he pushed the door closed behind him. 'I was afraid you'd run off somewhere.'

Aisly did her best to make it appear as if she hadn't been trying not to cry. Drawing herself up straight, she backed up to the worktable and gripped the edges. The discomfort of the rough edges of the wood biting into her fingers distracted her from thoughts of tears, making the ache in her throat ease up just enough so that she could talk. 'I'm not a fool. There's nowhere to hide here in the village if you wish to find me and I wouldn't run off into the forest.'

He nodded and took a deep breath, his hands hitching on his hips. 'I know you're not a fool. I just wanted—' He bit off the word and passed an agitated hand over his brow. 'I want to talk to you before I go.'

'There's no need.' She didn't want a drawn-out conversation when the only logical conclusion was that he was leaving. 'What does anything matter now?'

'It matters. We need to talk about what just happened. Who I am.'

'I heard enough. Your name is Magnus and you're a Dane from the settlement. I suppose Alstan will be gratified to know that he was right all along.' How she spoke without her voice breaking, she didn't know. She was gripping the table so hard her knuckles must be white from the strain.

'I know what you're thinking. I didn't lie to you.' He took a few steps across the space as if he was approaching a skittish animal.

Her heart beat faster and her rabbit instinct told her to run to save her heart from breaking even harder. She could only watch him, hoping that he stop, because she'd never hold herself together if he dared to touch her.

'I didn't know that I was a Dane, especially a Dane from the settlement.'

'You didn't know at all? Did you suspect?' She didn't know why she tortured herself by even asking.

That brought him up short and guilt flashed across his eyes. 'I thought it was likely. Particularly after I found the rebel Danes. I heard them talking and understood them with ease. I recognised it as the language from my dreams.'

A coldness washed over her, tingling its way across her skull, down her spine and to the soles of her feet. He'd told her that he'd overheard the rebel Danes discussing him. Of course they would've been speaking in their own tongue. Had she assumed it was her own language? Nay. She hadn't even bothered to think about it. She'd wilfully not thought about it. She'd been lying to herself, because she hadn't been interested in the truth if it took him away from her. 'I've been a fool.'

'Nay, fair one, not a fool.' He crossed to her then, but stopped short of touching her when she jerked away.

'Aisly…' His voice trailed off and she was struck by the genuine hunger in his eyes.

'I've wanted things I've had no right to want. Things I didn't even know I wanted, or maybe I'd forgotten I'd wanted…until you,' she said.

His eyes narrowed in on her and a flash of pain crossed his features, twisting them slightly. 'It's the same for me.' He raised his hand so slowly that she had plenty of time to back away or stop him, but she couldn't. Despite herself, she wanted to feel his touch one more time. When his fingertips touched her cheek, it was all she could do not to shiver with the yearning that worked its way through her body from that touch.

'I want you.' His voice was rough and it scraped over her skin, abrading it and making her remember that it had been only moments earlier when he'd held her against the table. She still ached from how deliciously rough he'd been.

'Do you even know who you are?'

He shook his head. 'Not entirely. I know the men, but my memories are still hazy.'

'You're their leader, M-Magnus.' She couldn't help but stumble over the word. It didn't seem to belong to him. 'You're the reason Godric is dead.'

For a moment, only their breaths filled the space between them. Finally he moved closer, crowding her against the table until only a hair's breadth separated them. He kept a hand on her face, while the other pressed into the table beside her. 'If that turns out to be true, is that the only thing keeping us apart?'

She turned her head, but it didn't make her less aware of him. His scent surrounded her and she loved it. Craved it. 'Do I want to be tied to a Danish warrior? Is that what you're asking?'

He didn't deny it, but it didn't lessen his intensity. Daring to meet his gaze, she saw the flicker of longing within them. She couldn't deny that it sent an unwelcomed thrill through her entire being. 'I want you, fair one.'

There was a pause and all she could hear was his breath, all she could feel was the heat from his body. She wanted him, too. She couldn't deny that, but she wanted the Magnus who'd lain beside her at night and the Magnus who had held her close and made her feel that everything would be fine.

Not this one. Not the leader of Danes. Not the murderer of her husband. Not her enemy.

'Come with me.'

The low command sent exquisite chills through her body. 'I cannot.'

He looked away, shoulders bowing in momentary defeat, but when he looked back at her, none of the fire in his eyes had been banked. They were vivid, the gold flecks sparkling with intensity. 'You can.'

'You're still a warrior. That hasn't changed. The Danes roam the countryside. Would you take me with you only to leave me for months while you fight?' She had him there. She recognised the surrender when she saw it, the fading of that intensity. They didn't suit, regardless of him being a Dane. Her heart was raging.

Finally he moved back just a little. Just enough that she could take a breath, and his throat worked once, twice, before he said, 'Let me know when you find out if you're with child.'

'Nay.' She shook her head and her stomach clenched in on itself. If there was a baby and he decided he wanted it, there was very little she could do to stop him from taking it. She'd been so terribly foolish. 'Your debt is paid.'

'This isn't about the debt, Aisly. I want to know. I won't abandon you with a child.'

'That wasn't the agreement. I don't need anything else from you.'

He must have seen the panic in her eyes, because he took a step back and his hand fell to his side. 'I have to go. I need to get back to who I am. I'm their leader and have neglected my responsibilities.'

She nodded and a weight lifted from her chest with the growing physical distance between them. However, she also wanted to weep from the loss of his touch. She was so confused in her feelings that she couldn't determine which emotion was the right one. 'Goodbye.' She managed to say that much before the ache swelled in her throat.

'Make sure you do as I've asked.' When she frowned, he elaborated. 'The dugout. If I'm not here to keep you safe, I need to know that you're taking defensive measures.'

She nodded, having already forgotten he'd mentioned the safety measure to her. There'd been no need to heed his advice before and she realised it was because she'd known that he would be there to protect her. There'd been no doubt in her mind that she could rely on him.

'Aye, I'll do it.'

He nodded. 'I'll have men in place to help defend the village. Keep vigilant around Wulfric. You cannot trust him.' He looked as if he wanted to say more, but changed his mind. Turning, he walked to the door and gave her one last lingering look. 'Come for me if you need help.' Then he walked out of her life.

Chapter Seventeen

It was all so vivid now, the scene so clear…

She was dying.

No one had said the words, to say them would invite Death in on the howling wind to take all of them, but Magnus knew. Her screams of the week before had long since faded, but they lived on in his memory. He huddled back into the limbs of the fir tree, hiding himself from the buffeting wind coming in across the water and the people stirring in the small village below. Drawing his knees up to his chest, he wrapped his thin, right arm around them and tried not to shiver too hard. His left arm he kept cradled against his ribs. It was the only way he'd found to ease the near constant pain in them.

Despite how he'd prepared himself for the moment, he couldn't stop the jolt of terror that bolted through him when the door to the small house opened and his father stepped outside. He despised that cowardly emotion, so he forced himself to watch the man walk down to the dock where his boat was moored, not looking away once. His father hadn't left to go fishing for a sennight and Magnus half-feared that the gentle snow would keep his father home again today. But after talking for a long time with several of the other men he usually fished with, they all set about preparing their boats for the day.

Magnus breathed a sigh of relief and his chest lightened as he watched the men push away from the dock. He forced himself to wait until they'd disappeared down the river towards the inlet before crawling out from under the branches, the sharp needles jabbing him through his clothes. Glancing around once to make sure no one would see where he'd emerged from, he took his first step out of the forest in a sennight. The pain on his left side tried to slow him, but he ignored it. There was no telling how long he had, so he must make the most of it.

Still...he hesitated when he reached the door of his home, afraid of what he might find inside. His hand was shaking when he reached out to push the door open and his heart was pounding in his ears. A blast of hot, stale air warmed his cheeks. The heat was nearly stifling as he stepped inside, though to look at the woman huddled under a pile of blankets on the bed, it might as well have been freezing.

Closing the door behind him, he forced himself not to limp as he approached the bed. He didn't want to worry her needlessly. He'd heal just as he had in the past. He worried needlessly. His mother's eyes were closed as if she were asleep, though her mouth was too tense for sleep. She was battling pain. Her entire face was drawn with it, so that she was almost unrecognisable to him.

Thoughts of his mother always conjured to mind the smiling visage of an exceptionally pretty woman with a plump face, fair hair and bright blue eyes, not this broken creature with sunken cheeks, lined skin and hair so stringy and faded it bore no resemblance to the silk he remembered. He disgraced himself by gasping at the change and her eyes opened. They were the only part of her to retain a recognisable shadow of the woman she had been—a clear blue that always warmed when she saw him, as they did now.

'Magnus.' Her hand reached out and touched his face. The act nearly caused the ache in his throat to overwhelm him. 'I knew you'd come back.'

'I'd never leave you.' His voice came out too scratchy as he hurried to assure her.

But his words didn't reassure her at all. To his surprise, her eyes filled with tears and her voice was sad when she said, 'Aye, I knew you wouldn't. Not while I'm living.'

He sensed the words had some profound meaning that he couldn't grasp. When she merely stared at him as if she were trying to commit his face to memory, his gaze went to the other side of the bed, looking for a smaller bundle at her side. It wasn't there. He wondered if the babe—who'd been born months too early for the spring birth his mother had planned—had lived or if it had joined the others. He didn't ask. The others had left her sad and nearly despondent—he didn't dare bring it up.

'I want you to know that your father cared for you very much, Magnus.' Her thin voice drew his attention back to her. It was so small and fragile that fear flamed to life again inside him and he grabbed her hand, squeezing it hard, as if that alone could infuse some of his life into her. She didn't seem to mind and only smiled as she continued talking. 'He'd sing to you when you were in my belly. I called him a fool, but he insisted you could hear and would heed his words. They were always songs about

warriors and their heroic deeds. He knew you would be a great warrior. He knew you would do great things.'

He frowned and wondered if she'd already begun to slip into the next world. Magnus couldn't reconcile that man with the one who'd beat her and then turned his fists on him when Magnus had intervened. *'Why would he think that? I'm a fisherman like him. I—'*

Still smiling that odd smile, she shook her head. *'Nay, not Vakr. Vakr is a fisherman and a poor one at that. Your father was a warrior. I should have told you the truth before, but I thought it might be easier if you thought Vakr was your father. I thought it might help if... It's time for you to know the truth.'*

'What are you saying?'

'Your father was killed before you were born. It's why I named you Magnus. It was his name.' Raising her other hand, she made to touch his face, so he went down on his knees beside the bed to make it easier for her. He wanted to be a man now, but he couldn't deny the way her touch soothed him like a child. *'Even though you're only ten winters, I see him in you. You have his eyes, his brow, his mouth and soon you'll have his strength. It's why Vakr is jealous.'*

It was too much to take in at once. He picked the one thing he knew to be untrue to argue. *'I'm not strong. I couldn't save you from Fath—'* Calling him that seemed wrong now, but to say his name seemed even more so. *'I couldn't save you. I couldn't fight back. Everyone says I'm too thin.'*

She ran her fingers through his matted hair and he couldn't help but turn into her touch. *'You're perfect, Magnus. You did what you could. I love you.'* The ache in *his throat cracked, giving way to the tears that had been threatening all along, proving that he wasn't strong at all. A warrior wouldn't cry. But she didn't seem to mind and rose up to kiss his tears, her body shaking with the effort. 'I want you to know that your true father and I loved you very much. We wanted you from the very first moment I suspected you grew within me. It is your birthright to be a great warrior. I want you to leave here and make that happen.'*

'Nay! I'll not leave you.'

She ignored him and pointed to the far corner. 'Move the chest there and dig below. You'll find a small satchel of coins.' When he protested, she looked to the door, reminding them both that their time was limited. Vakr had forbidden him from coming back when he'd thrown him out the last time. 'Hurry, Magnus. If I'm to die, I want to die knowing you'll be safe.'

He hesitated but did as she directed. Digging with his hands, he quickly found the pouch and replaced the dirt before moving the chest back to cover their secret. Moving back to her side, he took her hand again, unable to keep from touching her. 'I have it.'

She nodded. 'Your father's master was Jarl Hegard. Travel northward along the coast and you'll find his hall. Tell him that you are Magnus's son and he'll take you in. I should have let you go before, but I was selfish and wanted you for myself. Please forgive me, Magnus.'

Tears ran down his cheeks again and he nodded, hiding his face against the blanket so no one saw them.

'If he refuses you, then offer him the coins,' she said, her hand gently resting on the back of his head. 'But only if he refuses. You'll need it to buy your sword and armour.'

* * *

It had taken them two days to get to the settlement. Over the course of those days Magnus had spoken at length with Vidar and the other warriors, coming to small realisations about his life. The memories had come back disjointed, like pieces of a broken urn he needed to fit together, turning them different ways until he found the right way that would make them all fit.

This one of his mother was the first of them to come back fully formed. He had just dismounted to stand on the bank of the River Tyne outside the settlement. The boats docked along the river had caught his attention, jarring that first memory loose of watching Vakr with his boat, bringing back that first portion of a dream he'd had in Aisly's bed. But it was the cool gust of wind bringing with it the fresh scent of the fir trees on the other side of the river that brought the rest of the memory to life.

'Magnus?' Vidar walked over, loosely holding the reins of his horse with one hand. His other hand went up in a greeting to the men just bringing in the boats from their day out on the river. 'Are you unwell?'

Magnus's heart was pounding so hard from what he'd just remembered that he wasn't at all certain he was well. It nearly brought him to his knees to have to relive her death over again. After he'd left her that day, he'd waited in the woods, half-starving, but unwilling to leave her completely as long as she lived. It hadn't been a long wait. On the morning of the second day there'd been a flurry of activity and they'd brought her body out wrapped in a shroud. He'd left then, unable to stay and know that she wasn't there.

'Aye, I've just had a memory.' He forced his gaze away from the fishing boats and to the walls of the settlement.

'It's good they're returning.' Vidar smiled. He'd been coming back to the jovial man Magnus remembered with each mile that took them away from the Saxons. 'You just need to be home. We'll get some mead in you, not that Saxon piss they were feeding you. They'll all be restored in good time.'

Magnus nodded, for the first time feeling as if he were coming back into his own. 'We need to find Heir, the man I told you the rebels were talking about.'

'I've sent for the traitor. We'll deal with him tomorrow, after you've had a chance to settle in.'

Magnus's gaze went over the walls—high enough not to be easily breached—and then the settlement beyond as they walked towards it. The houses were in a similar style to the Saxons, but everywhere he looked he saw warriors. This felt familiar. This was home.

Vidar let out a cry of victory as they entered the gates. Everyone within hearing distance looked up from their tasks, their faces revealing surprise and recognition. Immediately they were swamped with men and the few women who lived there, each welcoming him back from the dead.

He was the leader of the settlement. Vidar had told him as much and the men had treated him with deference on the trip home, but this was the first time he'd truly felt it. As he greeted each person by name—aye, their names were coming to him—he had very clear memories of the path that had led him to this role.

Half-afraid that Vakr might come looking for him, he'd run for days after his mother had died until he finally arrived at Jarl Hegard's hall. The Jarl had taken him in and that was how he'd met the Jarl's bastard son Gunnar. To say they'd shared similar childhood experiences would be an understatement and they had bonded quickly. It was probably the best thing that had happened to Magnus—up until Aisly found him in the forest—as it had shown him a different way to live. He'd become a warrior like his father had wanted and amassed a modest living working on Jarl Hegard's longboats.

He, Gunnar and Gunnar's brother Eirik had eventually made the crossing to the Saxon lands. But three winters ago Gunnar had been injured. He'd been so wounded that Eirik, now a jarl, had sent him home to their father, because it had been assumed he would die. Gunnar had lived, but he'd stayed in their homeland and married. Upon Jarl Hegard's death, he'd assumed his place as a jarl rather than coming back to resume his place as leader here in the Saxon lands.

Magnus had been given his place here. He was leader despite Vakr's taunts that he'd never amount to anything. As he looked into the faces of these people so joyful to welcome him home, he realised that he'd been a very good leader. He saw himself leading men in battle and counselling them at his table. He remembered the pride he felt in taking a group of men and teaching them how to excel in battle. There was an intoxicating sensation of gratification and contentment to be found in watching the settlement grow and flourish under his command. He'd grown to crave it in a way that made him realise he'd never have been completely content in the Saxon village.

This is who he was.

He was smiling as they walked through the settlement, but not so much as he did when he saw the hall looming before them. It was nearly as large as Jarl Hegard's back home to accommodate long winters with many warriors and entertainment. It was at least three times as large as the Saxons'. He could smell the freshly cut wood they'd used and remembered helping to design and build it. It was his.

As he stepped inside, a wave of familiarity passed over him. There were three large posts made from tree trunks down each side of the building, holding the vaulted ceiling up high. Beams crossed overhead where smoke from the two hearths wafted up to the slits in the top. Tables and benches lined the walls for all of his warriors. The back held a loft for storage, with chambers beneath it, three on one side, two larger ones on the other. Pride swelled within him as he walked in, his fingers stroking the harsh wood of a post. He only wished that his mother could see the warrior he'd become and how he'd earned all of this.

That brought forth another revelation. He missed Aisly.

Nay, 'missed' was too tame a word for the emotion that twisted inside him. He needed her with him to fill the hollow ache in his chest. He wanted to show her his world and all that he had accomplished. His boots scraped the wood floor as he walked to the dais further in the room near the back where a table was set and a woman was busy putting out pitchers of mead. Perhaps in time Aisly could come to see that he was the same man she'd come to care about, not the Dane who'd destroyed her life. But that was only likely to happen if she was with him. He half-thought of going back to her one night, scaling the wall and bringing her here. She'd hate him at first, but he was certain he could remind her of how good things were between them.

He nearly groaned aloud as another memory came to him. This one was a face, a man with dark hair and a sinister smile that he recognised as belonging to Godric. The fool had led a small group of warriors into the settlement at dawn one morning. Magnus suspected their plans had been to attack the night before, but they had found the fortifications such that they couldn't. Danes on watch had found the small group and brought them inside the next morning. Godric had told them that their maidens had been taken, but when he'd been brought inside to speak to Magnus, he'd led his warriors on a senseless revolt that had included setting fire to a few houses.

Women and children had been threatened, and in the ensuing struggle to maintain order, Godric had led his men in a fight to the death. There had been no execution. No cold-blooded murder. It had been a senseless clash led by a fool that had resulted in three of Magnus's warriors being wounded and the Saxons' deaths.

Try as he might, Magnus couldn't regret the action that had brought about the man's death. Godric had been too full of himself to make good decisions for his warriors or for Aisly. Magnus shuddered to think that she'd ever been at the mercy of such a man. If his exacting justice had saved her from that tyrant, then he couldn't regret it. He did regret that he might never be able to explain to her what had happened, or how he'd reacted afterwards. Instead of taking the time to talk to the Saxons, he'd reacted in anger and had sent Vidar to level a retribution tax for the actions of the few warriors.

He'd been so angry with Godric specifically that he'd impulsively ordered Vidar to dispense an exorbitant penalty to the man's family. It had been a short-sighted move and one that had been dangerous to her. Because of him, she was almost destitute and at the mercy of Wulfric. While she might not appreciate his interference, his first

order of business was to figure out what had happened
to the coin, wool and tapestries taken from her and see
them returned. Returning it also carried the hidden advantage of making sure she was provided for. The wool
would give her resources and he felt better knowing that
she wouldn't be facing Wulfric while destitute.

Vidar and two other warriors, Arn and Leikr—he'd
immediately recognised them as confidants—joined
him at the table and took their designated spots on the
benches, leaving him the one in the middle. He sat and
took up the mead they offered, savouring the rich com-
bination of bitter and sweet on his tongue. By the gods,
he'd missed it without even realising it.

'It's good to have you back.' Vidar raised his tankard
again and threw back the rest of its contents. The other
men joined in. Someone from the door yelled out another victory cry and more warriors filled the room. They
all had questions about where he'd been, so once they'd
found seats, he stood and called for quiet.

'I've a tale, my friends. You won't believe it, but I assure you it happened. It starts with battle and death...'
The room started to quiet as his voice rang out. Even the
few still filing in hurried to find a seat, their eyes on him.
'But it ends with a fair maiden with hair like fire and
eyes like moss.' He kept his face stoic as he imagined her
face, refusing to allow his feelings for her to be known.

There were cheers and someone said, 'A fire maiden.'

Magnus smiled. The name suited her in more ways
than one. 'Aye, I owe my life to the fire maiden. I'll only
tell the story once, so listen closely.'

For the next several moments he spoke, telling them
about how he'd awakened about to be burned, and going
all the way until Vidar had spotted him. Of course, he

left out the fact that he'd made a deal with Aisly to get her with child, but he was certain his admiration for her was clear for all to see. It didn't matter. The men loved a good story and he was happy to give them one. It'd give them something to talk about through the long winter.

Finally resuming his seat, he noticed Vidar watching him with a measured gaze. 'What?'

'The fire maiden. Was that the woman walking with you?'

Magnus stiffened and rolled his shoulders, realising he was overdue for a bath and change of clothes. He didn't want to talk about her. The story was one thing. The men loved stories and it gave his trip the aura of a saga. He didn't want to talk about Aisly, but to refuse would only prompt more questions, so he nodded and picked up his tankard.

Vidar frowned and a knot of unease twisted in Magnus's gut. A woman put down a bowl filled with roasted root vegetables and fish before him, so he murmured his thanks.

Vidar didn't speak again until Magnus had already taken a few bites. 'The marriage has been arranged.'

Magnus nearly choked. He'd been right. He wasn't married or even attached to a woman. Not yet. 'What do you mean?'

'Eirik...' Vidar's voice trailed off and he grimaced. '*Jarl* Eirik...' he put emphasis on the 'Jarl' as only a younger brother forced to show deference to an older brother could '...has arranged the marriage you wanted.'

'The marriage *I* wanted?'

Vidar smirked. 'I imagine the bride would be put out to hear you say that. You truly don't remember?'

Magnus sat back, his mind churning to find the an-

swer. There was no woman he could remember. There
was no one for him besides Aisly.

'The peace-weaver,' Vidar prompted.

Then the pieces began to fit. Jarl Eirik had promised
him that his hard work would be repaid in the form of a
Saxon bride. Jarl Eirik had himself married a high-born
Saxon bride. Such brides were known as peace-weavers
and Magnus's marriage would help sow seeds of peace
amongst the native Saxons and the Danes. Of course, that
bride would have to be high-born so he'd be linked to a
well-respected Saxon family.

'When did this happen?'

'He arrived just after you left to go after the rebels. Do
you remember we'd received a message from the south
claiming the villages were being plagued by the rebels?
You took ten men south to meet up with the settlement
leaders there, while I rode to the Saxon village to collect
from Godric's family. At some point, the rebels overtook
your group. That's the battle that left you wounded.'

Magnus closed his eyes as an image of the ambush
came back to him. They'd been in unfamiliar territory
and the rebels had come from nowhere. One of his own
men had turned on him, slashing Magnus across his temple with a sword. Heir's brother. He remembered the coward now amongst the rebels he'd trailed to the north just
days ago. Both men were traitors. It was the only reason
the rebels had stood a chance against them in that battle.

'I remember now,' Magnus replied and relayed the
details of the battle that he remembered.

Vidar asked a few questions, but once the subject
was played out, he said, 'The marriage has been set for
spring.'

Before that battle, Magnus would have been overjoyed

at the news that Jarl Eirik had arranged a marriage. It would mean that all he'd done to leave his destitute childhood behind had finally come to fruition. He was someone now. Despite Vakr, he was a leader.

Yet it meant that Aisly would never be his, whether she forgave him or not. There was no room for her in his life. At least, not in a way that she'd find acceptable. He still wanted her, though. Every step that had taken him further away from her, each passing mile had just felt wrong. He wanted her for his own—if that meant keeping her as a mistress, then it was what he would do. The only problem with that would be Aisly. She wouldn't accept that from him. She wouldn't accept anything less than everything he had to give her. It was one of the things he'd come to love about her. If he was being honest, he didn't want anything less for her than the family she wanted for herself.

He could not give her that. Not in the way she wanted it.

He had to leave her alone. His breath left his body, leaving that hollow ache inside him to expand until it was almost unbearable. It wasn't until that moment that he realised he'd been holding to some hope that if he just gave her time, and sent her gifts, and perhaps even visited her a time or two, that she'd remember how much she loved him. She'd never said those words to him, but he knew love in someone's eyes when he saw it and he had seen it in hers.

But it wouldn't help them. If he said no to the marriage, he'd be turning his back on everything he was and everything he'd worked for. And it wasn't just his own dreams. Their position in the Saxon lands was precarious. There had been many deaths since his time here, both Dane and Saxon alike. His marriage could lessen the futility of those deaths and perhaps even save lives. His marriage could help them figure out a way to live with the Saxons in a truce.

He had to let her go. She'd be happier that way. He'd have to watch out for her from afar. Knowing that he needed to leave her in his past didn't stop the knot of dread from settling heavy in his gut as he struggled with acceptance. What if she was with child? Had he seriously thought he'd be able to rest knowing she and their child were out there facing the world alone and not under his roof, under his protection?

Realising Vidar still watched him, he nodded. 'I'll send word to the Jarl. I need to discuss with him the past few years, in case there are gaps in my memory.'

'Already taken care of, my friend. I dispatched a messenger while you were walking around reacquainting yourself with people you've known for years.' Vidar grinned and winked.

His tone was teasing and Magnus had a memory of his friend as a mischievous boy always causing trouble as he'd followed his older brothers around. 'Thank you for taking care of things while I was away. Seems you're ready to be a leader in your own right.'

Vidar laughed and looked out across the hall. 'A leader on a ship, aye, a leader here, on land…it's too restrictive. I value my freedom too much. There's too much left to see of the world.'

'The Jarl might disagree.'

'The Jarl can go stuff himself. I've been telling him that for years before he was Jarl.'

Magnus chuckled as another memory surfaced, this

one corroborating Vidar's words. The laughter felt empty, though. Now that he realised Aisly was truly far out of his reach, he wondered what joy there would be to life.

Chapter Eighteen

A chill swept up her spine, prickling the skin at the back of her neck and setting her cowardly rabbit heart to beating in her chest. The pounding echoed in her ears, momentarily drowning out the words being spoken around her. She'd been summoned to Wulfric's home. Summoned. He hadn't stopped by and asked her to share a meal. He'd sent a boy to knock at her door just as she'd been about to go to bed.

Her heart had leapt for just a moment as it always did when she thought that perhaps Magnus had returned. It was foolish. He'd been gone a sennight with no indication that he'd ever return. What need was there for him to return? She'd given him no indication that she wanted to pursue anything with him. Indeed, she'd actually made it very clear that she wanted nothing to do with him, proving how big a fool she really was. Had she really thought that she wouldn't miss him?

'Aisly.' Wulfric's sharp voice intruded on her thoughts as he successfully gained her full attention. He sat on the bench near his hearth as if he thought standing to confront her would be a sign of weakness. 'I wanted to give you another opportunity to declare your innocence.'

Arte sat next to him but looked away from her. She looked at the three other men present, wondering how much aid she could expect from them. Two were elders like Wulfric and the other was a warrior who held some rank with the others. Aside from Arte, they all looked at her with impassive eyes. Nay, she'd get no help from them.

Taking a deep breath, she tried to remain calm as she recited the same thing she'd told them all in Cuthbert's hall on the evening of the day her foreigner—Magnus, she must remember him that way—had been found out. She hadn't known that he was a Dane any more than anyone else had known. She had come upon him nearly unconscious in the forest. She didn't know why he'd come to their village. It was really all very basic and she couldn't understand why they wouldn't believe her. But she swallowed her pride and the anger that threatened, and made herself argue her innocence.

'You must know this is getting tiresome.' Wulfric sighed.

'Aye, I agree. It's very tiresome.'

He cut his eyes at her and rapped his knuckles on the table. 'I've had enough of your insolence.'

Keeping her hands folded in front of her, she made sure no one could see how they trembled. She knew it was smarter to placate him, but the more interaction she had with Wulfric, the more she realised there wasn't any way to placate him. He wouldn't be satisfied with anything short of her leaving, never to return. 'What do you want of me? I've answered your questions, but you are obviously determined to maintain that I colluded with a spy.'

Arte finally looked at her again, giving her a glimpse of pity in his eyes. Wulfric appeared thoughtful, his hand running absently along the length of his beard. The way he stroked it was almost sensual and it made her skin crawl. She glanced around the home again, looking for some sign of their wives, but it appeared that just the men were present.

'What's obvious to us is that the Dane was enamoured of you,' Wulfric said, accusation in his tone.

She did her best not to flinch. 'He was grateful for my kindness.'

'How grateful was he?' His cold eyes flicked down the length of her body, but he'd never dare to say aloud what he was thinking with the others present. Nevertheless, her cheeks flamed at the insinuation and how close to the mark it was. It didn't help that she knew how easily he could get rid of her if he tried. A part of her questioned why he hadn't already done something as horrendous as what he'd done to get rid of Beorn and Rowena.

'Let us not draw this out any longer,' Arte said, a quiet admonishment to his friend.

Her breath quickened, and she realised that while he hadn't done anything yet, this was the moment that he would.

A grin split Wulfric's face, all too eager to oblige. 'Certainly. Let us skip over the unnecessary banter. You see, Aisly, we know that there was more to your friendship with the Dane.'

The air squeezed from her chest as she thought back to all the times she and Magnus had been together. Perhaps they'd been too careless in public and all had been revealed on their faces. Or it could have been that someone had seen him leave her home one night. Or perhaps they didn't know at all and this was a bluff.

'We know you took him as a lover,' one of the other men who'd been silent up until now clarified.

The words hung heavy in the air, taunting her. Blood rushed in her ears and it was all she could hear. The idea that they knew about those precious hours spent with him simply made her furious. She should be ashamed and should probably beg them not to cast her out. But she was angry that they'd dare to sully her time with him.

'You know nothing,' she managed to say between clenched teeth.

Wulfric didn't wait a moment before saying, 'Bring in the girl.'

The warrior of the group rose and walked to the door. She must have been very close, because in moments he returned with Wyn. The girl's eyes were wide as he led her into the room. Arte stepped forward and took her arm, leading her over to stand next to Wulfric. 'Tell them what you saw.'

Wyn visibly swallowed, her eyes landing on Aisly for only a moment before skittering away to settle on the fire in the hearth. That moment was long enough for Aisly to read regret in their depths and on her face.

It was true. Somehow someone had found out about them. Dread settled like a heavy, wet blanket on her shoulders.

'I saw them together twice.' The girl's voice was very small.

'Speak louder and tell us when you saw them,' Wulfric commanded.

'Once in the forest. I saw them leaving together, and

I followed, thinking to help gather Aisly's larkspur. But they were... They sat against a tree and were...'

'Rutting like beasts,' Wulfric finished speaking for her, looking entirely too pleased with himself.

Wyn spared a glance at Aisly as if to say she was sorry, before turning her attention back to the fire.

Aisly gripped her fingers together even tighter as she remembered that foolish mistake. She'd been too drunk on Magnus and the horribly delicious things his touch did to her to even consider that they might have been followed. He'd been the one to suggestion caution on that day, but she'd brushed his concerns aside. She was a fool.

'And the second time, my dear,' Wulfric prompted her, his grin firmly in place.

'The day he was found out. They left the hall together...and I followed.' Her voice lowered on that last and she lowered her face in shame. 'They went to her home and I can't say what went on inside.'

'But you will say what you heard.' Arte touched her shoulder in encouragement.

'I heard them...sounds...something like a table or bench knocking against the wall repeatedly and—'

'Enough!' Aisly couldn't bear to hear her transgressions laid out for all to hear. They'd probably been discussing them for days, determining their plan. The very idea of them discussing her—*discussing that*—made her feel sick to her stomach. Those hours with Magnus had been just for them. She hated that Wulfric was able to use them against her. 'I won't listen to any more.'

'Oh, you will,' Wulfric said.

'I won't. You have no proof but the word of a jealous girl.'

Wyn gasped as if Aisly had slapped her. 'It's true. I

was jealous, but I didn't mean to tell them. I told a friend because I was hurt and angry, and she told my mother. Please believe me, Aisly. I didn't want anything bad to happen.' Wyn made a move to go to her, but her father kept his hand on her shoulder.

'It hardly matters how anyone found out. The fact is that this horrible thing happened, Aisly. We need to know why. Have you been giving the Dane information about us? What did he promise you in return?' Arte asked.

Unwilling to admit to any of it, but certain there was a reason Wulfric had set this trap, she glared at them all. 'Magnus was no spy. You know that, Arte. You saw him and even helped carry him inside. He was badly wounded and near death.'

'It's true and perhaps it means the plan wasn't premeditated. I believe he was injured, but he recovered quickly enough and used the excuse of having lost his memories as a way to stay and gain information.'

She couldn't deny the ring of truth to that. They were the exact words she'd repeated to herself over the past week. 'I was as surprised as you were when that Dane called out to him.'

'That hardly matters now,' Arte said, raising a hand to ask for her silence.

But the warrior who'd retrieved Wyn had apparently had enough of silence. 'His name is Magnus. Magnus is the name of the leader at Thornby, the man who killed your husband.' He sneered and looked at her as if she were dirtier than filth.

'Aye, I'm aware of his name. But I didn't know it when I saved him.'

'Nevertheless, we do believe you knew it soon after you saved him,' Arte continued.

For the hundredth time she asked herself why she hadn't pressed him harder for his name. He'd known it when he'd returned from scouting out the rebels. But he hadn't seemed to want to tell her and she hadn't pressed. What a fool she was. 'I didn't know. I swear to you that I didn't know his name.'

Arte opened his mouth to answer, but Wulfric rose to his feet. 'It doesn't matter if we believe you or not. What matters is that Magnus is fond of you. We need you to go to him, infiltrate his inner sanctum and bring back his secrets.'

Her blood ran cold. They couldn't possibly be asking what she thought they were asking, but even as she tried to deny it, there was no other explanation that made sense. 'What do you mean?'

'Go to him. Open your legs for him again. Say please and thank you and anything else he wants to hear until you find out his plans for attacking our village.'

'Wulfric!' Clearly appalled at his crudity, Arte walked Wyn to the door and shooed her off.

'I won't do it.'

'Why not? You've done it before for less.' Wulfric wasn't grinning now, he looked positively livid. 'Or were you hoping for a child? A bastard to pass off as my blood? You must know that were you to bear a child now, I'd believe it to be that Dane's spawn. I'll not accept it as Godric's and you'll not stay in that house.'

'Aye, you've made certain of that, haven't you? What did you promise Lord Oswine to get him to destroy the marriage contract?'

Wulfric laughed, mirthless and sinister. 'Don't you worry about that. Rest assured there is no marriage contract. If you do as I've asked, then I can sign it over to you. If you don't, there's always the abbey. They'll take in faithless whores.'

There was no way out for her. There was no way she'd keep her house, her livelihood. Wulfric would find a way to take it away from her no matter what she did. This explained why the villagers had been rather cold with her all week. Cuthbert's wife had accepted the mended tapestry back just the day before without a word or nod of thanks. Even her apprentices had been mysteriously ill, albeit she'd been too despondent to notice. This was why. They believed that she had deceived them. Magnus's betrayal had spilled over on to her because they all knew how friendly they'd become.

Or did they know about what Wyn had seen? *Please not that.*

'I refuse to go live at the abbey.'

Wulfric shrugged. 'Then go to Thornby and bring us his secrets.'

'You're asking me to…to *use* myself…to give my body to him for information. Do you hear yourself, Wulfric? Arte?' She looked back and forth between them. One of them sneering and the other appearing suitably horrified at the suggestion, though it wouldn't stop them from demanding it of her.

'Aye,' Wulfric said.

She shook her head and stepped backwards. The warrior made a move to either grab her or block her exit, but Arte made a gesture that he should stay seated. Were they going to physically drag her to the Dane and give her to him? Her stomach turned at the mere thought, even as she reasoned that it was Magnus. No matter what she thought of him and his possible deceit, he wouldn't harm her.

Then another horrible thought plagued her. What if

she refused, only to have them demand something even more despicable? She made a last desperate plea for sanity. 'What you're asking is sinful.'

'I'm not asking any more than what you've already given the Dane. Let's not make this out to be more than it is.' Stroking his beard again, Wulfric appeared bored.

'It's for a better cause, child. Once this is done, you can beg forgiveness and the Lord will grant it. Life in an abbey could certainly help your soul,' Arte stated quietly.

So that was their plan. Use her and then send her off anyway. Squaring her shoulders, she stood her ground and stared them down. 'I won't do it.'

Wulfric stared right back, trying to determine if she was bluffing. Finally he rose and for the first time she saw real anger in his eyes as they narrowed at her. 'You place too much importance on yourself, whore. Rest assured that we have other plans, other ways to reach him. But don't think for a moment I'll allow you to pawn his bastard off as Godric's child.'

Shaking with outrage, she turned and fled his home. She didn't care that they hadn't dismissed her. If she had to spend another moment in his presence, she might very likely run him through with his own sword.

She allowed herself to cry when she returned home. Falling to her knees next to the bed, she buried her face in the blanket and sobbed until she didn't have any tears left. Only then did she sit up, her gaze wandering the room. For the first time, she observed it with a sense of detachment. The cooking utensils across the hearth were familiar, but they weren't hers. The worktable in the front—currently free from any work because no one had commissioned anything—sat abandoned, drained of the life she'd once poured into it.

She realised then that Wulfric had more power than she'd realised. She was still here, still in her home, yet because of his influence they all had forsaken her. Cuthbert's wife hadn't come by, neither had Lora, and they'd spoken just the week before about a new tapestry. Wulfric had made it known that he was displeased and that was all it had taken. If that influence would extend to Lord Oswine's manor and the abbess, she didn't know. She could only assume it must if he'd somehow convinced Lord Oswine to destroy her marriage contract. The way everyone had turned on her made this place not seem like home at all.

What was left for her here? The house meant nothing to her if she couldn't continue to do her work. If she couldn't do her work, then she might as well go to her brother. At least with him she'd have an ally. He infuriated her sometimes, but she was certain he'd protect her.

Fingers tightening in the blanket, she remembered how tightly she'd gripped it when Magnus had been there with her. This house had felt like home then. Even knowing he was a Dane, she couldn't bring herself to regret what had happened. He'd felt like home.

She still felt horrible for how cold she'd been to him when she found out his identity. After all he'd given her, the least she could have given him in return was some understanding. But she'd turned away from him just like the people of Heiraford had turned away from her. She had to go warn him of the horrible things Wulfric had planned and she needed to apologise.

A small part of her still imagined a life with him as her husband, but she knew that it was only a dream that could exist in some other world. He was a Dane and she was a Saxon. They were destined to be enemies, because there was no place they could exist together. She'd never be at home with the Danes and he was a warrior. What sort of life would that be? So it was a thought she tucked away deep in her heart.

Rising to her feet, she dragged over a stool and climbed atop it to unfasten her mother's tapestry from the ceiling. If she was leaving, it would have to be tonight. She'd not risk another day in this village and allow Wulfric more time to bully her. For all she knew, he might stoop to locking her up. Laying it out on the bed, she grabbed an extra underdress and hose, along with the bits of golden thread she'd had left over from Lord Oswine's commission back in the summer. There wasn't much else that held any value for her. Rolling them up in the tapestry, she wrapped it with a hide tether.

Grabbing the knapsack she used while foraging, she filled it with root vegetables and the leftover loaf of bread she had bought for the week. Then she tied it to her belt along with her scabbard and sword, and wrapped her cloak around herself. Tying the rolled-up tapestry to her back, she headed for the door and peeked outside. It was late enough that no one was about.

She shut the door quietly behind her and made her way towards the front gate, using the shadows to keep her hidden. Cuthbert had increased the men on watch since Magnus had reported that the rebel Danes were planning to come back. They kept watch at the gate and had been posted in the forest on the back side of the village. Soon the horn would sound and it'd be time for the watch to change. It was risky, but she had to sneak out then. It would be her only chance to find the gates open before morning. She had to put miles between her and Heiraford by then. She had only the vaguest notion of where the Dane settlement was, but Alstan had mentioned once that there was a road and she knew its direction. She'd just follow the stream until she found it.

Chapter Nineteen

'Her name is Gwendolyn of the house of Alvey of Bernicia.' Jarl Eirik's voice carried across the table, just loud enough to be heard over the din of conversation throughout the hall. Eirik had only arrived in Thornby that afternoon. Magnus had questioned Heir and discovered the location of the last of the rebels to the north. He'd leave in the morning to find them. Eirik would stay and determine a suitable punishment for the traitor.

Magnus stiffened upon hearing the words. The subject hadn't been broached yet, but he knew who Eirik was referring to. His intended wife. Resting his elbows on the table, he leaned forward to peer down into his tankard of mead. A hundred thoughts vied for his attention, but the vision of Aisly won out. He didn't care who this woman was if she wasn't Aisly. Still, he had to offer something as the Jarl sat waiting.

'The family. I've heard that name before.' Bits and pieces of his memory were still returning. Often when a new piece of information was revealed to him, he'd have to think about it for a while to figure out how it fit. It was frustrating, but with every passing day his memories were becoming clearer.

'Aye, you have. The Picts and the Scots to the north have been intermingling for decades. They'll unite soon and may come south. Her family is old and have strong allegiances. They defend the northern land that keeps the tribes from coming down to challenge us. We need their allegiance before an enemy takes it.'

Vidar plopped down on the bench beside his brother. 'We don't *need* allegiances, brother. We take what we want. If you want that land, tell me and you'll have it.'

Eirik spared a glance at his younger brother and his jaw tightened in annoyance. 'We're stretched thin with our battles to the south. There's no need for battle if a marriage can accomplish the same goal.'

Taking a big drink from his tankard, Vidar grinned as he lowered it. 'Why sacrifice all the warriors, when only one will do?'

They all laughed, but the jest rang hollow to Magnus. He was the one being sacrificed. It was his duty and he'd sworn allegiance to Eirik, but he didn't relish the task. The more he thought about Aisly, the more he was sure that given enough time, he could've overcome her reservations about the fact that he was a Dane. It didn't help that her husband had led the revolt against him, but he was certain he could make her understand the truth of what had happened.

But he wouldn't get that chance.

'When?' he asked.

'The ride north will be easiest after the thaw in spring. We'll need the passes clear to transport all the gold her father demanded,' Eirik said, frowning as he ran a hand through his hair.

'How much did he charge you to marry his daughter to that ugly bastard?' Vidar laughed, nodding his head towards Magnus.

'Too bloody much,' Eirik grumbled and threw back a swallow of mead.

Shaking his head, Vidar shrugged. 'Or we could go in and take the land.'

'Too risky,' Eirik countered.

'Or we take the girl. She'd be ours, the old man would give in to get her back and she'll go home married.'

Eirik's scowl deepened as he stared at his younger brother. 'And Magnus would find his throat slit the first time he dared to close his eyes. And if he didn't return with her, we'd face rebellion.'

'The Jarl is right, Vidar,' Magnus interjected when the younger man opened his mouth to argue. 'Why take when there are other ways to get what you want? We save the aggression for later and gain allies in the process. There may be those within the house of Alvey who would oppose our rule. We save the fight for them.'

Eirik inclined his head in thanks. 'This is why he's the leader of Thornby and has been chosen for the marriage,' he said, smirking at Vidar. 'You could learn from him, little brother.'

Vidar scoffed and scowled. 'I don't want your forced marriages and responsibilities. Give me the sea and a sword any day.'

'One day you'll have to settle down and take on more responsibility,' Eirik said.

'One day.' Vidar conceded. 'But not now.' Then he gave Magnus a look that was filled with such pity for his upcoming marriage that Magnus couldn't help but laugh.

Shaking his head, Magnus said, 'You're old enough

for marriage and children.' A vision of Aisly round with his child flashed through his head and he tightened his grip on the tankard. He'd find out if she was with child before he married. If so, he'd make sure to leave her gold. Even if she wasn't, he'd make sure she was provided for. The idea of her raising his child without him gnawed at his insides. It felt so wrong that something deep within him screamed out.

When Vidar answered back, Magnus struggled unsuccessfully to focus on his friend. It was useless. Anger tore through him fierce and swift. There was no good reason for it. He was getting everything he wanted: a high-born wife, influence, enough power to show Vakr that he'd been wrong. Magnus was worth something. He was as great a warrior as his father had hoped. With this marriage, he'd rule the territory to the north like a king.

But the victory was hollow. Blowing out a breath, he mumbled something about a walk and got to his feet. As soon as he stood, the large oak doors of the hall opened, letting in a gust of cold wind. He could hear a female's voice but couldn't make out the words above the talking in the room. Others heard as well, and as two of the warriors on guard duty walked in with a small woman between them, all the eyes in the room began to turn towards them. The doors closed behind the small group with a loud thump that settled into the growing quiet.

The woman was Aisly. At first he didn't dare to believe the vision before his eyes. The woman's cloak had fallen back and either wind or a struggle had made her hair fall in tangles around her. The tresses were long and dark, the firelight catching its deep red highlights. She jerked at her arms, which were held in stoic silence by the men at her sides.

Somehow her gaze found his out of all of the others in the room and she startled in recognition. Her eyes widened and that was the moment he allowed himself to believe that she had come. His heart pounded and relief weakened his body. If she was here, then she was safe.

'Let her go.' His command silenced the remaining murmur of voices. The men at her sides hesitated, but when he began walking towards them, they released her and moved back, though they stayed close.

She wavered. Looking around the room as if she'd just realised she was in enemy territory, she drew herself up to her full height, but he could see the uncertainty in her eyes when she looked back at him. He wanted to pull her against his chest and tell her everything would be fine, but he didn't. Her soft green eyes reached right into him and squeezed his heart. When he came to a stop just before her, he managed to keep his hands at his sides. She appeared so frail and vulnerable. The tip of her nose was pink with the cold.

'Aisly.' His voice didn't work, coming out harsh and rough. Swallowing, he tried again. 'Why are you here? Was there an attack? Are you alone?'

One of the guards spoke up. 'Lookout spotted her about a league out. She was alone.'

Magnus nodded, but he didn't look away from her face. He couldn't.

'I needed to see you. T-to talk to you.' The sound of her voice was soothing to some primal part of him.

'Are you in danger? Is the village in danger?' He'd had men watching for the rebels, but it was possible something had happened.

'Nay, the village is fine. I just... It's Wulfric...' She gestured to the guard on her left and he noticed the man had a bundle slung over his shoulder. It looked suspiciously like a rolled-up tapestry.

'Is that your mother's tapestry?' When she nodded, it was as if a fist clenched itself around his heart and squeezed. Something horrible had happened if she'd left her home carrying the one thing she valued most. 'Did he hurt you?'

'Nay, I came to warn you that he's planning something. I don't know what, but he wanted me to…to…' She looked around with unease. 'Can we speak privately?'

'Aye.' He grabbed her arm gently, because he couldn't not touch her any longer, to lead her to his chamber. There was nowhere else he would even think for her to go. She was his and she needed to be where he could keep her safe.

'Who is this?' Eirik had walked up behind him.

Magnus stopped. He'd forgotten all about Eirik. Keeping his grip on her arm, he faced the Jarl. 'This is Aisly, the woman who cared for me.' Eirik had already heard the story from the men and Magnus had relayed the story of his time there as well. He'd even told him about Wulfric and his suspicion that the father had encouraged Godric's rebellion.

'From Heiraford?' His blue eyes narrowed in suspicion.

'Aye. She's come to us with information.' Before Eirik could even demand to hear it, Magnus continued, 'I'll speak with her privately.'

The Jarl looked down at her with an impassive expression, his arms crossed over his large chest. When she returned his stare, he nodded and stepped aside. Magnus led her to his chamber, for the first time noticing how she shivered. It had taken him two days by horse to make the trip from her village. How long had it taken her on foot? As they passed a small group of servants near the passageway, he ordered hot water and food brought to his chamber. The men had started talking again. He heard the phrase 'fire maiden' spoken more than once and smiled to himself. She'd become a legend.

Pushing open the door to his chamber, he allowed her to precede him inside. He followed her but didn't close the door behind them. If he did, the urge to pull her close would be too great for him to resist. He'd touch her, but later.

'Do you think you were followed?' he asked as she walked slowly into the room, her eyes taking in the space.

Shaking her head, she turned back to face him. 'Nay, I left in the middle of the night, sneaked out when they were changing the guard. They may have an idea that I'm headed here, but i don't think they'd be that foolish again. It's clear you have them outnumbered.'

He stared at her, trying to find something in her tone, in her eyes, that would tell him how she was feeling. Now that they were in his chamber, the fear that had coloured them was faded, but he couldn't tell what had replaced it. She was guarded. 'That would be foolish. I hope they've learned that lesson.' As soon as the words were out of his mouth, he wanted to call them back. Reminding her of her lost husband wasn't the best way to start their conversation, especially not when he was responsible for the man's death. He planned to tell her the truth of that encounter now that she was here, but that would be later tonight.

Other than a brief tightening of her lips, she didn't react. Instead, she pulled her shoulders back as if steeling herself for the task and said, 'Wulfric wanted me to offer myself up to you for your secrets.' His heart thumped and his groin tightened at the memory of the last time she'd offered herself up to him. The way she'd clung to him as he'd buried himself inside her against the worktable. He could still hear her soft cries and feel her hands clutching his shoulders. He must have taken too long to reply, because she elaborated. 'Get information from you about the settlement, by becoming your mistress.'

He had to clear his throat to reply. 'Aye, I understand.' He tore his gaze from her and ran a hand over the back of his neck, the skin there suddenly feeling too tight. 'I'm just not certain I understand why he would suggest that.'

'He found out about us. I suppose it was no secret the way we...well, the way we favoured one another. But someone saw us together.'

That got his attention and his eyes snapped back to hers. They'd always been so careful. Well, mostly careful. By the gods, he'd put her in danger.

'That day in the forest,' she answered his unspoken question. 'It was Wyn, Arte's youngest. I think she wanted you and followed us, unsuspecting. Then she heard us later.' Her cheeks reddened when a servant came through the door bearing a steaming pot of water, and another followed with a meal.

'Eat and there's warm water for you to use. I'll leave you to refresh yourself. I need to go talk to the men who found you and prepare in case the warriors from the village are close behind. This is my chamber and no one will harm you here. You have my vow.'

She nodded, but her gaze was already devouring the food.

Closing the door behind him, he stood outside his chamber and took a deep breath. Despite how he'd longed for it, he'd never imagined she'd be here. Now that she was, he didn't know that he could keep his hands away from her. He should. He could still make her no promises, but as he walked away he knew that he wouldn't.

Not unless she made him.

Chapter Twenty

Aisly was feeling better after a meal and a change of clothes. A servant had brought in her rolled-up tapestry, so after stripping off her dirty clothes and washing, she retrieved the extra underdress she'd packed. She was too tired to put on the heavy wool overdress. Instead, she found a supple velvet cloak hanging on the wall and wrapped herself in it. It must belong to Magnus, because it smelled of him. Her sword had yet to be returned, but she'd ask about it tomorrow.

She wanted to curl up in his massive bed and go to sleep, but she was in his room and currently uncertain of her welcome. He'd seemed surprised but happy to see her in the hall. She'd nearly been overwhelmed at the relief and exhilaration she'd felt at seeing him again. Relief because somehow she knew that everything would be all right as long as he was around to protect her. Exhilaration because she'd missed him terribly. She hadn't realised how much until she'd seen him again, yet she'd never seen him like he'd been tonight.

When she'd spotted him standing behind the table, her eyes had almost passed over him. Except his very pres-

ence had held them. He'd obviously been a leader. It was
only once they'd settled on him for a moment that she
realised he was Magnus. His hair and beard had grown
out just slightly more, but there was something in his
very presence that had changed. She hadn't talked to
him enough to know, but she would wager more of his
memories had returned. He looked like a man possessed
of himself.

Then when he'd walked towards her, she'd realised
that his clothing were much richer than any in her village. He'd been dressed in a tunic of some dark brocade
with silver embroidery along the hem and his breeches
had been a very fine hide. He was a man of some wealth.
As leader of the settlement, she had assumed he would
be, but it was just odd to see him in that role, however
well it suited him.

She couldn't keep herself from walking around his
spacious chamber, taking in the many trunks that undoubtedly held treasures and the shelves that held
armour and weapons. Seeing these bits and pieces of his
life made her wonder even more about him. How had he
come to be at this place? Where had he come from? They
were questions she had no right to ask him. There was no
point in her knowing the answers, not when there was no
place for them. Not when the answers would only leave
her yearning for more.

The door opened abruptly and she whirled to see him
standing there, his wide shoulders filling the doorway.
Her heart fluttered foolishly before she got a handle on
the thing. His eyes widened when he noticed her wearing the cloak and she had this notion that it must be important and she'd been awfully presumptuous to wear it.

'I'm sorry, I just saw it and it looked comfortable. I

shouldn't have taken it.' She was pulling it off when he closed the door behind him and stepped inside.

'It's fine, Aisly. Keep it.' He stepped further into the room, but he seemed agitated. His hands raked over his hair on either side of his head and, except for that initial moment when he'd walked in, he seemed unwilling to look at her. His eyes lit on the small fire.

She shrugged out of the warm folds of the cloak and placed it across the end of the massive bed. She still couldn't get over how large it was. It could easily fit two of him. 'Perhaps I shouldn't have come,' she said, when he hadn't moved. 'I didn't mean to cause any trouble.'

That got his attention. 'You're not causing trouble. I left men behind to guard the village, just in case the rebels came back. One of them followed you here, so you were safe the entire time. He didn't make himself known, because he wasn't certain of your intentions. He confirmed that you weren't followed. Whatever they're planning, it isn't happening yet.'

She nodded. She'd had no notion that one of the Danes was following her, but she wasn't particularly surprised. 'Nevertheless, now that I'm here I realise how foolish it was. I don't have specific information for you, only his vague threats. Only that he'd requested I spy on you.'

'Wulfric frightened you. I'm glad you thought you could come to me.' Though his words were comforting, his jaw seemed tight, as if he were holding back.

He was right to hold back. They should hold back. Things were different than they were when they touched whenever they were alone together. It wasn't the same now. But her body didn't know that. A coil of heat began to unfurl in her belly as she became aware of how broad he was. She hadn't quite remembered that part correctly.

She did remember how solid he felt against her. How safe she felt when he held her. A gentle throbbing began between her thighs and she pressed her legs together to keep it from worsening. That part of their relationship was over.

'I'm glad you're doing well, M-Magnus.' Something changed in his eyes when she said his name. A barrier came down. It had been difficult to say, but she was happy she'd tried. 'Have your memories returned?'

'Much of them.' He paused, started to speak, then paused again, running the edge of his thumb over his bottom lip, before that hand messed the blond hair at the back of his head. The muscles in his arm flexed as it moved, drawing her attention. 'I want you to know the truth of what happened the day Godric came here.'

She wasn't sure what she'd expected him to say, but it wasn't that. It was a blow, a reminder that she really should not have these feelings for the man. He was her enemy. 'I do not think—'

'Hear me out, Aisly…please?' He moved as if to touch her but stopped himself and dropped his hand back to his side. 'He came here with his warriors to fight. It wasn't about the women. It was about destroying us. He meant to kill as many of us as he could, even the innocents.'

'I don't…' This was not the conversation she'd imagined. She didn't want to talk about Godric or imagine the confrontation between him and Magnus. She turned to blot him out, but he walked up behind her.

'You should know, Aisly. They weren't murdered savagely.' Finally he touched her. It was only his fingertips on the curve of her shoulder through the linen of her dress, but it might as well have been naked flesh for the spark of heat that flared beneath his touch. He drew in a shaky breath, making her think he felt it, too. 'It was battle. They burned houses. Women and children were threatened, innocents who could've been killed.'

The awful truth of that washed over her. She had no trouble believing it, because Godric had spoken often enough of the need to kill them all. He'd said the Danes needed to be wiped from the land before they could pollute the Saxon race by mating. He wouldn't hesitate to harm innocents if they stood in his way. Deep down she'd known that about him.

And she'd married him.

A shudder of revulsion moved through her entire body, leaving nausea lingering in its wake. She'd married that depraved man, yet had felt shamed when she'd found out Magnus was a Dane. He'd been nothing but kind and good, and she'd turned from him. A gasp tore from her, trying to bring with it tears, but she fought them back. She pressed her hand against the ache in her chest and tried to stop them, her body trembling from the tension.

But he was there. Drawing her back against his warm, strong chest as his arms went around her. That same feeling of peace she always had with him came to her now, making everything better and somehow worse at the same time. She couldn't draw herself away from him. She turned her head so that she could hear the steady and reassuring rhythm of his heart against her cheek. 'Please forgive me for doubting you. I know you are good and just, but I let my duty to him sway me. I turned my back on you and that was awful of me. It was so wrong of me to do that after everything you've given me.'

His lips brushed the top of her head and his arms tightened so much it was nearly uncomfortable, but she didn't want him to let her go. 'I understand, fair one. You don't have to explain.'

Of course he understood, further proof that he was everything she didn't deserve. Not that she could've had him had she actually deserved him. The muffled voices of the Danes in his hall penetrated the safety of his chamber. Their words were foreign, but she imagined they were retelling stories of battles, battles they'd fought against her own people. Magnus had led them in those battles. Though she believed with her whole heart that he'd never harm innocents, she could never stay here with him. He could keep her safe, he could make her feel precious, but he could never truly stay with her. His battles would call him away.

He was an enemy. Alstan could disown her. It would mean turning her back on everything she knew.

'I'm sorry that I ordered my men to take so much from you. I was angry and allowed that to rule my judgement,' he continued. 'I have the tapestries still. I want you to have them back.'

She gasped and turned in his arms. 'My mother's?'

He nodded. 'I'm sorry.'

He was. His eyes had gone soft and warm, just as she remembered they could. This was her foreigner. His wound looked nearly healed. There was a red line bisecting his eyebrow and slashing up into his hairline where the blade had cut, but it was only a little scabbed over and there was no swelling. The masculine beauty of the unmarred side of his face had always been startling, but now that it was matched by the other, he was breathtaking. And he'd been hers. She wanted him to be hers again. She adored the way the firelight caught the gold in his eyes, matching the gold highlights in his hair, the way his soft, perfect lips parted just a bit. 'I want—'

'Wait.' The one word cut her short, but he softened it by pulling her against him and cradling her face with one hand. His thumb traced over her lips, making them tingle with anticipation. 'You should know that I'm to be married.'

The words hit her like a blow. They left her reeling, forcing her to take a deep gasping breath. It hadn't even occurred to her that there might be a woman who claimed him, not after she'd arrived and he'd been so kind. *Kind.* She'd stupidly mistaken kindness for some lingering affection. 'My apologies. I didn't think.' She tried to draw herself away, but he wouldn't allow her to go.

'It's not like you think. I've never met my bride.'

'Oh.' She blinked and forced herself to look away from his face so she could think. Her gaze settled on the midnight of his tunic. Did it make it better that he'd never met the woman? Aye, it meant that she wasn't someone he was longing for. She wasn't someone Aisly had unknowingly usurped. Well, perhaps she had, but it wasn't as if he had genuine affection for the woman.

Before she could finish thinking of the implications, he tilted her head up so that she met his gaze. 'Let me tell you about my life. It will help you to understand.'

'You remember?' She couldn't help but smile that he was coming back to himself.

'Aye, a bit.' He smiled then, too, and it was the first genuine smile she'd seen from him since they'd been apart. It warmed her and filled her with butterflies at the same time. 'I want to tell you.'

She was nodding before she'd even thought about her

answer. She wanted to know of his life. She wanted to know everything.

'Come.' His expression sobered as he released his hold on her to take her hand and lead her to the bed. She faltered a little when she realised that was his destination, but he simply swept her up into his arms and placed her squarely in the centre. He paused only to rid himself of his boots, making her stomach flip over on itself as she watched, before he climbed in beside her. How she'd ever thought the bed that had seemed so gigantic when unoccupied could hold two of him, she didn't know. When he settled his wide shoulders against the headboard, she had to scoot over to give him room. He didn't allow her to go far and pulled her against his side, where she fit perfectly.

They talked into the night. Long after the voices in the hall had drifted away as the men found their beds. Magnus told her about growing up with Vakr as his father. He told her about his mother and all the babies she'd lost, which he now realised had been due to Vakr's brutality. Guilt ate away at him, despite the fact that he'd only been a child. Aisly had stared into his eyes the entire time he'd relayed the story and not once had she flinched away from him. Not once had a shimmer of doubt or blame clouded her soft green eyes. They'd shown only love and understanding, and her hand had pressed gently against his heart.

When he spoke of the marriage Jarl Eirik had arranged, it nearly shredded him to see the flash of pain that had crossed her face. Yet it somehow managed to hurt him even more when she nodded her understanding. Pressure squeezed tight in his chest, moving its way up to form an ache in the back of his throat. His arm tightened around her and his hand gripped hers where her fingers had closed over his heart.

'It's my duty, fair one. I have to see it through.' The words were needless, because she merely nodded again in understanding.

'Your father would be so proud of you. Do you know that?' She raised up on an elbow, her copper tresses falling down around her to pool on his chest. Somehow they'd slipped down in bed as they spoke and his head lay cushioned on the down-filled pillow.

'Aye.' While somewhere in the back of his mind he cared about that, she was more important to him now. It was frightening how easily she'd slipped into that role. Nay, that was understandable. She was easy to love. It was much more frightening to him how easily the urge came to him to turn his back on everything he was. For her.

She must have read his mind, because her voice lowered to a gentle rasp when she spoke. He'd heard that voice many times. It never failed to warm his blood and send it pulsing straight to his manhood. 'I'm proud of you.'

'Aisly,' he whispered, his hand shifting so his rough fingertips skimmed over the silky skin of her inner wrist. Her pulse raced.

'Please don't think me wicked, but…' Her voice trailed off and she flushed, but she didn't have to say the words for him to know what she wanted. The longing was in her eyes.

An instinct, a *need*, he couldn't control tore through him. He'd flipped their positions before he'd even realised it. His larger body settled over hers and her smaller one fit itself to him, knowing just how to shift and flex to give them optimal contact. Her soft gasp when the fullness of his erection pressed against the thigh he straddled nearly drove him to the brink of madness.

'You're not wicked.' He was the wicked one, enticing her when he had nothing to offer her.

'I just…' Her brow furrowed as she tried to control herself, but then the words poured out of her. 'God help me, I want you, Magnus. I know that I'm not entitled to you. I know that we're enemies and I could never be yours, wife of a Dane. I know that we can never have more than this stolen night, but I want that. More than anything, I want to steal a night with you. Just once more before we have to walk away in the morning.'

He crushed her mouth beneath his. It wasn't a practised or gentle kiss, just desperate and searching. She opened beneath him and their mouths ate at each other, seeking solace and closeness. When the need to be even closer caused him to pull away to undress, she stared up at him disoriented. He sat up on his knees, jerking at his tunic and undershirt. She did the same, sitting up to lift the linen dress over her head before tossing it away. His gaze was drawn to her perfect, round breasts with their pink nipples already hardened for him, until she lay back and spread her thighs for him. Then he looked there. That beautiful mound between her thighs.

'Magnus.' Her voice was a plea as she held her arms out to him, her hungry gaze eating up his chest as it made its way down to the bulge in his breeches. 'I need you. Please.'

Greedy for her, he impulsively said, 'You won't leave tomorrow. You'll stay longer.'

She looked puzzled for a moment but then nodded

her agreement. It was all he needed. He tore at the fastenings until he sprang free, pausing only long enough to push the leather down his hips before he was on her. Her hand found him, guiding him to her, and he pushed inside in one deep thrust that tore a cry from her lips. The pleasure of her tight, hot grip was so intoxicating that he couldn't think for a moment. He could only feel her soft body beneath him, her wet heat surrounding him as he throbbed within her, begging for release. When he finally could latch on to a coherent thought, he realised that he'd hurt her. She was so small and he hadn't checked to make sure she was ready.

'I'm sorry.' He managed to give voice to the words, though it took effort.

She whimpered, making him take his face from her neck so he could see her face. Her eyes were closed, and when he'd drawn up enough that he wasn't crushing her, she rolled her hips beneath him. 'So good...please.' She rolled her hips against him again, her inner muscles clamping down on him.

He groaned and somehow lengthened inside her. Despite the way his shaft throbbed and begged for release, he didn't want to take her harshly. Taking her hands in his, he drew them over her head and pressed them against the mattress, lacing their fingers together. The position spread her out beneath like an offering and he took advantage, pulling a nipple into his mouth and sucking deep until she cried out, grinding her body against him. He groaned at the sensation and gave an involuntary thrust into her. It was hard. Deep. By the gods, he'd missed this. His entire body pulsed with need for her.

'Look at me.' His voice was so harsh and raw that he didn't even recognise it.

She obeyed immediately, revealing eyes so dilated with need that the green was a mere sliver. His hips gave another reflexive thrust against her, drawing a soft cry from her lips.

'I love you,' he said, tightening his fingers around her hands, not daring to break her stare.

Her eyes widened in surprise but softened immediately. 'I love you, Magnus. I love you so much it hurts.' Her voice cracked with emotion, tearing at his heart. He kissed her then, soft and deep. His vicious need for her had abated just enough for gentleness now that he was inside her and as close to her as he could get. When they pulled apart, gasping for breath, he pressed his temple to hers and thrust deep. His low gasp mingled with hers. He couldn't hold back any more and moved against her, setting a gentle but deliberate rhythm.

She moved with him perfectly, calling his name as if it wasn't the name of an enemy. He loved hearing it wrenched from her lips in pleasure. When the cries became demands that transformed to need, he sped up his thrusts, making them hard and deep, until her body clenched him so tight it was nearly painful. 'Aye, let me hear you as you come apart.'

She obliged him, tumbling over the edge, her voice soft against his ear as she found her release. He followed her quickly, pumping his hips hard against her until he came deep within her. He still held her hands, her fingers tight around his, as he fell over her. He was shaking in the aftermath, and as his eyes met hers, he saw the bewildered feeling of wonder that he felt reflected back at him. Something small but profound had changed between them, while nothing had changed around them.

He was still a Dane, an enemy. He was still destined to marry for power and duty. But between them they'd found something they'd each lacked, something they'd been searching for all along.

They'd found each other.

Chapter Twenty-One

Aisly had been exhausted from her walk to Thornby, and even more so after making love with Magnus. She had fought sleep for as long as she could, though, preferring to spend the night talking with him and revelling in their newfound closeness. The uncertainties that had kept them from finding that closeness back in her village were gone. Perhaps it was the knowledge that they'd have only one night, or perhaps it was how things should've been all along for them, but Aisly found that she just didn't care that he was a Dane.

He was Magnus and she loved Magnus.

When she finally did close her eyes and succumb to sleep, it was with him wrapped around her. His arms were holding her to his chest and his legs were entwined with hers. There was no need to worry that he'd have to leave soon so that no one would see him. For a few blissful hours, there were no worries at all.

But that all changed with the morning.

Aisly awoke with a start. Disoriented, she clenched her fingers in the blanket and pulled it up to cover her nakedness. It smelled like Magnus. A delicious warmth moved through her, soothing her as she remembered him and why she was naked. Her entire body ached a bit from the many ways he'd had her last night, but the pleasure was worth the leftover pain.

He was already gone. The bed was cool where he'd lain and the sounds coming from the hall told her it must already be late into the morning. She'd been too tired to hear him leave. It was probably just as well, because she'd only have tried to get him to stay. That wasn't how they needed to start the day.

She had nothing to offer him that could compare with the life of a king and that was what waited for him with his bride. He deserved that.

Rising from bed, she dressed quickly and ate the cold breakfast of porridge and bread that had been left inside the door of the chamber for her. Then she retrieved her gold thread and left the tapestry in the corner. It was time for her to go. If she saw Magnus in the hall, she'd take the time to explain to him, if not, then she'd try to leave on her own. It would be easier to escape unnoticed if she wasn't lugging the tapestry about on her back.

Truth be told, she rather hoped she didn't run into Magnus. It would take very little for him to sway her decision and she didn't want to put him in that position. He wanted to marry for power. She didn't blame him for it. It was what he'd strived for his entire life. It would simply be easier if she didn't have to convince them both of that. He was too kind and would try to do the right thing by her if confronted. If she left without a confrontation, she had no doubt that he'd proceed with his plan with his northern bride.

If she thought it would be easy to blend into the people of the hall, she'd been sorely mistaken. As soon as she emerged into the main room, men and women alike paused to stare at her. She wasn't certain if it was because she was Saxon, or because she'd spent the night with their master in his chamber. Likely both. Her cheeks flamed, but she couldn't find it in her to regret her time with Magnus.

Neither Magnus nor the men who'd been at the table with him last night were present. Good. Ignoring the stares as best she could, she approached one of the women who hadn't given her a second glance. She was working at the hearth, preparing a stew for the next meal. Loaves of bread were warming on one of the low stone walls of the hearth near her. Aisly asked for one, but the woman only gave her a puzzled look. Remembering that there was a language barrier, Aisly indicated what she wanted and the woman nodded. Aisly took it and dropped it into her knapsack, before making her way outside.

She wasn't Magnus's prisoner, but given her reception last night by the Danish sentries, she hadn't been certain what to expect when she stepped outside. Just like in the hall, people looked at her, but she couldn't read their expressions and they seemed content to allow her to walk around unmolested. As she made her way to the front gate, she was surprised at how similar the settlement was to her village. There was a disproportionate number of men—most of them warriors by the weaponry they all seemed to carry—but their work was the same. A blacksmith's hammer rang in the distance, a woman stirred a large, bubbling pot of laundry, young children chased each other, darting amongst the houses. The conversations around her were in a language she didn't understand, but as she walked, she had the sense that they were very much the same as the ones back home.

Perhaps she could convince Alstan of that. Perhaps something good could come from all of this. Cuthbert was reasonable. Alstan could talk to him and convince him that living with the Danes would be the better option. They'd all known Magnus as a foreigner before they'd known him as a Dane and they'd all liked him. Why did that have to completely change now?

She watched for him as she approached the gate, but he wasn't to be found. She knew that it was good, but she couldn't help but feel disappointed that she'd not get one last look at him. She wished there was someone she could ask about his whereabouts, but there was no way to do that without rousing suspicion. So she kept her head down and walked right through the gate, along with the other people coming and going.

A group of warriors seemed to be returning from a training exercise, they dragged their weapons behind them and wiped sweat from their brows. A group of women carried buckets, leaving Aisly to assume they were going to the river for water. It was easy to blend in with them, especially since she'd pulled up her cloak to disguise the fact that she'd lost her headrail.

The snow had stopped falling and left only small piles in the shadows, so she didn't worry about leaving tracks. As soon as she was out of direct sight of the walls, she darted into the forest, keeping near enough the road that she could follow it without being seen from the road. She didn't know where Magnus had gone, so she had no idea how long of a head start she'd get should he decide to follow her. Therefore, she moved as fast as she could.

* * *

Magnus stared down the length of his sword at the man who dared to taunt him. Even with most of his men dead around him, the fool still refused to be cowed. Blood and spittle combined to dribble down the twin tails of his beard.

'Kill me now, heathen. I'll not rest until you and all of your men are wiped from the earth,' Wulfric said, his words holding little meaning as his arms were being tied behind his back.

The sentries had come to Magnus at first light. It turned out that Aisly had been followed, though not by men from her village as they'd anticipated. The group of rebel Danes had returned and caught her tracks. Only luck had kept Magnus's men from doubling back on them. They'd seen the rebels from a distance and had managed to lay low until Magnus and Jarl Eirik arrived with more warriors to confront them. It was only after they'd ridden into their camp that Wulfric had been discovered with them.

'Then you'll not rest before your death.' Magnus held his sword steady as his horse shifted beneath him. His men had already dismounted to dispatch the fifteen dead and wounded rebels. Wulfric had survived, primarily because Magnus had been so surprised to see him there that he'd called for his life to be spared. 'Why have you forsaken your village?'

The man must be mad, because he only grinned. 'I've not forsaken them. Cuthbert is a weak leader who believes in antiquated principles such as diplomacy with the Danes. Diplomacy will get you nowhere with people set to rule you. You Danes know nothing but aggression

and power, so we have to turn it back on you. *I* wanted
to use the rebels against you, but he would hear nothing
of it. I did what needed to be done.'

Magnus frowned down at the man. 'And what needed
to be done?'

'We needed to make peace with the rebels. They
wanted women, so I gave them women.'

'You are responsible for the kidnapped maidens?' His
stomach turned as he imagined the maidens at the hands
of the ruthless rebels.

Wulfric shrugged. 'They were but a small price for
the safety of all my people.'

'That's why Godric never came to plead with us to
find them. He came to fan the flames of war.'

'Nay, Dane, he came to talk to you. You killed him in
cold blood. That death is on your head.'

Godric had spoken with the same misguided hatred
as the man kneeling before him now. His own illusions
had led him to believe that he and a handful of poorly
trained Saxon warriors stood a chance against a Danish
army. Now Magnus understood why. Wulfric himself
lived with illusions and he'd passed those on to his son.

Instead of answering Wulfric's allegation, which
would have been pointless, he said, 'You'll come back
to the settlement as my prisoner. I'll arrange a meeting
with Cuthbert and you can answer to him for your poor
decisions.'

Wulfric laughed. 'Rest assured that, no matter what
happens to me now, I will triumph in the end. The rebels will avenge me. They'll kill you and your men, and
they'll purge your seed from the earth. Just as you have
done to mine.'

Magnus's heart shuddered in his chest. 'I have no

child.' Not yet, though it was possible Aisly carried his child even now.

'They have orders to kill your whore on sight. That should solve the problem,' Wulfric countered.

'Bind his mouth,' Magnus ordered, sheathing his sword and riding over to Vidar, who'd been questioning a wounded rebel. 'What have you found out?'

Vidar stood over the prone rebel. 'This was most of them. There is a small handful that split off. They've been given orders to take Aisly if they can and await orders from Wulfric.'

Magnus nodded. Though his heart pounded, he knew that she was safely ensconced within the walls of Thornby. Nevertheless, he felt a desperate need to get to her as soon as he could. 'They won't get to her.'

'Who is this woman to you, Magnus? I know she's the one who tended you, but...' His voice trailed off and he scratched his head, raking his hand through the length of his hair. His brow furrowed and he shook his head. 'We have bigger problems. These villagers are no threat to us. The rebels have all but been annihilated. The few left won't make it through winter.'

'She's everything to me.' Magnus had never spoken truer words.

'Everything except your bride,' Vidar said, his voice insistent, as if that detail had escaped Magnus's attention.

It was the one detail that Magnus couldn't ignore, though he refused to address it just yet. Giving orders to Vidar to finish the task of seeing to the dead rebels and the prisoners, Magnus turned his horse around, Leikr and Arn flanking him, and headed back to her as fast as he could.

* * *

'Halt!' Drawing his horse to an abrupt stop, Magnus listened for the sound to come again. His heartbeats pounded out the moments.

'Magnus?' Leikr whispered, but Magnus only held his arm up for silence.

The afternoon sun glinted through the trees, but he couldn't see anything out of the ordinary. Just when he thought he'd imagined the bird call so late in the season, the call of a hawk reached his ears. It was far in the distance and authentic enough to be taken for the real thing by someone unsuspecting. It came two more times in rapid succession. It meant there was trouble and they'd need to proceed carefully.

They were only an hour away from home. Instinct told him the matter concerned Aisly. His stomach churned as he turned in the direction of the call.

Aisly prayed fervently for Godric's sword to appear in her hand, but that prayer continued to go unanswered. She'd never have been able to leave the settlement without rousing suspicion with it, so when it hadn't been returned to her, she hadn't thought about it again. If it would help her now, she didn't know, but anything would have been better than nothing.

It seemed that she'd barely got out of view of the settlement when she'd felt eyes on her. She'd assumed it was some of the Danes. They seemed to be everywhere. It was no surprise that one of them would have been curious about her leaving and followed. As long as they didn't intervene, she was fine with it. But as the afternoon had worn on, she'd begun to feel apprehensive. The presence felt menacing. She was being stalked.

Unable to stop herself, she'd picked up her pace a few times. The distant sound of leaves crunching under boots echoed her own steps. Her heart pounded and she scanned the trees for somewhere to hide. There was nowhere, especially not when she was so obviously being observed. They'd see where she hid. Any tree that she was able to climb, they'd be able to climb.

She should've stayed in the settlement and waited for Magnus. He would've given her an escort to Alstan's home. But she hadn't, because she'd been too afraid that she couldn't face him and still walk away.

A twig snapped to her right and she jumped, her gaze frantically searching for the source. There was nothing. It happened again, this time to her left. They were surrounding her, toying with her. Her mind raced for some way out, but there wasn't one. Then a figure emerged from beneath the canopy of branches just ahead.

It was a man. He stood there grinning, displaying the dark grooves carved into his teeth. She turned, but they revealed themselves to her until she could see there were four of them, each only thirty yards away. She had no hope of making it, but she refused to stand docilely while they closed in on her. She screamed and ran, aiming for the clearest path directly between two of them.

One of them laughed, his mocking voice following her as she ran. The two nearest her ran, their legs eating up the distance until she was sure one of them would reach out and grab her, but he fell, his cry of pain echoing through the forest. She had no idea what had felled him, but she couldn't stop to look as the other one promised to reach her soon. She pumped her legs, nearly sliding on the wet leaves when his fingers brushed her shoulder. He almost took her down, but he cried out in pain. Over her shoulder, she saw the bulk of his body as he fell.

Sounds of footsteps closing in spurred her onward and another cry of pain made her flinch. But then a body crashed into her, sending her rolling with a heavy body on top of her. She caught a quick glimpse of the rebel who'd smiled at her, just before they came to a stop and he pulled her to her feet. One hand tangled in her hair, while the other wrapped around her waist in a strong hold she had no hope of breaking, though she tried. He jerked her hard back against him and yelled something she was certain was a call for her to be still.

She did still, but only because she saw the reason the rebel's friends had fallen. An army of Danes emerged from the trees. She had no idea how so many of them could have been hidden, but she was certain there were at least a score of them. There was a thud and she was jerked to the side along with the rebel holding her. Only, he was falling and he was taking her with him. The flash of the hilt of a sword in the sunlight told her he'd been hit with it.

Strong hands went around her, freeing her from his grip just as he crumpled to the ground in an unconscious heap. Ready to fight her new adversary, she jerked but heard the most precious sound she could imagine: Magnus's voice.

'It's me, fair one. You're safe.'

It took a moment before she could believe that he was there. It seemed so incredible, yet there he stood staring down at her, the gold flecks in his eyes catching the sun. And he was smiling.

'We've got them all. You're safe.'

She flung herself into his arms, not caring that the other Danes watched them. She was so overcome with happiness and relief that the strength left her legs and tears rolled down her cheeks. Magnus held her, murmuring soothing words as he stroked her.

'Why did you leave?' he whispered, when her trembling had abated a little.

'Because I couldn't bear to tell you goodbye. I know what this marriage means to you, Magnus.' She pulled back just enough to look up into his eyes. 'I won't force you to choose anything less than everything you've worked for, but neither can I stand by while you marry someone else. I thought it best if I just go.'

He looked so pained she wanted to take it away from him, so she stroked him. His shoulders, his chest, anywhere she could to try to take that away. 'While I marry someone else?' he asked. 'Does that mean you could consider marrying a Dane? The man responsible for your husband's death?'

'I could marry you, Magnus. Not a Dane. Not a warrior. But you. You're so much more than any of that.'

He smiled at that and pulled her hard against his chest. She allowed it because his arms was the only place she wanted to be, but it didn't change anything. Did it?

'I'm still a warrior,' he finally said.

'I know.' She closed her eyes and burrowed deeper. She'd have to come to terms with that and accept that she wouldn't have as much of him as she wanted.

'Jarl Eirik.' His voice surprised her when he called out.

She jerked away as far as he would let her, to see a large blond man approach on horseback. He was the same man she'd seen in the hall the previous night. He wore chain mail and a mantle, and when he dismounted, he was as tall as Magnus, but his expression was fierce. Magnus had mentioned him the night before. This was

the man responsible for Magnus's marriage. This was
the man Magnus had to answer to if he disobeyed. Fear
tightened in her belly, but she didn't acknowledge it as
she drew herself up to her full height.

'I want to marry Aisly.' Magnus's voice was firm and
he surprised her by speaking in her language.

'Magnus!' She looked up at him. 'Nay. This is what
you wanted.'

He only shook his head as he spared her a glance. 'It's
what I thought I wanted. I want you, Aisly. I don't need
to be King. I have nothing to prove to anyone but myself…and to you. I'm the warrior my father wanted…
I'm the man I want to be… Now let me be the husband
you want.' He turned back to the Jarl.

'Magnus, this isn't a question of want,' the Jarl said,
surprising her with his grasp of her language. He spoke
with barely a hint of an accent. 'It's obligation. The
Alveys expect an alliance.'

'Aye, I know they do and I'm certain we can find
someone for them. Remove me as leader if you need to.
Appoint a new one and let him marry the woman.'

'That person is you.' Eirik crossed his arms over his
chest and widened his stance.

Undeterred, Magnus shook his head. 'It was…once. I
don't want that life any more.'

'Magnus,' Aisly said, tightening her grip on his waist.
'Please don't give this up for me. You've worked too long.
It's what you've wanted.'

'Listen to her, brother. This is what you've earned.'

Magnus only smiled, a strange peacefulness coming
over his face. 'Aye, I have earned it and I do want to lead
my men, but not if it means losing Aisly. She's what I
want. A life with her.'

Jarl Eirik blinked, then looked at her, *really* looked at her for the first time. She couldn't help but think he must find her lacking. What did she have that could compare to the bride Magnus was giving up? Nothing. She had absolutely nothing to offer him.

Looking up at Magnus, she pulled herself away from him, needing distance. With a little distance she was certain he'd come to his senses. 'Please don't do this, Magnus. I can't offer you what she can.'

Magnus only smiled wider. 'You're right. You can't offer me a kingdom, but you can offer me what's important. All the little things that I forgot I needed. I want you, Aisly. I choose you.'

'What of your duty, Magnus?' She wrapped her arms around herself, lest she fall apart.

'The only duty marriage to you disqualifies me from is marriage to her, an alliance.' Turning his attention back to the Jarl, he said, 'Someone else will have to do that, while I keep the peace in this region.'

The Jarl was so quiet, she was certain he was about to dash the foolish hope that had begun to grow within her. But then he smiled at her. She noticed that he was quite handsome when he smiled and she was certain that the three of them had gone mad together. 'Merewyn will be overjoyed to welcome another Saxon woman to her table.' To Magnus, he said, 'You're right. You can keep peace in this region, it's why I appointed you leader of Thornby. Your marriage to this Saxon won't disrupt that and you'll stay on as leader.'

'But what of the Alvey marriage?'

'Vidar was my first choice. As my brother, he'd create a stronger alliance.' The Jarl surprised her by laughing. 'He refused initially, but he won't disobey a direct order.' Turning back to mount his horse, he said, 'We'll tell him tonight.' Then he rode back towards Thornby.

When Aisly noticed her hands were shaking, she clutched them into fists, but that didn't do anything to stop them. Magnus stroked his fingertips across her cheek, brushing her hair back from her face. 'You'll marry me, won't you? You can have your own place to work and do your embroidery if you wish.' He didn't seem particularly unsure of himself, as his voice was more coaxing and gentle than that.

'You just gave up everything for me.'

'I didn't. I still retain my position as leader of the settlement.'

'But your future…'

'My future is with you…if you'll have me. If I am fortunate enough to live out my days as leader of Thornby with you at my side, I'll die a happy man.'

The hope doubled, tripled, within her, but she still couldn't bring herself to believe that this great man wanted her as his wife. 'Are you certain, Magnus?'

He laughed and picked her up, his arms tight around her waist as he brought her up to eye level. 'Aye, I'm certain. I can't change the fact that I'm a warrior, but as leader I'll have duties that keep me at the settlement. I can arrange it so I'll rarely be gone for more than a fortnight.' His eyes softened, and his fingers tightened at her hips. 'Marry me.'

She nodded, and the laughter spilled out of her. 'I love you. Aye, I'll marry you.'

He kissed her then, his lips sealing over her vow. The Danes cheered around them, but she didn't care. Magnus was hers. He was everything.

Epilogue

Aisly ran her fingers through the thick waves of his golden hair. It had grown out quite a bit since winter. She was finding that she quite liked it this length, down to his neck so she had something to hold on to. Her fingertips disappeared in it, only to re-emerge as she stroked downward along the golden skin of his back.

'At least tell me what you're saying.'

He grinned at her and kept talking in his language. So many of the people at the settlement knew her own language, and had been considerate in using it when around her, that she hadn't mastered his yet. She could get by, but he was speaking so low and fast that she couldn't keep up.

Finally he finished and leaned forward to place a kiss on her growing belly before lying down in bed beside her. 'Only how lucky I am to have stumbled upon his or her mother near that stream.'

She took his hand and moved it to the spot on the upper right where there was movement. 'The baby can hear you, I think. It kicks every time you talk.'

Magnus smiled wide and his eyes practically shone with joy as he spread his hand wide to feel it. It was early summer and the baby wasn't due to be born for another couple of months, but they were both excited. Aisly had worried that Magnus might regret his decision, but so far he hadn't. He managed the settlement and left for small trips to visit other Danes or handle disputes, but he was home far more often than he was away. It seemed too much to dream for, yet it was working.

Alstan hadn't been entirely happy to learn that she'd married a Dane, but he hadn't disowned her. She'd visited him once when Magnus had gone to visit Lord Oswine about Wulfric's involvement with the rebels. Lord Oswine had claimed ignorance of Wulfric's deception, just as he'd claimed no knowledge about her marriage contract. Magnus had been suspicious, but there was nothing to do without solid proof. For his part, Alstan had vowed to keep an eye on his master and he'd hugged her, all the while vowing to harm Magnus if he harmed her. They wouldn't be having him over for a visit any time soon, but she was confident that eventually he'd come to see Magnus as the fair man he was. Just as she was certain that Cuthbert would make the villagers see that the Danes didn't have to be their enemy. He'd already graciously accepted Magnus's payment for harbouring him during his injury.

The only casualty had been Vidar. He'd spent the winter at Thornby and she'd got to know him a bit. He'd been easy-going and likeable—he'd even offered her a bolt of deep blue silk she took to be an apology for stealing her tapestries—but he'd been upset about his marriage. Guilt gnawed at her every time she thought of him.

'Do you think Vidar has reached the north yet?'

Shaking his head, Magnus brought his hand up to smooth out her brow with his fingers, before kissing her there. 'Probably, but don't fret. Vidar will be fine. He's survived a father who makes most men tremble in their boots and two older brothers who learned at their father's knee. He can survive a bride.'

'It's not that. I just worry for him. Doesn't he deserve a chance at what we've found? What Jarl Eirik and Merewyn have found?' She'd met them once when Magnus had taken her to visit them at the beginning of spring. They'd clearly been in love. 'How can he have that with an arranged marriage?'

'It's not like this for everyone, fair one. Aye, he deserves a chance, but if it's not what he wants, then he'll marry the girl and be on his way. He may be happier that way.'

She frowned. It didn't seem right. 'And will she be happy?'

Magnus was quiet for a moment, twirling a length of her hair around his finger. 'Perhaps—if they're very lucky—they'll be happier than they ever thought possible.'

* * * * *

*If you enjoyed this story,
you won't want to miss these other
great reads from Harper St. George*

*ENSLAVED BY THE VIKING
ONE NIGHT WITH THE VIKING
THE INNOCENT AND THE OUTLAW*